NEW BEGINNINGS AT CHRISTMAS TREE COTTAGE

GEORGIA HILL

BLOODHOUND
— BOOKS —

For Lynn as she so generously 'gave' me Jago.

CHAPTER 1

'DECEMBER WILL BE MAGIC AGAIN' – KATE BUSH

Friday 19th November

Violet clouds, shot through with apricot, chased across the wide Dorset sky. The day was nearly done. One day closer to a Christmas none of them wanted to celebrate.

Jago Pengethley opened the attic window and inhaled the salty sea air. The window was a fancy one that opened up onto a balcony, so he went out to stand on it, not quite trusting it to bear his weight. He breathed in the view. This was why he'd agreed to the house. From its position a little way up the hill, he could see across the tumbling roofs to the little town of Charmouth and West Bay beyond, stretching over the sea to Portland in the east. Beyond the raggedy houses snaking down to the sea, he glimpsed one side of the harbour wall curled round and the fishing boats bobbing in the high tide against the walls. The halyards on a few dry-moored yachts clinked wildly; the boats were chained up for the winter on a scrap of yard behind the RNLI station. Thankfully, the station building itself was out of view.

In the bowels of the house he could hear faint noises. His mother was making one last round of tea before the removal men headed back on their long journey to London. His little sister was busy in her new bedroom. She was supposed to be unpacking her overnight case but, from the rhythmic thumping sounds, he suspected she was trampolining on her bed. Merryn had been beside herself with excitement about the move to the coast, but he knew under the excitement lay a febrile anxiety. It was the same with all of them. The sense that, even while grabbing at happiness, there was every chance it would slip away like something intangible in the night. Love for his family surged fierce and hot. He'd love and protect them as long as he lived. That was the promise he'd made to himself. He'd go down and help soon but was content for the moment to contemplate the view and the dying light. A glorious sunset was spreading across the late November afternoon, with the sky crimson over a midnight-blue sea. His fingers tingled to get his sketchbooks out, but they were still all packed up. From here, frustratingly, he wouldn't be able to see the moment the sun finally sank into the sea in the west, but it was only a short stroll to the seafront, the promenade and the beach. If it was clear tomorrow, he'd do it then. There was too much to do today.

He glanced round at the room behind him. The space was crowded with boxes piled up neatly, but it would soon become his working and living room. The attic flat stretched the length of the house and had been converted for use as a holiday let. It had a small shower room, a kitchenette, a decent-sized bedroom with the rest devoted to a vast living space. With four windows and a balcony facing onto the sea it was full of light, even at this time of day and year. It had influenced his decision to move in with his mother and sister.

With half his equity gone after the divorce, there hadn't been a great deal of money left. Besides, being self-employed meant a mortgage was difficult. Up here he'd have complete privacy whenever he chose, it was an ideal workspace, but he'd also be near his family. After all they'd been through, he wanted to keep them close.

He was itching to unpack his crafting gear, desperate to get settled at his workstation and get creating again – there was something about this town that set his creative juices going – but he needed to go downstairs. His mother had been keeping herself deliberately and frantically busy over the last few weeks and he knew that, unless he stopped her, she'd be unpacking boxes into the night. Apart from making up the beds there was nothing that needed doing immediately, but his mum wouldn't see it that way. He'd have to force her to stop ripping open boxes with the promise of fish and chips. At least they wouldn't need cutlery for those. Opening the door which led to the narrow stairs he glanced around. They would be happy here. It was a new start. They *needed* to be happy here. He ran downstairs.

As the removal van belched diesel with the effort of crawling up the steep hill, Jago waved it goodbye. It was the final link between them and their old life. Feeling foolish, he stuck his hands in his jeans pockets and ignored the heap of unpacked boxes he could see in the hall. He concentrated on gazing at the house, their new home. Although it was called Christmas Tree Cottage, there was little of the cottage about it. Instead, it was a solid square Victorian villa, set sideways onto the road, with a terraced garden behind and a tiny parking space in front. Both rare things to possess this close to the harbour and seafront they'd been told by Ellie, the efficient woman from the estate agents, when she'd shown them around.

The irony that the house was called Christmas Tree Cottage wasn't lost on him. He didn't think he'd ever feel the same about Christmas again. He'd make the effort this year for Merryn and his mother, but it would feel hollow. As his glance slid sideways to their immediate neighbours, he could see they already had their Christmas tree up, decorated and festooned with twinkling lights. He swallowed a sigh. That was the trouble with Christmas, it was hard to ignore.

As Avril came out of the house to stand by his side, he slipped an arm around her. 'No regrets then, Mum?'

He watched as she took a deep breath of sea air, half-closing her eyes in pleasure. Even though it was nudging December, it was still mild. One of the gifts of being in the southwest.

'None.'

'Happy we bought here and not in Cornwall? Don't you think Dad would have wanted us to go back to his hometown?'

'He might have, I suppose. Your dad and I were happy there when we first married before we went to London, but I needed a fresh start. We all needed a fresh start somewhere new.'

'I wish I could remember living in Fowey better.'

'Well, you were tiny when we left.' She leaned into him.

He sensed her exhaustion. 'I'm a proper city boy. Definitely lost my Cornish roots.'

'You are,' she reproved gently. 'Living here might be a challenge for you. No Ubers, no Deliveroo, but it'll suit Merryn and me. I can feel it in my bones. Cornwall was one step too far west. Living here means we can visit the family in Fowey, or what's left of them, it's only an hour or so away. And Lullbury Bay's well-served to get back up to London if any of us need a city fix.'

'True.' He contemplated the view again. 'Although I'm not sure I'll ever want to leave here.'

'You might. I think you'll miss the city more than you realise.' Avril peered up at her rangy son. 'Are you sure you're going to be happy sharing with your old mother and little sis? Won't it cramp your style?'

Jago laughed. 'There's been none of that going on since the divorce.' He felt his mum's arm tighten around his waist. She was so tiny, it was the only place she could reach when they were both standing. 'And it made sense to pool resources so we could buy what we wanted. You and Merryn have the house and the attic flat will suit me absolutely fine. It's got masses of light so I can work. If I get any done – think I'll spend all day looking at the view.' Like his mother he sucked in a lungful of salty air. 'I think this was the right move, Mum. The right move for all of us.'

CHAPTER 2

'DO THEY KNOW IT'S CHRISTMAS?' –
BAND AID

Monday 22nd November

Honor smiled at the line of children impatiently waiting to come into her class. They twitched and bobbed like yachts on the sea, their woolly hats and scarves flying. Now Bonfire Night was done, there was only one thing on their mind: Christmas! She loved her job, challenging though it had been over the last couple of years. And through the exhaustion of a hectic autumn term shone a creeping excitement. She loved Christmas too. With a passion.

'In you go, folks. Get your reading books out and I'll be in in a moment.' She turned to the woman standing to one side clutching the hand of a skinny girl. 'Hello,' she said, addressing the little girl. 'You must be Merryn. Welcome to St Winifred's Primary School. I'm Miss Martin and you'll be in my class. We're delighted to have you with us. We're just about to start practising for the Advent Service so I hope you'll enjoy joining in.'

'I'm Mrs Pengethley, Merryn's mum. Avril.' They shook hands.

'Honor Martin. It's lovely to meet you,' she said, over the top of the child's head. The woman looked anxious and had put emphasis on the word *mum*. An older mother, maybe in her late forties? Perhaps she was often mistaken for the grandmother. 'Welcome both. I understand you've just moved here?'

'Only on Friday. I was keen to get Merryn into school.'

'Oh my goodness, you must have been busy. Well, welcome to your new school.' She smiled gently at Merryn, who looked terrified. 'And it's hard making new starts. I understand.' She reached out a hand and was relieved when Merryn took it. 'I know because I moved here from the Midlands. But, do you know, Merryn, I think Lullbury Bay is the friendliest town in west Dorset. I wouldn't live anywhere else. Are you ready to come in now? I'll show you where you can hang your coat and PE kit and then we can meet the class. You've arrived in town at the absolute best time. There are lots of Christmassy things going on.' Over the child's head, she mouthed to her mother, 'She'll be fine.' Too many new parents hung anxiously on, prolonging the agony. And there had been a flurry of new children recently. Some settled quickly but some didn't. Either way it meant disruption to class routine as the dynamics shifted and changed. The sooner Merryn got into class and met her new classmates the better. Thankfully Mrs Pengethley took the hint.

Giving her daughter a huge hug, she said, 'Off you go now, Merryn. The day will fly by and I'll see you at three thirty. We can go for a hot chocolate in the café on the seafront you liked the look of.'

Honor looked seriously at them both. 'Only with marshmallows though. It's the only way to drink hot chocolate at the Sea Spray Cafe.'

'You can only have it with marshmallows?' Merryn looked up at her, eyes wide.

Honor winked. 'Absolutely. It's the law. And in November and December, you have to have it with a chocolate flake too. So come on in then. Tell me all about your new house. Did you get to choose the biggest bedroom for your own? It's Christmas Tree Cottage, isn't it? The one on Harbour Hill with the fabulous views? What a wonderful place to live.'

She steered the little girl towards the classroom. Merryn was so busy telling her all about her new bedroom which she planned on having painted turquoise, Mum was forgotten. Honor gave a subtle thumbs up to Mrs Pengethley who smiled and went.

'And they have a class hamster. He's called Chestnut and you get to look after him in the holidays. Holly had him all through half term. And I had chicken pasta for lunch. It was delicious. Holly didn't eat all of hers but I did. Holly wants me to go to tea. Can I, Mum?'

Avril pushed the mug of hot chocolate nearer. They were sitting in the cosy fug of the café. Right on the seafront, it was decorated in yellows and blues and smelled sweetly of cake and pastry. 'Of course you can. Introduce me to Holly and her mum tomorrow morning and we'll sort out a date.' She grinned at Jago over the child's head. 'Think she's enjoyed her first day.'

'I think she has.' Jago ruffled Merryn's hair. 'Did you ever stop talking? Your poor teacher. What's her name?'

'Miss Martin. She's so beautiful.' Merryn sighed happily. 'She's got eyes like the sea and hair like honey. We did similes in literacy,' she added, importantly. 'Miss Martin says my similes make her smile.'

'Impressive.' He chuckled. 'How would you describe me then?'

Merryn put her head on one side, studying him. 'Hair like bubbles and eyes like green sea glass. Like the bit we picked up off the beach on Saturday.'

Jago laughed and tugged on one of his dark curls. 'Even more impressive. Maybe I should get it cut though?'

'No. It makes you look like a pirate. We had a pirate story at home time. Miss Martin tells stories so well. She does all the voices. It was really funny.' Suddenly distracted, Merryn pointed out of the window. 'Look at that dog!'

Avril and Jago turned to see what she was staring at. An enormous man with an equally large dog were loping along the promenade, past the café.

'I've never seen such a big dog,' Merryn cried. 'It looks like a wolf!'

'Irish Wolfhound I think,' Jago explained. 'Or deerhound maybe. Huge but gentle giants.'

'Can *we* have a dog, Mum? Can we?'

Avril hesitated. It had been a request repeated ever since the child had learned to talk. Their London house had had a long strip of garden but she'd never thought their lifestyle was right. Her husband had worked all the hours known to man, and so had she. It would have been cruel to have a dog they wouldn't have time for. But now, with the move to Dorset, it might be possible. With savings, Kenan's pension and her redundancy money, she didn't need to look for work straight away. Maybe it was time for a puppy? Merryn had been the bravest of all of them through this, perhaps she deserved a reward?

The girl picked up on the fact her mother hadn't squashed the idea flat straight away. 'Can we, Mum? I'll look after it, I can walk it on the beach. I promise.'

'Well maybe. Not for Christmas though,' Avril added firmly. 'Christmas is not the right time to get a puppy.'

'And possibly not an Irish Wolfhound,' Jago suggested. 'Maybe something smaller?' He saved Merryn's mug from being knocked over as the child leaped to her feet and threw her arms around her mother's neck. 'Jolly-wow! A dog,' she cried. 'I'm getting a dog!' Bouncing back to Jago, she landed, half on his lap.

❅

The movement caught Honor's attention as she walked past. She never once took for granted that she could walk home from work along the promenade. She could take the route uphill from school and then down the high street, but it was much prettier this way. Plus, it was good to get the fug out of her lungs from a day in school, and she needed the exercise. Even today, with the light going and mist hanging over the sea, it was beautiful. Stopping outside the café, she wondered about going in. She often did at the end of the day. It was easier to grab something quick to eat rather than cook for one at home. But it was Monday and she had a pile of marking to do. Through the steamed-up windows she glimpsed Mrs Pengethley and Merryn. The girl had settled easily into her new class and had already made a friend. Holly Carmichael hadn't been in Lullbury Bay long either. Lots of new people had moved into town. COVID had forced people to re-evaluate, and many came in search of a better quality of life, which Lullbury Bay offered in buckets and spades. Seeing Merryn hug her mother, she thought she'd leave them to it, not wanting to intrude. A man got up from their table. He was tall and lanky and looked much younger than his wife. Honor shrugged. In twelve years of teaching, she'd learned families came in all shapes and sizes. Pulling up her collar against the damp, she shifted her heavy workbag onto her shoulder and turned to go. If she got a move on, she could throw something together to eat in front of *It Takes Two*. This year's series of *Strictly* was the best she'd watched and she was obsessed. Trying not to dwell on the fact that she was thirty-two and the highlight of her life was a reality dance show, she made her way home.

CHAPTER 3

'O COME, O COME, EMMANUEL' – TRAD.

Sunday 28th November

Jago hadn't been in a church since school. He'd never been sure of what he believed. Had rarely given it a thought before losing his father. He had a vague notion of there being some kind of great being somewhere, but his father dying had made him question everything. There was no way a god could exist when such sorrow had been inflicted on him and his family. He hadn't wanted to be here, he had a commission waiting to be finished, but his mother, with unusual sternness, had insisted he support Merryn. The church smelled old and the dense cold was making the inside of his nostrils burn. They'd dropped Merryn off at the side entrance where she'd been gathered up by her new best friend Holly, and were now sitting on the third pew from the front. They were lucky to get the spot. Even though Avril had insisted on arriving early, the church was filling up. Good. It might make it warmer. The primary school was a Church of England one and boasted proud links with the church. It had made Jago uneasy but, as it was the only school in town and fed into a prestigious secondary, it made sense for Merryn to go there. And to be fair, it had done an amazing job of settling her in. There had been a few wobbles, but she'd taken to it like a duck to water. Jago suppressed a grin. The literacy lessons on similes were catching. Or was that an idiom?

'Glad to see you looking more cheerful,' his mother hissed. 'Especially when I had to practically drag you here.'

'It's not my usual habitat.'

'Can't see why. Look at all the stained glass.'

Jago had to admit the windows were superb. He'd come back at some point when the church was empty to have a proper look. The building and its purpose were separate for him, however. Whilst he could appreciate the craftsmanship that had created it, he was ambiguous about the religion it housed.

Avril huffed a bit and turned away. She was soon busy chatting to Mrs Carmichael on the other side. The two mothers had become friends. He was glad she'd made a friend. Groaning silently, he cursed himself for treating her like Merryn. Around him he was aware of a shushing and a call to attention. Merryn's class were walking into the church from the vestry. He was impressed at how seriously they were taking it. At the same age, he'd have been convulsed with giggles and poking the pupil in front. They filed into the choir stalls. It had obviously been rehearsed as they all knew exactly where to sit and what to do. They held service programmes like the one he'd been given on entry, only the children's were decorated in green and red with a glittery red tinsel bow. Merryn's teacher stood at the side, making sure they were all in place. Her blonde hair caught the light and Jago could see her silently making gestures to a little boy who was peering out into the church, presumably to see if his parents were there.

The vicar took the pulpit. She was so tiny she could barely see above the impressive eagle-shaped lectern. She was a beige, nondescript person so when she spoke with a warm voice bubbling with humanity and humour, it took Jago by surprise.

'As some of you probably know, I'm Verity Lincoln, your vicar. May I extend a very warm welcome to St Winifred's Church on this most glorious of occasions,' she said, and smiled at the full congregation. 'I'm delighted to see so many of you here. You'll be glad to know this is all you'll hear from me. Because I'm an extremely lazy person,' at this some laughed disbelievingly. 'I've very happily handed over the church to Starfish Class who are going to lead the service this evening. I'm sure they'll do a far better job! It just remains for me to repeat my warm welcome to you all, or as warm as I can make this old place. I have put on the heating and I can only apologise for its lack of efficiency. Please warm yourselves up by singing as loudly as you can. And now, over to you, Miss Martin and the children of Starfish Class.'

A tall red-haired girl came to the front of the choir stalls and spoke into a microphone. She wore an enormous pair of silver tinsel wings. *Do not be afraid,'* she began in a loud clear voice. *'For see – I am bringing you good news of great joy for all the people...'*

'That's Holly Carmichael,' Avril explained in a whisper to Jago.

The other children stood as one and turned to their parents. Jago saw Miss Martin hold up her hands to focus their attention and then nod to a pianist at the side. They sang a song about it being a magical time of the year. It was simple but, even to Jago's ears, the childish voices were uplifting.

A reading followed about how excited everyone became at Christmas, how everyone was impatiently waiting. One by one a child stood up holding a painting.

'I can't wait for roast turkey!' one shouted, waving a picture of the bird.

'I can't wait for all my family to arrive,' whispered a tiny girl in glasses, flapping a painting of several blobs Jago assumed were her relatives.

Another shouted out, 'I can't wait for Christmas pudding.'

'And I want to see my granny!' said the little boy who had been peering out into the congregation before the service started.

Everyone went, 'Ah.'

Then Merryn bounced up. 'I can't wait to open all my presents,' she yelled, making everyone laugh with her enthusiasm.

Another reading followed; this time read importantly by a serious-looking boy. 'Even though it's a busy, exciting time of the year,' he read out, ponderously, 'we're really waiting for the best present of all. The present of a baby boy born in a manger who was God's gift to the world.'

The congregation rose to sing 'O Little Town of Bethlehem'. Several more readings and songs followed, with prayers, one read out by Merryn.

'I didn't know she was going to take part,' Avril whispered to Jago. 'I'm so proud of her.' She sniffled a little and he put an arm around her shoulders. The service finished with Miss Martin guiding a pupil to light one candle on the advent display and then the parents shuffled out to collect their children.

The chilly damp air hit them hard. It was raining slightly. Even though the church had been cold, it felt colder out here. They'd been instructed to wait on the drive in front of the church so they could be reunited with their offspring.

Ciara Carmichael shivered next to them. 'Well, that was super, wasn't it?' she said to Avril. 'Oh here comes Holly. Running as usual. I'll give you a ring. She's been pestering me to have your Merryn over. I'd be delighted but I've just been so busy lately.' Waving at one of the teachers, she called out, 'I've got her!' and then she grasped her daughter by the hand. 'You did marvellously, darling, I could hear every word. Come on, let's get home, it's too cold to hang around. See you, Avril.'

Merryn was one of the last pupils to come out of church. Honor Martin brought her over. 'My apologies for keeping you waiting,' she said. 'Merryn lost her painting and I promised them all they could take them home.'

Merryn ran into her mother's arms.

'I was so proud of you, my little mermaid,' Avril said. 'Is this the painting of your presents?' she asked as Merryn thrust her painting into her face. 'We'll have to find a spot in the kitchen to hang it up. Fish and chips for tea as a treat?'

'I'm starving.'

Jago laughed. He ruffled her hair. 'Tell me something new.' Turning to Honor, he said, 'Thank you.' He didn't know what else to say, so settled for a lame, 'It was a really... erm... interesting service.'

She grinned, appearing to enjoy his discomfort. 'Glad you thought so.'

'The children obviously worked very hard.'

'They did. I'm very proud of my class.'

'And thank you for including Merryn, especially as she hasn't been with you for very long.'

'My pleasure.' Honor smiled with genuine warmth and Jago was taken aback. In the light spilling from the open church door, her golden hair glowed ethereally. She was wrapped up in a white wool coat and was holding Holly's silver tinsel wings. He wouldn't have been at all surprised had she sprouted angel's wings of her own and flown away. An image of a simplified angel with glass wings and a halo flew into his imagination and his fingers itched to cut some glass again. He hadn't had that urge for too long.

'Are you all right, Mr Pengethley?'

'Sorry?'

'You were miles away.'

He shook his head. 'I was. Sorry. Inspiration struck.'

She looked bemused. 'Erm... good.'

'And it's Jago, please.'

'Jago. Lovely name.'

'Thank you.' He couldn't stop staring at her.

'Well, must go, it's too cold to stand around and I need to help tidy the church.'

'Yes, it is.' *Good going with the witticisms, Jago man. You've really knocked her out with your witty repartee.* He still couldn't move.

Merryn tugged at his arm. 'Come *on*, we need to get fish and chips. I've got a tummy roaring like a tumble-drier.'

Honor laughed. 'I hope we'll see you all at the school nativity,' she added. 'Merryn has a part in that too.'

'Then we'll be sure not to miss it,' Jago answered, even though a primary school nativity play was the last thing he wanted to watch.

'I'll see you there then.'

As Honor turned and entered the church, he had the strangest sensation she was taking all that was light and good with her.

CHAPTER 4

'JOY TO THE WORLD' – TRAD.

Thursday 2nd December

Avril yelled up the stairs. 'I'm going out now. Be back for tea.' She cocked an ear but heard nothing. She wasn't sure if it was because Jago hadn't heard – the walls of this old house were thick – or whether he had his head down working and wearing his earbuds. It was no matter, they didn't live in each other's pockets. Shutting the front door behind her, she walked briskly down the hill towards the harbour and headed left to Sea Spray Café. Since Merryn had taken such a liking to it, they'd been regulars. It was no hardship. The hot chocolate was wonderful and, if she or Jago didn't fancy cooking, so was the food. As she walked, she breathed in deeply. Inhaling the cold, salty air took her straight back to her Cornish childhood. There was something deeply and instinctively soothing about being near the sea. She hadn't realised how much she'd missed the endless rhythmic shush and roar until she'd move here. Even though it wasn't Cornwall, it felt strangely like coming home. It blunted some of the nerves she had about what lay ahead. It was ridiculous. A year ago, she'd been a confident wife, mother and working woman, getting on

17

with things, busy with life. Now it felt like a layer of skin had been removed. With Kenan dying, her confidence and certainty – and maybe complacency – with life had been lost. After so many years married to the same man, everything was hard-going, everything felt like a mountain to climb – only with metaphorically decreased lung capacity and a weighty rucksack on her back. She had Jago, of course, and thanked whoever it was up there who looked after them, for him daily. But she couldn't rely on him. She refused to rely on him. He had his own life to build.

Passing a shack called Blossoms which purported to sell candy floss and another called the Ice-cream Dream advertising the finest ice cream in west Dorset, both currently closed, she headed over the open space outside the yacht club. Her stomach was churning, tears were never far away and, not for the first time, she wondered if she was doing the right thing. As her hand landed on the door, a gull swept over her, laughing. It came so close she could feel the air its wings brushed away. Its cry mocked her.

She turned to watch. It caught a thermal and its coolly-shaded grey-and-white body lifted away against the winter sky. Part of her yearned to join it. 'I'll show you, you stupid bloody bird,' she muttered, her courage rising. 'I can do this!' A year ago, she wouldn't have thought twice about walking into a room full of strangers. This was what they didn't tell you about grief. The way it dissolved your old self into a formless blob and you had to build yourself back up into something different. She took a deep breath and pushed open the door, pausing for a moment to calm her breathing and imbibe the sugary scents to give her confidence. Or at least the *appearance* of confidence. 'Fake it until you make it, babe,' Suz, her neighbour in London, used to say.

The hug took her by surprise. She was engulfed in Tracy's trademark earthy fragrance. A larger-than-life character, with a mussed-up mop of curly pink hair, she managed the café during the day. Both Cornish-born and of similar age, an instant friendship had sparked between them. Having travelled for a few years, Tracy had not long taken over the café and was always interesting to talk to. And it was Tracy who had suggested Avril join the Knit and Natter Group who met at the café once or twice a week. As she explained, they met ostensibly to knit but there was always far more nattering going on.

'Glad you could make it! I'll bring a coffee over. The group are set up in the window.' Tracy noted Avril's anxious expression. 'Don't worry, maid, they're a friendly bunch and you're joining at the right time. They have some project or other they want to get going on. No idea what it's all about,' she added cheerfully. 'And, to be honest, I don't want to know. As long as they're spending money in the caff I'm happy to host. Do you want me to introduce you?'

'No. I'm a big girl.' Avril unwound her scarf and grimaced. 'And getting bigger thanks to Merryn's obsession with The Codfather's chips.'

Tracy ran a hand over her own generous curves. 'Well, they are to die for. Folk come from miles around to eat at that chippy.' She winked. 'Off you go and make friends. I'll bring you cake if you're a good girl.'

'No calories?'

'None whatsoever,' Tracy replied with a straight face. 'And then I'll finish up decorating the tree. Café looking festive enough, do you think?'

Avril took in the silver and blue tinsel streamers across the ceiling, the white fluffy angel fairy lights dangling across the serving counter, the yellow and blue giant gnomes on the tables, each with a fair isle sweater, bushy beard and enormous woolly hat. Then there was the enormous half-decorated Christmas tree. 'Well, I don't know…'

'I know. I know. But you can't overdo the Christmas decs, can you? I'm going full-on this year, seeing as it's my first Christmas here and luckily Maisie the owner agrees with me. She's over there with the group so you'll get to meet her. One of my favourite people in town, is Maisie, and not just because she was daft enough to employ me.' She prodded Avril. 'Off you go. I'll go and put some music on. Get you in the Christmas mood. It'll be that or I'll come at you with a sprig of mistletoe.' Wagging a finger, she added, 'Don't say I didn't warn you!'

With leaden feet, Avril made her way over to the group of women at the two tables shunted together in the window. Paul McCartney singing 'Wonderful Christmastime' belted out of the stereo. Turning back to Tracy, she winced and the woman made an apologetic face and turned it down.

Avril had left behind a close circle of friends in London and a wider group of work colleagues. Taking voluntary redundancy from John Lewis and making a new start was all well and good in theory; what she hadn't counted on, now most of the moving stuff was done, was how lonely she'd find it. Taking another deep breath, she stopped by the friendliest-looking woman and said, 'Hi.'

The woman, possibly in her seventies and very chic with a sharply cut silver bob and long dangly earrings, looked up and smiled. 'Oh, my lovely, you must be Avril. We've been expecting you. Scoot up the rest of you. Sit yourself down Avril, and I'll introduce everyone. I'll start with me, I'm Brenda Pearce.'

Avril sat down, unbuttoned her coat and hung it on the back of the chair. There were about fifteen women in the group and all looked at her with curiosity. The age range was wider than Avril had expected, she'd anticipated them to be mostly older. As Brenda introduced them, she only took in a few names.

'Next to you is Lucie Wiscombe, Brenda stopped and corrected herself. But of course, you're Lucie Taylor now you've married the lovely James, or have you kept your name?'

'Hi there,' Avril said. She knew Lucie, a young woman in her twenties with vivid chestnut hair. When buying the house, she'd mostly dealt with the manager of the estate agents, a ferociously efficient woman called Ellie, but she'd often been made a cup of coffee by this friendly girl.

'No, I'm still a Wiscombe. Just can't seem to shake 'em off. Hi, Avril. Hope you're settling into the new house?'

'Yes thanks. Still lots of boxes to unpack though.'

Lucie rolled her eyes in sympathy. 'I can imagine. Good luck! Give us a ring when you've emptied them, we can put you in touch with someone who needs packing boxes. There's always someone looking for them and it saves you a trip to the tip.'

Avril was surprised at the kind thought. 'Thank you!'

'On my right here is Marion Crawford,' Brenda continued. Marion nodded coolly and looked superior. 'Next to Marion is Lucie's mum, Debbie, and next to her is Clare Cheney who runs Cheney House in Bereford and Maisie who kindly lets us meet here.'

Brenda reeled off several others, but Avril lost track.

'This is Avril Pengethley. Just moved from London and keen to join us Natterers. We're a few missing today, as not all of us can come to every session,' Brenda apologised. 'And I'm sure I've completely bewildered you with all the names, but you'll get to know us one way or another. We're all friendly. No point in being otherwise, is there?'

No, Avril thought and, Marion aside, they did indeed look friendly. Some of her nerves subsided now she'd done the hardest part. In London her friends had evolved gradually. Some from the primary school Merryn had attended and where she'd been a parent-governor, a few from work, and Suz next door who she'd become close to. She wanted to make a fresh start in Lullbury Bay, wanted to carve out a social circle that didn't depend on her children or work but had more to do with her and who she was. Tracy's suggestion of the Knit and Natterers seemed a good start. She'd knitted a lot years ago but hadn't had time to do much recently. She said as much to the group.

'Oh, don't worry yourself,' Maisie, a young dark-haired woman, said. This must be the owner of the café Tracy had mentioned. A warm smile spread over her face. 'I used to knit but I can't remember a thing. I'm here to learn. I'll be relying on your help, Avril. That's if you've got the patience.' She pulled a face and the others laughed. 'And you might need a lot!'

'I'm here to learn too,' Lucie put in. 'I'm writing a book and one of my characters is a knitter, so I thought I'd learn too. You know, I've always thought your surname ever so unusual, Avril.'

'I've always been told it's Cornish, but it might be Welsh. It's where I'm from originally, Cornwall that is. But I've lived in London for most of my adult life.' Avril paused and said, slightly tremulously, 'Not sure where I belong these days.'

Brenda gave her a quick hug. 'Well, now you belong to Lullbury Bay,' she said comfortingly.

Maisie beamed. She seemed a welcoming, uncomplicated sort of a person and warmth exuded from her. 'It's easy to learn to belong to Lullbury Bay, Avril. You're very welcome. I hope you'll be happy here. No, I *know* you'll be happy here. It's a wonderful place to live.'

Avril came close to tears. These women had welcomed her unquestioningly and were being genuinely warm. Tracy had been right, it *was* a good group to be part of.

'I've always *so* loved Cornwall,' Marion said, in a nasal, pinched sort of a voice, which cut through all the bonhomie. 'Such divine little houses. Always hankered after a *pied-à-terre* there. In Padstow or maybe Rock? I do *so* adore the Rick Stein place.' She sniffed slightly. 'I attended a cookery class there once, you know, and was asked for my curried gurnard recipe. I was told it was very highly thought of.'

Lucie made a strange snorting sound and Maisie hushed her. Brenda cleared her throat and Avril noticed one or two of the group exchange knowing glances. She suppressed a smile. She'd met Marion's type before, often at the school gate. She had her sussed.

'Shall we get down to business, Knitters?' Brenda said. She looked around dramatically as if to see who was within listening distance and then bent nearer and whispered. 'Now, Avril, I know you've only just joined but I'm going to have to ask you to promise an oath of secrecy. Quite possibly on a matter of life or death. Promise I won't make you sign in blood though, or make you sign the official secrets act.'

Lucie spluttered. 'I bet if Aggie was here, she'd make you do that, or possibly a satanic ritual at midnight on a full moon. Naked. There would probably be whips involved. Rumour is, she still has a stash in the wardrobe.'

'Haven't we all,' Marion chortled, to Avril's surprise. Perhaps she was more fun than her first impression implied.

'Just as well she's out of town, then,' Maisie said, more reassuringly. 'Avril, you've plenty of time to meet our lovely Aggie when she comes back from her holiday. She's Lullbury Bay's most, shall we say, notorious OAP and once met never forgotten, but she has a heart of gold.'

Avril nodded, mystified. This wasn't turning out to be the cosy but possibly dull group she'd anticipated.

'Right then,' Brenda commanded. 'Gather round troops, be discreet, we don't want this getting out, but we need to discuss our cunning plan!'

CHAPTER 5

'ONE NIGHT, ONE MOMENT' – NATIVITY! THE MUSICAL

Friday 3rd December

It was another soft misty afternoon. Jago waited outside the primary school in the fading light, feeling self-conscious amongst all the, mostly female, parents. He felt one or two eye him up and smiled back nervously. He'd only occasionally picked up Merryn from her London school, where a man was apparently less of a rarity at the school gate. Avril always warned him about getting involved in school gate politics and cliques and he had no intention of doing so here either. Suspecting the other adults might be studying him with forensic detail, he concentrated on the enormous Christmas tree he could see in the school entrance. It half blocked the doorway and was chaotically decorated with what looked like child-made ornaments. It dripped with lights, which glowed warm and cheerful against the dank December afternoon. Seeing a couple of women whisper behind their hands, he was thankful he didn't have to wait long. Merryn came running out, dark curls flying, her coltish legs looking skinnier than ever.

She threw her arms around his waist. 'Mum didn't tell me it

was going to be you picking me up.' At the sound of her name being called she looked back to the school entrance. 'Hang on. Miss Martin wants me.'

Beside him he heard a woman say to another, 'You can't mistake who the father and daughter is there, can you. Not with those curls.' He didn't have a chance to correct them as Honor came up to them, hand in hand with his sister.

'I've a huge favour to ask you. Merryn suggested you wouldn't mind.'

'Please, please say we can, Merryn pleaded. Pleeeese!'

'Merryn has asked if she can be the one to look after Chestnut.'

Jago looked at her blankly. 'Chestnut?'

'The class hamster. It would be for the Christmas holidays. To be honest he doesn't need much looking after and he'd come with full instructions.'

She smiled and Jago felt something twist inside. Today she was in some kind of navy cord pinafore and white polo-neck. It should have looked frumpy. Except it didn't.

Merryn tugged his hand. 'Pleeeese!'

'Can't see it being a problem.' Jago studied Merryn. There was something missing. 'Have you forgotten your coat, Mer? Go and get it.' After she'd run back into school, he turned to her teacher. 'Is there anything we should know about, erm, Chestnut, Miss Martin?'

'Honor, please. And no, hamsters are pretty easy to look after. I'll supply a list of instructions, it's nothing onerous. A tip, though, put the cage somewhere he won't disturb you at night. They're mostly nocturnal. I really appreciate you taking him on.'

'You're welcome.' For a moment neither of them spoke. Something electric fizzed in the air. He felt heat rise in his face and saw Honor blush slightly. It was extraordinary. When they'd met outside the church after the service, he'd dismissed his instant attraction to her as simple hormones; she was devastatingly beautiful. He'd always scoffed at the concept of love at first sight, putting it down to lust disguised as love. But now, he again felt this visceral pull towards her. And it was caused by something other than a hormonal surge; he *yearned* to get to know her.

Emanating from the depths of the school he could hear childish voices rehearsing a song. It was vaguely familiar. Something about a night and a moment. It fractured what was passing between him and the woman in front of him.

Honor cleared her throat slightly. She blinked hard. 'That's the choir. They're rehearsing a song for our nativity. It's from the film. *Nativity*, I mean. One of my favourites. I watch it every Christmas. I'm a huge fan.'

'Of the film?'

'That, and of Christmas generally. I just love everything about it.'

'Everything?' He couldn't resist teasing. 'Traffic jams, crowds in shops panic buying, terrible muzak, TV Christmas Specials, overpriced office party meals?'

'Absolutely everything.' She smiled at him, and he wanted to dive into it.

Merryn ran out of school and hung off his arm. She had her coat worn as a cloak, only buttoned at the neck. Tearing his eyes away from Honor, he looked down at her and said, 'Are you going to promise to look after Chestnut?'

Merryn beamed. 'You said yes! Of course I'll look after Chestnut. I'm a very good looker-after-erer.'

'I'm sure she will,' Honor put in, with another enchantingly twinkly smile. 'Merryn is a very responsible young lady.'

'Good to hear. Maybe you deserve a trip to the Sea Spray then?'

'Yes please! Bye, Miss Martin.'

'Bye, Merryn. Bye, Jago.'

He turned to go but something made him look back. He was

desperate to catch one more glimpse of her, but she'd been swallowed up by a crowd of parents.

The café was packed. The steamy interior hummed with the sound of voices and wrapped a vanilla-sugary-scented hug around him the minute he pushed open the door. Standing at a loss for a second, not able to see an empty table, he sensed Merryn's disappointment.

'If you don't mind sharing with me and this big fellow, you'd be welcome to join me,' said a deep voice to their left.

Jago turned to see the man they'd spotted walking the Wolfhound along the prom on their first visit to the café. They were sitting in the window. The dog was sitting on its hind legs but its enormous head still poked above the level of the table. It was grinning, with its huge tongue lolling out.

'Tiny's very friendly,' the man said with a smile. 'He only eats people when there's an x in the month.'

Merryn went to sit down so Jago followed.

'I'm Tom Catesby.'

'Jago Pengethley.' The men shook hands. 'Thank you,' Jago added. 'For letting us share the table, I mean. Crowded in here today.'

'Yes, I wouldn't have come in had I known.' He nodded to the dog. 'He and I need a bit of space as you can see. The grammar school had a Christmas concert today and it looks like most of the audience have piled in afterwards.'

Tom was well matched with his dog, both being enormous and both having shaggy greying hair.

'Is your dog a Wolfhound?' Merryn asked.

'He is.' Tom smiled at her. 'It's very clever of you to know his breed.'

'May I stroke him?'

'Of course. Thank you for asking first. He likes being tickled under the chin.'

Merryn put out a tentative hand. The dog whickered and laid his massive head on her lap, his wise eyes blinking at her adoringly through a silvery-grey fringe. She slipped down to sit on the floor next to him and stroked his long back. Rolling over, he offered his tummy, his endless legs splaying out.

'He likes you. You've made a friend for life. Once Tiny takes to you, he'll never forget you.'

Jago met Tom's eyes. 'And that will suit Merryn down to the ground. She's dog-obsessed.' He caught the attention of the young bleached-blonde waitress.

She jogged over. 'I'm *so* sorry to keep you waiting,' she said, looking harassed. 'There's only me and Tracy in today and we've been manic.' She pulled a face. 'And we're usually fairly quiet at this time of day.'

Jago smiled, said they'd only just walked in and ordered for him and Merryn. Noticing Tom had nothing in front of him he asked, 'Have you been served? Can I get you anything?'

'A coffee would be great, thank you.'

'Oh, I'm so sorry, Tom, have you been waiting long? Hasn't anyone taken your order yet?'

'It's not a problem, Alice, honestly. I was happy to wait. I could see you had your hands full. If Tracy has any of her Christmas shortbread left, I'll have a slice of that too, please.'

'Okay. Two hot chocs and a coffee coming up, a special biscuit for Tiny, some shortbread and I'll see what else is going, to thank you all for being so patient.' She dashed off.

'Mum's promised me a dog of my own,' Merryn piped up. 'But I can't have a puppy for Christmas. It's not the right thing to do.'

'That's true,' Tom replied. 'You sound as if you're being very sensible about it. I don't agree with giving puppies as Christmas presents either. I think it should be a considered decision. Christmas is a hectic time and it can be scary for a little puppy.

Imagine being uprooted and put in a completely different environment, away from your mummy and brothers and sisters. Then imagine being tiny and on the floor and all around you is crackly paper and noisy people, lots of visitors coming and going. It's not the ideal time.'

'I know.' Merryn nodded sagely, her eyes wide and serious. 'I've been reading up on it online. There's loads of Christmas food that's poisonous to dogs too. Chocolate and dried fruit. And it's really sad how many puppies are given back after Christmas when people don't want them anymore. I think it's very, very traddit,' she mispronounced. 'Dogs are hard work and a big responsibility.'

Jago hid a smile as Tom looked impressed. 'You sound as if you're going into it well-prepared. I think any dog would be lucky to find a home with you.'

Merryn beamed.

'And speaking of animals finding homes, that's what I do.'

'You get dogs a new home?' Merryn asked.

'Sometimes. I run the Lullbury Bay Animal Sanctuary just out of town.'

'Oh jolly-wow!' Merryn leaped up.

'Now you've gone and done it,' Jago said, laughing.

'My dream job!' she said. 'That's what I want to be when I'm grown up.' She considered her answer, chewing her lip. 'Or a vet. Or a Shakespeare actor.' She jigged up and down and Jago shifted her out of the way of a party of five leaving.

'All very sound ambitions,' Tom said. 'You must come and visit us.' He glanced at Jago. 'As long as Dad agrees.'

There was a tiny but uncomfortable pause.

'Jago's not my dad,' Merryn protested. 'He's my big brother.'

Tom looked from brother to sister. 'I apologise.'

Jago shook his head to dismiss the faux pas. 'Easy mistake.'

'I'll ask Mum if we can come,' Merryn added, excitedly. 'What animals have you got?'

'At the moment? A couple of donkeys, two reindeer, a small herd of alpacas, lots of ex-battery chickens, a few goats and ducks and quite a lot of guinea pigs. Nothing too exotic but they all love being made a fuss of, especially the guineas.'

'Guinea pigs,' breathed Merryn. 'I love guinea pigs. Jago, do you think we could have a guinea pig?'

'Hold on, Mer. See how you get on with looking after Chestnut the hamster first. Then we'll see.'

She pouted. 'I'll be excellent at looking after Chestnut. I'll be as good as gold. That's a simile.'

'No, think it might be a–' but Jago was interrupted by Alice bringing them their drinks. As his grammar knowledge was being stretched, he was glad to see Merryn was thoroughly distracted by the three enormous slabs of chocolate cake and a plate of shortbread heading their way too.

'Don't tell Mum,' he hissed as his sister perched on his knee and spooned the thick cream off her hot chocolate.

Honor, walking home, glanced in. In amongst the Christmas decorations festooned from the ceiling and the crowds of customers, she saw Jago, with Merryn on his knee, laughing and talking to Tom from the animal sanctuary. Something inside her softened. He seemed such a devoted dad. She must have imagined the frisson that had sparked between them earlier. He simply couldn't be the sort of man who would cheat on a lovely woman like Avril and betray a sweet little girl like Merryn. Pausing, she stared in. He was an attractive man. Tall and loose-limbed, with a sense of inner burning energy that was very sexy. Something inside her stirred which hadn't done for too long. Since she'd broken up with her boyfriend, there hadn't been anyone she'd felt any attraction for. Until now. She'd promised herself she'd be cautious about starting a relationship with anyone and wouldn't throw away her affections on a man she didn't think worthy. Not after being hurt so badly. She gave a snorting laugh which made the family coming out of the café stare at her curiously. She certainly wasn't going to fall for a married man, even if he did possess a pair of luminous green eyes and a kind soul. Married men and parents of children she taught were as far off limits as to be in a different universe. Ramming her woolly hat over her ears as punishment for even contemplating Jago Pengethley's sexiness, she turned decisively on her heel and carried on walking.

CHAPTER 6

'DO YOU HEAR WHAT I HEAR?' – TRAD.

Saturday 4th December

Jago crept into St Winifred's, hardly daring to breathe. The church felt very different to the other evening when it had been full of hopeful childish voices and light. Now the atmosphere was hushed and he had the sense someone – or something – was watching. Not liking the shadowy musty-smelling corners, he went to stand in front of the stained-glass windows he'd admired during the service. He wanted a closer look.

Stained glass was something he'd like to get back into, but he'd need space in order to make any. He'd made a name for himself on the gallery circuit with his large decorative glass panels, but studio space had been expensive in London, so he'd had to abandon them. Then the pandemic had shut everything down. Instead, he'd concentrated on making small objects with coloured glass fused together. His light-catchers in the shape of birds, suns with rays of light, delicate silvery moons and stars sold well. A bonus being he could make them at home with minimal space and equipment needed. To make his larger works he needed a workshop, and to retrieve his kit out of storage. His glass kiln and storage drawers alone took up too much room to keep at home.

It was a cold, bright day outside and the hard winter sun illuminated the image of a woman dressed in robes and holding a sword. The artistry was astonishing and the glass glowed jewel-like, pooling a warm liquid light on the tiled floor. He perched on a pew and gazed at it, lost in its beauty. He'd never get over how glass art could make him feel. He could well understand why it was chosen for churches; it was literally awe-inspiring. A relatively simple process, it took immense skill to make it well and to make it as stunning as the example in front of him. His fingers, with their bumps and scars from incidents with glass cutters and soldering irons, itched. He needed to make big again. Something as beautiful as this inspired him to make on a grand scale.

'St Winifred herself.'

The voice made him jump a foot.

'I'm so sorry. I should have realised you were in contemplation. Would you rather I left you in peace?' It was Verity, the vicar. She was dressed in black trousers and a neat grey sweater, her clerical collar showing above it.

'No please. It's your church.' Jago tried to keep the irritation out of his voice.

'And yours too. But sometimes it's good to be still and quiet and alone.'

Jago shook his head. 'I don't want to be alone. I wasn't praying. I came for a closer look at the windows. I work in glass so it's an interest.'

'You're connected to Merryn Pengethley, aren't you? I've seen you collect her from school. She's quite a character. I take assemblies at school once a week and she often asks me the most challenging questions.'

He mustered a smile. 'That's my little sis. She keeps all of us on our toes.'

'I can imagine.'

He stood up, dwarfing the woman. Shaking her hand, he introduced himself. 'I'm Jago.' Embarrassed, he added, 'I'm sorry I don't know how to address you.'

'Verity will do fine.' She sat on the pew in front and twisted round. Tucking her light brown hair behind her ear she said, 'Our friend up there is St Winifred herself. Her lover chopped her head off when he discovered she wanted to enter a convent. Quite the racy story!' She grinned. 'She's a bit of a hero of mine. Where her head fell there appeared a miraculous spring. She's a Welsh saint so we're a bit of an outpost down here in Dorset. There's only us, and the church in Branscombe over the border in Devon, round here dedicated to her. We're old but not as old as the one there. Our tower's Norman, which you can guess from its squat square shape, but the window there is Victorian. Made by a local craftsman. She's rather beautiful isn't she? Especially at this time of day with the light streaming through. I often come and chat to her. She's a brilliant listener. Sit down, take a pew as the saying goes.'

Jago hovered, unsure if he wanted to stay and chat.

'Go on, I promise I won't try to convert you.'

He grinned and sat down. For a moment, they both gazed at the window. St Winifred wore a gown of rich dark blue, with a saffron-coloured cloak, her drapes luxuriously folded around. On her head of tightly curled golden curls was a crimson and pink halo. She was magnificent.

'I take it you're not a believer?' Verity asked.

'I'm not sure what I am. I'm not sure what I believe. Not anymore.'

She shrugged. 'Join the club.'

'But you can't have doubts. Not in your job.'

'I have doubts every day. One reason I talk to Winnie here. Wouldn't be human if I didn't have doubts. And this job can get,' she paused, 'wearying, sometimes.'

'You must be busy, especially at this time of year.'

'Just a little, but it's a joyful time too. Take the Advent service. Such joy and wonder in seeing the children lead it.'

Jago was silent for a moment. He thought back to the service and to the innocent childish voices. 'I have to confess I'm a little uneasy at Merryn attending a church school.'

'That's understandable. It's not for everyone. Before I joined the church I was a teacher. Taught in church and non-church schools. Always felt, though, the non-church ones had no shape to the year somehow.' She smiled kindly. 'But, as I say, it's not for everyone.'

'When we moved here, we thought Merryn going to the local school would give her a chance to make friends in the town.'

'And it's a feeder school to the grammar of course.' Verity's eyes twinkled.

Jago had the grace to look embarrassed. 'We've come from London. It's a battle to get into a decent school there, unless you can pay.'

'Whereas in this part of Dorset all the schools are pretty good. The grammar school is excellent and very academic. Merryn strikes me as a clever girl. It should suit her. And you're quite right, she'll have a cohort of friends from primary to go up with. How are you finding the move?' Verity put an elbow on the back of the pew and stared at him intently. 'Big change.'

'You're right, it's very different. I work for myself and can work anywhere, so that's not been an issue. Merryn has taken to it with enthusiasm. She seems to have settled into school, has made a friend and loves her new teacher. Mum has joined the Knit and Natter group and is knitting again. It seems to be taking up a lot of her time already.' Jago stared at St Winifred's feet. The artist had given her open-toed sandals and the detailed shading on her feet was exquisite.

'But?'

He looked across at Verity. 'Did I say there was a but?'

'No. I heard one though.'

'I suppose we've all been so frantically busy with the move, that now the boxes are unpacked and the admin is done, I wonder if the reality will hit us.' Jago wasn't sure what was keeping him here, in this chilly church, talking to a woman he didn't know, who was also a *vicar*. He'd never talked to a vicar before in his life. He wasn't sure he'd talked to anyone quite like this before.

'How did you decide on Lullbury Bay?'

'We stuck a pin in the map.'

Verity laughed. 'No! Really? That's marvellous.'

'Well, it wasn't quite like that.' Jago smiled. 'We looked at somewhere with a direct train to London. And Mum and Dad's families come from Cornwall so Mum wanted somewhere fairly close to Fowey to travel back there if she needed to. But we did actually stick a pin in a map, only we kept sticking it in until it landed on somewhere we thought we could live,' he admitted.

'And what about your father?'

'He died.' It was still hard to say the words.

'Oh, Jago, I'm so sorry.'

Verity must have said the same phrase over and over in her professional life. Her sympathy, easy and quick but sincere, should have irritated, but it didn't.

He swallowed. 'Thank you. It happened at this time of year. Last December.'

'My, you *have* been through a lot. Bereavement. A change in location and a big change in lifestyle. I'm not surprised you feel unsettled, unsure.'

'I didn't say I was.'

'No, you didn't say it. But I felt it.'

There was a pause. Part of Jago wanted to get up and leave. He didn't want to rake over his emotions. He just wanted to get on with living. Work. Eat. Sleep. But he'd drifted away from so many of his friends back in London, there had been no one to talk things over with. Not wanting to burden his mother, who was also grieving, he'd bottled it all up. He found he couldn't sleep now, and his work ethic had disappeared with it. He'd attempted making an angel inspired by Honor Martin and had only got so far. Instead, he'd made a tiny pendant. Letting his hair fall over his face to hide it, he said, 'My friends in London–'

'Go on.'

'Most were still in the going out having a good time, spending money, sleeping around phase. The others had coupled up, had small children. I was in neither camp. No one else I knew had gone through what I had. They all had living parents.' Now he'd started talking, he couldn't stop. The words tumbled out. He wasn't sure he was making much sense. Verity sat very still, listening. Her job he supposed, and she was good at it.

'Overnight I became the head of the family. With a mother who was in bits and a sister not quite eight and not understanding why her daddy hadn't come home. It made me grow up. Grow up properly, I mean.' He risked a glance at Verity. 'Plus, I was also dealing with my marriage ending. Working and living together in lockdown had just about finished Rose and I off.'

'You've had a lot to deal with, Jago.' Verity's voice was quietly sympathetic. 'Three of the biggest stresses in life.'

'Maybe. With Dad…' he took a breath to calm himself. 'With Dad dying, friends of mine, good friends of mine, just didn't get it. One even saw me coming and crossed the street to get away.' He still couldn't believe Aaron had done that. It had felt cruel and unnecessary, and it still hurt.

'It's a common response, Jago. People don't know how to respond to a grieving person. They don't know what to say. If they express their condolences, they worry they'll remind the person of what happened and won't be able to deal with the emotions brought up. If they don't say anything it feels callous.

Grief is a tricky journey to navigate and not just for the bereaved.'

'You're telling me. *I* don't know how to deal with it. But I could have done with being taken out for a beer, or something. They just ignored me.' He frowned at his trainer, noticing a scuff mark. 'Mum had some good friends, work colleagues, they saw her through the worst of the beginning. Merryn seems to be okay but I worry about what's going on underneath.'

'Children can respond very differently to loss. Sometimes they can be horribly practical, almost matter of fact.'

'Yes.' Jago gave a grim smile. 'Merryn went through a phase of asking questions about the *process*. What would happen at the crem, what the ashes would be like. It felt callous.'

'She was trying to make sense of it all and young children don't always have a social filter. They don't know what questions shouldn't be asked.'

'So what do I do, Verity? How do I get through this? I can't sleep, I'm struggling to work.'

Verity put a hand on his shoulder. 'Give yourself time. You haven't begun to grieve yet. I suspect you've been too busy looking after everyone else.'

'I'm so angry.' He glared at St Winifred who was smiling benevolently down, frozen in stained glass and time. 'I want to get back to myself. Back to how I was.'

Verity remained silent.

'But I won't ever be that person again, will I?'

'Possibly not. But you might become a different person. Maybe an even better one.'

'And how can a god exist if he let such an awful thing happen to us?'

'Ah. One of the biggest questions in faith.' Verity pulled the cuffs of her sweater over her hands to warm them.

'And what's the answer?'

'I can't give you anything pat, except to trust in God.'

'And how have you managed that?' Jago asked bitterly.

'I haven't always. When I was first married, I had a baby who died. I asked all the questions that are running through your head now.'

Jago turned to look properly at her. She was a slight woman with dusty salt-and-pepper brown hair. She reminded him of a sparrow, drab but quietly busy. Except she had a glow. The sort of glow which comes from someone sure of her place in the world and what she believed in. He had no desire to go down that route, he didn't want to find God, but he envied her certainty.

She smiled but he saw the pain. 'I had some of my blackest times. I berated God, I raged at Him, asking all the questions you are now. Eventually, after some time, He answered. I opened my mind and my heart and listened and heard.' She paused, her lips twisting. 'But that was me. That was my path through the grief. It's different for everyone. It'll be very different for you.'

He grimaced.

'And I'm sorry if that's not very comforting, not what you want to hear, but you've made the first step in your grief by coming here.' When he began to protest she chuckled. 'I don't mean to find God, although I'd be delighted if it was a by-product. I mean that you were so willing to open your heart to me, another human being and a stranger.'

'I don't have another option.'

'Ouch!' Verity smiled.

'Sorry. I didn't mean it to come out quite as ungraciously.'

'No offence taken. Be easy on yourself. Grief is knackering.'

He started. 'Are vicars supposed to use that word?'

'I've no idea,' she said cheerfully, 'but this one does. It's true though. Nothing so exhausting as grief. Coupled with all you've been through, plus you're not sleeping, it's not surprising you're feeling at a loss. My practical advice would be to get yourself checked over by the doctor. Get some pills to make you sleep or, if that's not your thing, go for long walks along the cliff tops. The sea air round here is famous for its ability to knock you for six. Pop by the church to talk to Winnie whenever you feel the urge, I try to keep the church open as much as I can. My number's on the noticeboard in the porch if you want to talk again. Or knock on the vicarage door if you ever fancy a coffee. It's only next door. I'm like a Catholic priest. Whatever you say is in confidence and I'm also non-judgmental and objective. If you give permission, I'll pray for you too.' She held up a hand. 'Don't worry, I'm not on a recruitment drive, although my Bishop tells me I should be. It's my way of being of practical help. The doc gives you drugs, I get on my knees.'

Jago laughed. She wasn't at all his idea of a church person. He wanted to hug her but wasn't sure it was the thing to do. Already he felt lighter, as if by simply unloading a little had eased his path through. 'Thank you.'

She smiled. 'Just doing my job, Jago.'

He wasn't sure it was the exact truth. He sensed she really cared.

'You take care now.' She rose to go. 'Stay with Winnie for as long as you like. She's the patron saint of joy and peace. I hope she brings you some. I have to go now.' She grimaced. 'Meeting. Besides, it's freezing in here. Tell Merryn the answer to her question is, of course he exists, and to make sure she hangs her stocking up and keeps the chimney clear. Oh, and he likes a mince pie and some milk. I'll be hanging up my stocking and she can come to the vicarage to check.' Then she left.

He sat for some time, staring at St Winifred, feeling a peace settle round him. A peace he hadn't felt for a very long time. He breathed out, watching his breath mist in the frigid air and turn yellow and crimson in the light pouring through the stained-glass window. 'Thank you, Winnie,' he said. 'You've been a great help.' He got up to leave and, as he did so, he could swear the saint winked.

CHAPTER 7

'STEP INTO CHRISTMAS' – ELTON JOHN

Monday 6th December

In an attempt to take Verity's advice on board, Jago decided to get some exercise. He'd never been a fan of gyms, so he took to walking around. It was good to explore and to get his bearings.

Lullbury Bay was cut into two parts, with the harbour and Christmas Tree Cottage at one end of the long promenade and the shops at the other. Both had steep narrow roads climbing up to the main road beyond. The main street served as the bus route to Axminster and the train station, and had a fair smattering of shops, including a gallery which he investigated with interest. To give his thighs time to recover from the steep hills, he strolled on the beach, unable to resist picking up shells and sea glass, adding to the collection on the kitchen windowsill. The shifting colours in the sea and sky fascinated him. As did the chasing clouds and the magical reflections on the wet sand at low tide. It was almost too much for his senses to cope with, but it was awakening his artistic instinct.

One walk took him along the cliff tops towards a nature reserve and a National Trust shop housed in a utilitarian hut. It was open and decorated with heavy swathes of gold tinsel and a miniature Christmas tree so he stopped, grabbed a Styrofoam cup of tea and some iced biscuits in the shape of snowmen, and enjoyed the view. From here, he could see a vast open expanse of churning sea and the narrow fingernail stretch of golden beach below. It was windy out at sea today, and the white horses were galloping in.

As he sat and made some rapid sketches, several dog walkers joined him and made small talk. Petting one exuberant but charming Staffordshire Bull Terrier, he thought a dog companion would be a good idea. He made a note to discuss breeds with Avril when he got home. It was important to find the right breed and the right breeder. He wanted to make it right for Merryn. For all of them. He'd enjoy having a dog too, especially as a companion on walks like this. Although breezy, it was no hardship to sit in the sun on the bench outside the hut, sipping tea and enjoying the view which was spread out before him. The Staffy owners departed and he was left on his own. Sitting motionless, he was enraptured as several rabbits emerged from the gorse scrub. Watching them with a smile on his face, he was enchanted as a small roe deer joined them. The sight soothed his soul. Surrounded by the soft green of plant life and the silver-blue of the sky and sea, his city life had never seemed so far away. He had no desire to chase it. It had been too long since he'd been able to sit and do nothing for a while, and it felt good.

The burden of grief was beginning to lighten. He didn't think he'd ever fully get over losing his father, and in such tragic circumstances, but with Merryn settled at school and Avril disappearing off with her new knitting friends, he felt the weight of responsibility for them shift and ease slightly. Moving to Lullbury Bay was beginning to look like a very good idea.

On his return down the steep lane which ran parallel to the main street, he ventured, out of sheer curiosity, into the less pretty part of town. He was well away from the seafront, the cafés and tourist hot spots near the prom and the souvenir shops which were strung along the high street. Strolling past some tennis courts, he came across a large white block of a building which looked scruffy and unappealing from the outside but which boasted an enormous and proud sign declaring it Lullbury Bay Art School. Thinking it was closed, he made a note of the phone number and walked on.

'Hello, my friend. Can I help you?'

He turned to see a middle-aged man in paint-stained dungarees and a beret addressing him.

'You're welcome to come in for a look-see if you want.' The man stretched out a hand. 'Dave Wiscombe. I'm the bloke in charge although it doesn't seem that way most of the time. Come in. Have a gander.'

'Thanks, I'd love to,' Jago answered, surprising himself with his enthusiasm. It would be good to make contact with the artistic community.

He followed Dave into an entrance hall where there was a tiny reception and a long white-painted corridor. 'What goes on here?'

'Mixture of things. Still building the place up, really, as we get more funding in. At the moment we run a lot of courses. Painting, pottery, photography, graffiti art. We've got studios which we rent out to artists. Plus, we've our jewel in the crown which is our central space. It's big enough for exhibitions. Had one or two very successful ones recently. It's a versatile space, as you'll see and our main earner.' He led Jago along the corridor. 'Some of our work's on show.' He gestured to the walls. 'You can have a wander round afterwards, if you want, take a closer look.'

Jago had a quick glance as he walked. Hung along the white-walled corridor were paintings, black-and-white photographs, and some really skilled pencil drawings. He was impressed.

'We're getting the big space ready for a lantern workshop and then we'll be doing the Christmas Craft Fayre, so the main studio doesn't look up to much at the moment, but I can show you the pottery room and some of the other spaces. We've got a decent staff room too. What are you? Painter? Sculptor?'

'How did you guess I did something artistic?'

Dave waggled his brows. 'Oh I dunno, my friend. Wild guess. You taking our number down was a clue.' He grinned and nodded to Jago's hands. 'And you don't get those scars from pressing buttons on a keyboard all day.'

Jago spread his hands out and surveyed them. They were scarred from getting too careless with a glass cutter or soldering iron. His fingertips were calloused from hours of pressing and shaping glass into place and there were nubs on the joints on the first two fingers of his left hand. His fingers were long and slender, and his hands were strong, but no one could say they were pretty. 'I make ornamental glass objects. Decorative stuff. Light catchers.'

'Do you now?' Dave said, sounding interested. 'You don't fancy a table at the Fayre, do you? We've had someone drop out, so we've got a spare. We've got, amongst others, painters, weavers, a wood craftsman, a couple of ceramicists, someone selling knitwear, a candle maker, but no one selling any glassware.'

Jago thought rapidly. It would mean unpacking a few dozen boxes, sorting through some stock and digging out the Christmas-themed stuff but it was too big an opportunity to miss. 'Yes, I'll take you up on that. I'd be delighted. Thank you. Weird. I wandered into this part of town by accident. It seems like fate I should stumble on you.'

Dave laughed. 'Things happen like that a lot in this town. Got any pictures of your work to show me?'

Jago got out his phone and scrolled through a few examples.

'Looks good, although it's difficult to see the quality on a phone. Reckon they'd sell a bundle at the Craft Fayre though. What's your name and I'll book you in. Got a card on you?'

'No card I'm afraid, but I can drop one or two examples of my work in if you like. Give you a better idea of what I do. I'm Jago Pengethley.'

Dave started. 'I know your work! You're London-based, aren't you? I was up town seeing a young friend of mine and I saw your glass panels in the gallery he's got some of his paintings in. Nice work, my friend. You might be too expensive for a small-town Christmas Craft Fayre though.'

'That's me. You're talking about the gallery in Islington, aren't you?' Jago laughed deprecatingly. 'Adya took several of my window panels. That's my high-end stuff though. I got a few commissions off them. I was very grateful to her.'

Dave nodded, thoughtfully. 'She knows her stuff, does Adya. Doesn't take any old rubbish.'

'At the moment, though, I'm just making the smaller objects. My bread-and-butter stuff. I've just moved into Lullbury Bay so I'm based in the south west now. In fact, I'm looking for studio space. I'd like to make more of the large stained-glass pieces, but I need a bigger place than I've got at home to do it.' The statement was uttered before he'd even formulated the thought properly. He liked Dave, had immediately taken to him and a workshop atmosphere might appeal. He spent much of his time working alone, it would be inspiring to work alongside other creatives. It might even ignite his work ethic which was still sluggish.

'Studio space? We can rent you space, my friend. We'd be delighted to. Come and have a look.'

Jago followed Dave, a slight smile playing about his mouth. The gut feeling that the encounter was fate was growing. Dave showed him the available workshop which, even on this silvered December afternoon, was flooded with light. It was a large square shape, completely empty and painted white. Jago stood in the middle, envisaging his glass kiln along one wall, his set of glass storage drawers on the other, a large worktable in the middle. There were even hooks on the wall next to the door where he could hang his goggles and aprons when not in use. It was perfect.

'Is the site secure? Some of my gear is expensive. I mean, it's insured but it's a pain if your kit gets stolen.'

Dave nodded. 'All work rooms are lockable and we've got CCTV on all the obvious access points and motion sensor lighting on the car park now.' He gave a rueful grin. 'Sacrificed re-tarmacking the car park to get it in, so watch your tyres on the potholes if you drive. I'll admit we're not in the most salubrious part of town, but it's generally a low-crime area. We don't get much hassle. A few of the tourists get drunk and lairy in the summer but they don't know we're here, so we're left in peace. And the School is a busy place, there's always someone around, evenings and weekends included.'

'Sounds great.'

'Come and see the main space then.'

Dave showed Jago into a large hall which was bare except for lines of naked trestle tables. The double-height ceiling, white walls and intense light begged for some glass art to be hung.

'I'll definitely say yes to both if I may. Yes, to the studio space but also to the Craft Fayre. I've a workspace at home but it's only suitable for the smaller stuff. I'd like to take on more commissions but I've,' he hesitated, 'had a quiet period over the past year. Need to build up my client base again.'

Dave shook his hand. 'Consider it done, Jago. Great to have you on board. You've got my number? Drop me your deets and I'll add you to the programme. It'll be mostly Christmas shoppers at the Fayre, but it'll be a good way to get your name out there in the local scene. We're quite a crafty lot here in west Dorset.'

Jago thanked Dave and, after having a more thorough look around the centre, exited to find darkness had drifted down. He walked back towards the town centre, keeping up a brisk pace as it was now bone-chillingly cold. He had a quick browse along the high street. The lit shop windows were like beacons of hope against the dank, secretive closing-at-the-end-of-the-day feel to the evening. He rechecked the town gallery and one or two of the craft shops. One sold some good silver jewellery and some high-end decorative items. He promised himself he'd call in and try to persuade them to take some of his stuff. Smiling, he decided it had been a good day.

He walked downhill to the bottom end of the high street, where it met the square and the promenade which led off it. Here the pavement split into two parts, the higher one with shops and the lower, narrower pavement, leading to the beginnings of the prom. In the square, a magnificent Christmas tree was already in situ, awaiting the lights switch on ceremony.

He went to stand on the raised part, at the top of some steps, which looked over the prom below. Standing against the railings, he gazed over the sea and to the Dorset coast beyond in the east. He watched as car headlights dipped and rose on the coast road. Someone driving home after a long day at work, maybe. It was calmer now, the wind having dropped slightly with the tide. All was inky dark with only the slightest glimmer of lighter sky clinging on in the west. Below him, he could hear the sea shushing in the darkness. One or two dog walkers passed him, but, apart from that, all was quiet. It all felt very different to the closed-in high-buzz city vibe he'd left behind.

The dark, shifting water pulled at his thoughts and his good mood deserted him. He shivered. It had been night when his father had died. Jago shuddered at the thought of his father helpless in the freezing treacherous waters of the Thames. It was why they had ended up living by the coast. His mother couldn't cope with the sight of the river gleaming sluggishly through the city. She'd needed to get away. He was glad the water here smelled different, fresh and briny. Invigorating. But he knew, because of the presence of the RNLI station on the harbour, the station they all pretended to ignore, that these waters were dangerous too. He blew out a bitter breath. If only people learned to respect the water more. For an island race, its population had forgotten its instinctive relationship to the sea. Feeling his mood dip, he shut his mind off. He refused to think about it. Enough, he thought. He didn't want to ruin what had been a positive day by dwelling on it any further. Turning sharply away, he collided with someone running up the steps.

'I'm sorry.' He caught her by the arms to stop her slipping on the wet cobbles. 'I'm really sorry. Wasn't looking where I was going.'

'Hello, Mr Pengethley.'

It was Honor Martin. His mood lifted instantly at the sight of her. It was as if she brought sunshine into the darkest of hours.

'Honor! Hi. And please call me Jago. Sorry again. I was lost in the view.'

'I can understand why. There's something special about the sea at night, isn't there?'

'There can be.'

'Were you on the way home?'

'No, actually.' He made the decision instantly. He didn't want the day to end quite yet. 'I was heading for something to eat. Could you recommend anywhere? I don't know the town very well yet.'

Honor wrinkled her nose as she thought. He was entranced and had a sudden urge to kiss the little crease between her nose and brow.

'What sort of food did you have in mind? There's not a huge amount open at this time of year.'

'Pub food in front of a roaring fire.' He shivered as a lick of breeze slid down the neck of his Barbour. The wind was getting up again.

'The Ship is good.'

'I'm after comfort food.'

'In which case The Ship is the perfect place. Its steak pies are the best sort of comfort food.' She pulled her collar up around her face and hunched her shoulders into it. 'And it's the right time of year for it.' She grinned, her nose looking pink with cold. 'Lenny the landlord likes to have the fire lit too. Ooh, it's making me hungry just thinking about it!'

'Would you like to join me?' he blurted out. *Where had that come from?* He fully expected her to reject him.

He saw her hesitate for a second, the nose wrinkle repeated itself as thoughts chased across her face. Then her shoulders dropped as she made her decision.

'Do you know, I'd love to. It gets to this stage of term when I really can't be bothered to go home and cook.'

His relief at her acceptance filled him with a warm glow and his good mood returned. What was this all about? He hardly knew her. But he wanted to. 'Let me just make a quick phone call and then you can show me where it is.' Honor nodded and moved away. He assumed to give him some privacy. He liked her thoughtfulness.

Turning back to the sea, he clicked on the home number. 'Hi, Mum, don't worry about cooking for me, I'm grabbing something while I'm out. Oh, you haven't? Good. What? Yes, it's been a really good day.' He glanced at Honor who was staring intently into Seasalt's window display. 'And it looks like it might be getting even better. Yes, I do sound more cheerful, don't I? Catch up when I get in. Bye. Love you.'

CHAPTER 8

'WARM THIS WINTER' – GABRIELLA CILMI

Honor led him up the hilly main road and along a narrow alleyway which led to an old coaching inn. 'Not many people remember this is here,' she explained, 'so it'll be quiet.'

When they entered the relief from getting out of the cold was immediate. They stood, blinking in the dim light, letting the cosy pub wrap its comfort around them.

Honor made her way to the bar and introduced Jago to a wiry, freckled man in a Motörhead T-shirt. After the introductions had been made and drinks bought, she asked, 'Lenny, can we have a table to warm us up and we'd like to eat, if that's okay?'

Lenny grinned, showing gappy teeth, and nodded to a table just the right distance away from the roaring fire in the enormous inglenook. 'Limited as to what's on offer tonight but I can do you a couple of steak pies and triple-cooked chips. That do you?'

'Perfect,' they chorused and grinned daftly at one another.

'No probs. I'll bring your drinks over. Go and get yourselves warmed up. Cold one tonight.'

After divesting themselves of all the outer layers of winter clothes they were both wearing, they settled at the table and had sat down just as Lenny brought their drinks.

Clinking his pint of Black Ven stout against her glass of mulled wine, Jago said, 'This is just perfect, isn't it? I had no idea it was here. Look at the thickness of those walls. The place must be eighteenth century at least.'

Honor smiled at his enthusiasm. 'It's probably older. Medieval in origin. Lullbury Bay was once a medieval port which traded cloth with Flanders. Lots of the bigger and more important buildings in town have medieval foundations.'

'I didn't know Lullbury Bay was an important port. The harbour doesn't look big enough.'

'It used to be, but that was an awfully long time ago. When the ships got too big for the harbour the town went into decline. Tourism saved it in the early nineteenth century. The fashion for sea-bathing crept along the coast from Weymouth. Since then, it's been reliant on tourists. There are a few local employers, there's a computer company and the local paper of course, but it mostly trades in buckets and spades nowadays.' Honor sipped her wine and grimaced. She put her glass down with a chink and looked mortified. 'I'm so sorry. There are some days I simply can't switch the teacher in me off.'

He laughed. 'Please don't be sorry. It's fascinating learning about where you live. I suppose you teach it as a topic?'

She nodded. 'Local history module. And you're right, it is interesting if you're into that sort of thing. And, if you are, I'd recommend a visit to the town museum. It's really good.' She picked up her glass again. 'What do you do, Jago?'

Jago told her. He got out his phone to show her the pictures of his light-catchers.

'They're so pretty! How do you make them?'

'I draw a design, then make the templates and cut the glass. Then the parts are all fused together using solder.'

'I'm sure there's a lot more to it than that.'

Jago grinned, deprecatingly. 'Well, maybe. I'd be happy to show you sometime.'

'I'd like that.' He watched, fascinated, as a blush stole over her features. She handed his phone back hurriedly and said, all in a rush, 'I love the little robins and the stars. They'd make great Christmas presents.'

'So did Dave at the Art School. He's offered me a table at the Christmas Craft Fayre.'

'It all sounds very promising. It must be very satisfying having a talent like yours. To create something with your hands.' The blush deepened and she picked up her wine and drank deeply.

'It is but I've let things slide a little lately.'

'Moving house takes a lot of time and energy.' Honor's voice was warm and sympathetic.

'I'm hoping the Fayre will give me the motivation I need. And then, after Christmas, I aim to go back to making my large panels. I looked at a space in the School which I could use.' The more Jago said it, the more excited he got. His mojo was finally returning. He scrolled through his phone and showed Honor the glass panels on exhibition at the gallery in Islington. He was trying not to show off but something deep inside him was desperate to impress her. 'The technique for these is the same as the one used to make stained-glass windows, like in the church here. An ancient craft using lead to fix the glass pieces in place.'

'Oh my goodness, they're stunning!' Honor's eyes went wide. 'Why did you stop making them?'

'Oh, various reasons.' He paused, not wanting to share the crisis in confidence he'd suffered after his father had died. He'd used the excuse of his kit being in storage to avoid working but really it was his nerve which had failed. Nothing about what he did had importance after his father's death. Settling for a practical answer, he said, 'The most pressing being space. I need a big space to make this stuff. I've a workstation at home in the attic for the small items but need a bit of elbow room for the stained-glass proper. My kit takes up a lot of room too.'

'I can imagine. And the School can provide that?'

He nodded. 'It's perfect. I'm hoping to get it all organised in the new year.'

'A new year. A new start,' she said, brightly.

He gazed at her. At her shining optimism. 'You don't know how true those words are.'

She frowned and he could see she wanted to ask more but, luckily, their food arrived and for a few moments they concentrated on passing each other the salt and vinegar, sorting out cutlery and eating.

'It's a big move,' she said, spearing a chip with enthusiasm. 'You've not just moved house, but you've moved area and lifestyle too. I'm sure you must have been busy. No regrets though?'

Jago contemplated her smooth skin and sparkling blue eyes. 'None so far.' He cut into his pie, enjoying how the rich gravy oozed out. 'This is delicious. Just what I needed. I hadn't realised I'd got so cold.'

'December's like that here. The temperature isn't low but it's the damp. It has a way of seeping into the bones. Catches you unawares.'

'Are you local?'

'Born and bred is the saying. No. I'm not local. I'm another blow-in. I'm from Worcester. My family have been coming to this area for holidays for as long as I can remember. One of the wonderful things about teaching is it's a portable skill. Once I'd trained and got some experience under my belt, I began looking for posts in Devon and Dorset. I've been here about ten years now.'

'And you'd never go back to the Midlands?'

'I don't think so. Think I'm here to stay. The place has a way of getting under your skin. Teaching in a small community can have its tensions, but it's amazingly rewarding too. I get to know families really well as I teach brothers and sisters, their cousins too.' She pulled a face. 'Although I'm beginning to think I've been here for a little too long now, I had an ex-pupil bring in her baby today. That was a shock.'

'I can imagine. She must be a young mum though.'

'Yes. Very.'

'My own had me when she was only nineteen. Mum and Dad were childhood sweethearts. Began going out at school and got married at twenty.'

'Oh, that's lovely. Family's so important. Are you close to them?'

Jago hesitated. He didn't want to bring the mood down by explaining about his father. 'To my mother, yes. What about you?'

She nodded vigorously. 'Oh yes. They still live in Worcester so it's not too far to drive to see them and they make every excuse to come down to visit, especially in the summer. I have a sister too, and she has family of her own now. Another baby due soon.'

'My sister drives me insane sometimes but I'm very fond of her.' He raised his glass again. 'To sisters!'

Honor raised hers to meet it. 'To sisters,' she said with a grin.

They ate in silence for some time. Around them the pub gradually got busier. They weren't the only ones seeking warmth and succour on a cold night. Quiet conversation and clinking of cutlery filled the space as people ate. In the corner near the fireplace, a Christmas tree glowed with gold tinsel and flashing red lights, and in the background the Elton John classic Christmas song followed Slade.

Eventually Jago sat back, replete. 'That was so good. I must bring the family in.'

'The Ship's pies have a reputation and sometimes it's the only thing that will hit the spot,' Honor answered. 'I've been too busy to eat at all today so it was much-needed. Thank you for saving me from eating on my own.'

'The pleasure's all mine. Why have you been so busy?'

'On top of all the usual madness that is Christmas in a primary school, we had another rehearsal for the nativity this afternoon. It was absolute chaos. I was trying to herd thirty Reception age angels at one point. They were all over the place.' She sighed and then giggled happily. 'I love it though. There's something very magical about working in a primary school at this time of year.'

'I can't wait to see it.' It was true. He *was* looking forward to seeing it – and he couldn't believe it. 'Merryn's talked of little else. That is, when she's not pestering us for a dog.'

'A dog?'

Jago filled her in as their plates were cleared and replaced by coffee.

Honor sat back, nursing her cup. 'She's a sensible girl. I think, for once, you can believe the "I'll look after it" promises.' Putting her cup down, she glanced at her watch. 'Oh my goodness, is that the time? The evening's flown. I really must go,' she added regretfully. 'At this end of term, I can't manage with anything less than nine hours of sleep. There's a reason teachers have a reputation for being boring. We're too tired to be anything else!'

Jago laughed. He couldn't imagine anyone less boring. She had a slightly old-fashioned quality he found endearing, but he'd never think she was boring. He got up and paid at the bar, refusing her offer to contribute. 'You can treat me next time,' he said and was perturbed when she looked uncomfortable. 'Walk me home? I'm heading down the high street and then along the prom.' He pulled a face. 'It's scary in the dark.'

She giggled. 'I can go as far as the bottom of the hill but no further. You'll need to pull on your big boy pants and walk along the prom all on your own.'

As they stood at the pub door, putting on coats and scarves and putting off leaving, Jago looked up. Some wag had hung a sprig of mistletoe over the door. For a second he considered using it as an excuse to kiss her then dismissed the idea as crass.

Honor followed his eyes, blushed furiously and became very busy tugging on her woolly hat.

The cold air, when it hit them, made them gasp. They didn't talk as they marched downhill and, all too soon, she pointed out the narrow lane off the high street that led to her flat.

'Are you sure I can't take you all the way?' He didn't want to leave her, didn't want to end the evening.

'Quite sure.' She smiled up at him. 'Lullbury Bay's a safe place and it's not late. Besides, I've taught most of the teenagers who hang around. They see "Miss" coming and scarper.'

He laughed and then didn't know what to say. 'Well goodnight then.'

There was a horrible pause. Neither of them knew what to do next. Eventually, Honor put out her hand and they shook awkwardly. 'Thanks for a lovely evening.'

'You're welcome. Thank you for keeping me company. I've really enjoyed it, Honor. Goodnight.' He turned to go.

Honor stomped bad-temperedly along the lane, cursing under her breath with a very out of character venom. A black and white cat approached, tail curling, looking for some fuss. It took one look at her and fled, disappearing into the shadows.

Oh, why was Jago so wonderful? She seethed silently. He'd been brilliantly easy to talk to and *interesting*. She'd loved hearing about his ambitions for the new year. He'd listened to what she had to say, too, seeming to hang on her every word. Although, goodness knows why. Why had she bored on about local history? Good going, Honor. Way to go! Why hadn't she scintillated with wisecracks and clever zesty remarks? Instead, she'd gone on about Lullbury Bay's history and the dull routines at a primary school. And she'd even *told* him she was boring! She kicked at a pebble and stubbed her toe. Ouch! Now she had a sore foot as well as a foul temper. Oh, he was so clever, talented and close to his family. He was about as perfect a man for her as possible. A dream man. And he was so *sexy*! At one point she'd found herself staring, fixated, at his long fingers, feeling long forgotten and unaccustomed lust heating her. If he had even slightly kissed her under the mistletoe she would have responded, and she was shocked by how much she wanted to. It had been a wonderful evening. She had a glow inside that had nothing to do with good food and drinking mulled wine. She also had an awakened sexual longing and a bad temper to boot.

Unlocking the front door and slamming it behind her, she ran up the stairs to her flat. Cursing all the while that, while Lullbury Bay may be full of gorgeous men, they all seemed to be firmly attached. Still in her coat, she threw herself onto the bed, lay on her back, and stared furiously at the ceiling.

She'd caught a snatch of the phone call he'd made before they'd walked up to the pub. She hadn't meant to; the wind had carried his words. He'd told the person on the other end of the call, she assumed it had been Avril, he loved her. She deflated. A wistful sadness gradually replaced the excited horniness and left her feeling flat.

She blew out a gusty breath. 'Dangerous waters, Honor my girl.' She addressed the navy-blue lampshade and the glittery handmade paper chain decoration that hung from it. 'You simply cannot, absolutely *cannot* develop feelings for a parent no matter how gorgeous he is and especially one who is obviously so happily married.' Closing her eyes to ward off any thoughts of how lovely Jago Pengethley was, a vision of his sexy green eyes and smooth skin flooded her imagination. Oh, why did he have to be so *nice*? She thrummed her heels on the bed in frustration.

'Repeat after me, Honor Martin, you will *not* fall in love with Jago Pengethley!'

As her downstairs neighbour banged on his ceiling to complain about the noise, she repeated it three more times for good measure.

CHAPTER 9

'THE HOLLY AND THE IVY' – TRAD.

Saturday 11th December

The Pengethleys' car rattled along the pot-holed track and parked up on a gravel drive in front of a dilapidated thatched house. An oversized wreath made of prickly holly with shiny red berries and dripping with variegated ivy hung on the front door. The air hung heavy with a hoar frost and when they got out of the car, their breath misted in the cold. Everything was iced-white and it felt very Christmassy. Spotting a sign pointing them around the back of the house, they followed it, with Merryn bouncing along in excitement and tugging on Avril's hand.

'Amazing house,' Jago said. 'I bet it's older than it looks.'

'Aw, Jags, the house is *boring*, I want to see the animals. Do you know they've got reindeer?' Merryn's face was aglow. 'Real live reindeer!'

Tom strode out of a door in the back of the house and intercepted them. He was wearing muddy overalls and a Santa hat perched incongruously on his head. 'Well, if isn't my favourite animal expert.' He ruffled Merryn's hair. 'How are you doing?'

'We've come to visit like you told us to.'

'Merryn!' Avril said, scandalised. 'Don't you mean as we were invited to?' She stretched out a hand. 'I'm Avril Pengethley. Pleased to meet you.'

Tom shook it, grinning broadly. 'Nice to meet you. I've heard all about you from Lucie and Ellie. Ellie's my sister,' he added as an explanation. 'One thing you'll find out about Lullbury Bay is that everyone is either related to one another or knows one another.'

'You're Ellie's brother?' Avril exclaimed. 'She was absolutely brilliant when negotiating our purchase. I'm so glad to meet you. Please, will you pass on my thanks? I'll pop in with a box of biscuits or something as a proper thank you soon, but I just haven't had time yet.'

'I'll pass on the message,' he said with a broad smile, 'but I'm not surprised she did a good job. That's my Ellie,' he said, proudly. 'Well, welcome to Lullbury Bay Farm. Good to see you've all got wellies on, it can get muddy round here, especially in December.' He rubbed his hands together. 'Going colder too, so you need your hats and coats. Where would you like to begin?'

'Reindeers. Reindeers. REINDEERS!' yelled Merryn.

'Think that's decided it then. Come on, Merryn, let's find Elsie and Morag the reindeers. I like your scarf with the Christmas pudding pattern, by the way.'

'Mum knitted it for me. She's ever so clever.'

The sanctuary was, quite clearly, a work in progress. It mostly consisted of fields with ramshackle stables and pens housing a few animals. But they all looked happy and well-cared-for and even the sullen mist which was lying low on the ground and the chill didn't dent Merryn's enthusiasm or insistence she see every single creature.

Reindeers' noses stroked, alpacas admired and the goats and ducks visited, the guinea pigs were last on the tour. They were housed on the lawn at the back of the house and nearest to it.

There were a number of the stubby little creatures, all scampering about in a long pen put over a grassy area. At one end was a robust 'house' to protect them from the cold and predators. When Tom demonstrated how to feed them a seasonal carrot and some sprout cuttings, lots more ran out, tumbling over each other, squealing and chattering and bringing most of their straw bedding with them.

'They're so cute,' Avril smiled. 'Have to say I've a weakness for guinea pigs.'

'Unfortunately, so does Mr Fox. We have to make sure they're all securely locked in for the night,' Tom explained. 'The tan and white piggie is really friendly. She won't mind you picking her up for a cuddle. When I've had a stressful day, this is where I head for. Nothing beats a guinea pig cuddle for putting things into perspective.'

Avril bent down and picked up the guinea pig, getting Merryn to sit on an upturned bucket so she could take the little creature on her lap.

While Avril and Merryn were preoccupied, Tom took Jago to one side. 'Don't know if I'm speaking out of turn here but I've had a dog come in and I thought of you all. I'd never normally rehome an animal just before Christmas, especially a dog, but I think this might be a good fit.'

Jago thought of how his walks seemed purposeless without a dog, of the inviting flat beach minutes from the cottage where it could run around. If Merryn bored of it, which he doubted, he'd be happy to take it on. In fact, ever since the conversation with Tom in the café, the idea had seemed more and more appealing. 'Tell me more.'

'She's not a tiny puppy. About nine months old, some cocker in her, maybe a bit of springer, who knows. She's been rescued from a puppy farm. Got a slightly deformed front leg but it doesn't affect her, except from giving her an endearing limp. There are no medical implications we can see, although obviously pet insurance would be a good idea. Because of it they couldn't sell her on and we got to her in time before they started breeding from her. She's a sweet little thing. Will need some training but she's clever, she'll pick things up quickly and she's already clean in the house.' He pulled a rueful face. 'Well, mostly, that is. I can distract Merryn if you want to talk to your mum about it. It's just that we've got her here now if you want to meet her.'

'It's all a bit sudden, Tom, we were going to get Christmas out of the way before we started looking. We wanted to research a breeder and what type of dog would suit us.'

Tom blew out a breath. 'I understand.' He looked at his feet. 'And, as I say, I'd normally never rehome a dog at this time of year, but this little thing needs someone loving to look after her.' He met Jago's eyes. 'She's only ever known a dark barn and hardly any affection but she's as gentle as anything. I wouldn't rehome her with children if I thought otherwise.' He stopped, obviously on the verge of tears. In the distance, a cockerel crowed, and a braying donkey joined in. 'It never fails to amaze me how they can come through the worst of neglect and still want to lick your hand.'

Jago was moved. He nodded. 'Okay, I'll talk it over with Mum. Thanks, Tom.' He watched thoughtfully as Tom took Merryn off with the promise of collecting eggs from the chickens. Could they take on a rescue dog? What if it didn't work out? What if they didn't know how to train it? Turning to Avril who had her arms full of guinea pig, he repeated what Tom had just suggested.

'I'm not sure, Jago. It all seems too much of a rush.' She put the animal back gently in its run and dusted straw off her hands. 'Although I don't mind about having to train her up, we had a springer as a kid so I can remember the basics, but we haven't a thing ready.'

'We don't but we can get that sorted. Merryn's done enough research on the subject.' He grinned. 'She's written a list. We just need to do the shopping. I think it's the right thing to do. We've got the first Christmas coming up without Dad,' he hesitated, not wanting to upset his mother. 'It might be a struggle to get through it. At least with a puppy around we'll be kept busy.'

Avril fixed him with a stern look. 'You going to do your fair share of mopping the kitchen floor?'

'I'm happy to chip in with looking after it,' he promised. 'The more I think about it, the more excited I get. I've really enjoyed walking around the area, getting to know it, getting some exercise, but I can see if the weather closes in, I'll find excuses to stop. With a dog, you have to go out.'

'You certainly do, and Merryn won't have time to walk it when she's at school, so it might be down to you. Have you got time to commit around your work?'

Jago watched as a fat wood pigeon landed not far from them and began pecking at guinea-pig feed scattered on the scrubby grass. 'I think,' he began slowly, 'that it would be just the thing to get us through this Christmas. It's not going to be easy, this first one. Mum,' he said, suddenly decisive. 'Let's meet it and then decide. If it's not right, then we'll walk away. Can't do any harm.'

'There speaks the man who's never viewed a litter of puppies!' Avril raised a disbelieving eyebrow. 'And do you think, once Merryn's cuddled a puppy, she'll let go?'

'Point taken.' He gave his mother sidelong glance. 'Might make her Christmas though?'

They found Merryn clutching a basket of eggs and standing by the hen coop. When they explained, Jago took the basket from her as she was quivering with excitement so violent he thought she'd drop them.

Tom led them back to house saying the dog was in the farmhouse being looked after by his mother. He warned Merryn she'd have to be calm and quiet so as not to frighten the puppy. They walked into the kitchen where an older woman was sitting at a huge, scarred table reading a broadsheet newspaper.

'This is my mother, Joan,' he explained. 'She's been keeping an eye on the pup.'

'Hello, greetings all,' she said in a low voice. 'The little one is over here. Hello,' she addressed Merryn. 'You must be the animal whisperer Tom has told me all about. Are you ready to meet her?'

Merryn nodded, wide-eyed.

'Come on then, through to the boot room. She's having a snooze in her bed. Come in quietly though.'

The others followed, standing in the doorway to give Merryn and the dog some space. A scrawny black and white spaniel was curled up, watching with twitchy defensive eyes. Joan knelt on the quarry tiles and beckoned for Merryn to join her by the dog's bed.

'Hello,' Merryn crooned.

The spaniel regarded the little girl, and Merryn sat perfectly still, waiting for the dog to come to her. Everyone held their breath. Time ticked by slowly. Eventually, she was rewarded by a sniff and then a lick and then, a tiny wag of a tail.

'Here,' Joan said gently, 'try a biscuit.'

Merryn held out the treat. The dog wolfed it down, frantically sniffing her bed for crumbs. Finding none, she licked Merryn's hand and then planted two enormous paws on the girl's shoulders and licked her face. Merryn responded by getting into the dog bed and cuddling her.

'Think it might be a match,' Joan said, standing up stiffly. 'You did exactly the right thing. You *are* an animal whisperer. If you ever want a job here at the sanctuary, you know where to come.' She glanced up at the others and said, with tears in her eyes, 'This little thing has been to the ends of hell and back but I think she's found her home.'

Behind him Jago heard his mother sniff.

'I think she has too,' Avril said.

While Merryn played with an increasingly confident puppy,

Joan took them back into the kitchen, made them all tea and distributed more biscuits, this time for human consumption.

'I'm sure Tom's explained she's a sweet little thing,' she said, as she poured tea from an enormous flower-patterned teapot. 'We've worked hard on her potty training and she's nearly there. She can be timid around strange men and new experiences but, once she's got the measure of you, she's fine. She'll soon be bouncing around at home with you all.' She held out a plate of chocolate digestives. 'Lots of socialisation, I think. Just as you would with a new puppy. And, if she shows any nerves, gentle reassuring and lots of treats and, if that doesn't work, take her out of the situation. That would be my advice.'

'We had a springer when I was a child growing up in Cornwall,' Avril said.

'Ah well, you know the spaniel breed then. I mean, they all vary but fundamentally they're all inquisitive, highly intelligent and eat like billy-o,' Joan tapped her nose, 'and have their brains in their noses.'

Avril laughed. 'Oh yes. I remember that about Pip. Pip was my springer. Ever-so biddable until she caught a scent. And then she was off.'

They listened for a minute as the sounds of Merryn trying to teach the puppy to 'give paw' floated through from the boot room.

Joan beamed. 'I think you'll all be very happy. And we're always here to answer any questions, don't forget.'

Tom kept hold of the puppy while they made an emergency dash to a pet superstore and bought a bed, treats, collar and lead, food and everything else needed. In the car on the return trip to the sanctuary to collect her, Merryn decided on a name.

'I wanted to name her Holly,' she announced. 'But that would be too confusing seeing as Holly is my best friend so I think we ought to call her Ivy.'

On the journey back to Christmas Tree Cottage Merryn sat in

the rear cuddling a whimpering dog all the way and talked to her softly.

As they released an anxious-looking dog into the kitchen, Jago said, 'Now remember what Tom and Mrs Catesby said. We don't want to overwhelm her,' he warned. 'Let Ivy settle in her bed, have a drink and a sniff around. Maybe, in a minute, we'll take her out in the garden to see if she needs a wee.'

Avril, hands on hips, looked at them all. 'Just as well we have tiles on the kitchen floor, is all I can say.'

'Why, Mum?' Merryn asked.

As Ivy sniffed around and then squatted, the reason became apparent.

CHAPTER 10

'LAST CHRISTMAS' – WHAM

Tuesday 14th December

The little dog settled in quickly. She soon learned to toilet outside and, thankfully, seemed to understand having a collar on. She wasn't keen on being lead walked and pulled like a train, but they solved the issue with a harness. After gaining her trust, Jago soon got used to early morning walks around the harbour walls and on the beach, with a second briefer one when Merryn got out of school.

On a steel-cold morning, when it felt barely light, he walked past the RNLI station to find the door to the boathouse open. It was lit inside and felt too inviting to ignore. Like a moth to flame, he stopped and read the list of rescues chalked up on the board:

Crew launched to two fishermen in water from capsized boat. One taken to hospital suffering from hypothermia.

Crew launched, along with coastguard and search and rescue helicopter, to locate two walkers and one dog cut off by tide. All brought back to shore by lifeboat and safe.

Crew launched to reported swimmer in difficulty.

Jago shivered. He knew there was a group of local women

who swam every morning, but couldn't see the appeal in December. Reading the board and noting the tide times for the day, a wave of longing engulfed him. He missed volunteering with the RNLI. He'd been based at the London Tower Station and had volunteered for them since turning twenty. He missed the adrenaline of a shout, the camaraderie of being part of the crew, the sense of doing something worthwhile. He missed it so much it felt like an actual pain.

A young guy came out to update the chalkboard. He looked to be in his twenties and had spiky jet-black hair. 'Morning,' he said, cheerfully. 'Nice dog.'

Ivy whickered and hid behind Jago's knees. They'd learned she was nervous when meeting all strangers, not just men. Jago was having to work hard with her.

'Hi. She's a bit skittish I'm afraid. A rescue. We've only just got her.'

The man nodded. 'Hold on a sec.' He rubbed out the details about the swimmer. 'False alarm,' he added as explanation and disappeared. When he returned he had a handful of dog treats. 'We keep some by just in case we get a call out to rescue a dog. Most of the time they're too distressed to take one but occasionally it can win them round. Would your dog like one? I'm Jamie by the way.'

'Hi, Jamie. I'm Jago. This is Ivy. You can try, I'm not sure how you'll get on.'

He watched as Jamie crouched and offered a biscuit. 'Hey there, little Ivy. See I'm not scary.' He continued making soothing, nonsensical noises until Ivy decided he was no threat and took the treat. She even submitted to a chin scratch.

'Thanks,' Jago said. 'That'll help her socialisation. We've no idea what she's been through but we're pretty sure she was mistreated at the hands of a man. You're very patient,' he added, admiringly.

Jamie stood up. 'I like dogs. Would love one of my own but

haven't the time. I come across one or two when I'm volunteering. Then it pays to have patience.' He grinned. 'Although a lot of the dogs are far easier than some of the humans we rescue.'

'Tell me about it,' Jago said feelingly. 'I was on a shout when we got a drunk out of the river. Swore and kicked out at us, then gave the paramedics an equally rough time when they tried to get him in the ambulance.'

'You're a volunteer?'

'Was. In London. On the Thames.'

'Wow. Different set of challenges up there. You don't do it anymore?'

Jago shook his head, not elaborating.

'Well, if you ever fancy returning, we can always do with experienced crew members. And, if you want to get to know a few of us, we hang out in The Old Anchor on the harbour here. We're having a carols and mulled wine event too, next week. Come on down and join in. Speaking of which,' Jamie grinned, 'I'd better get Welly Major and Minor out.' When Jago looked mystified, he added, 'Our mascot dogs made out of old yellow wellies. They're a hit with kids. Not as pretty as Ivy here but they attract attention and, more importantly, donations in the bucket. I'll see you around then, maybe in the pub?'

'Maybe.' Jago turned to go but yearned to stay. He felt a desperate tug to go into the office and sign himself up as a volunteer again. He hadn't realised, until this moment, how much he'd missed it. He stayed to watch Jamie put out two 'dogs' created from standard issue RNLI boots. One large, the other smaller. With their four welly feet and a head made out of two more wellies cleverly placed sole to sole, with an eye drawn on, they were endearing.

Putting up a hand in farewell, he walked to the furthest most point of the harbour, his mood uncertain. Finding a bench which looked back towards the town, he sat and watched as the day began to wake up. It was very calm but cold, with a fog clinging to the river valley and mist dancing on the tide. Above him a gull called mournfully. He shoved his hands into the pockets of his jacket and buried his nose in the collar. There wasn't much happening. The harbour was deserted, apart from one or two other early-morning dog walkers. No fishing activity going on, either they'd packed up for the winter or had gone out earlier. The only action in the harbour was a man on his yacht doing routine maintenance. His boat boasted a mini Christmas tree attached to its mast complete with fairy lights. The faint sounds of Greg Lake's 'I Believe in Father Christmas' floated over the water from the onboard radio. It almost made him smile.

Jago's thoughts were pulled back to the lifeboat station. As he glanced over, he could see an older woman opening up the shop next to it. Jamie had come out again and the two were having an animated conversation. The woman put a hand to Jamie's arm and bent over laughing at something he said. They looked close, they looked as if they were having fun. It drilled into Jago it was the community life of volunteering he was missing. Was craving.

Working for the lifeboat here would be very different to London, though. He wasn't stupid enough to think there were no dangers lurking in Lullbury Bay but the Thames was dark and treacherous, with swift undertows and hidden dangers. At night it could be lethal. As it had been for his father.

On Kenan Pengethley's last ever shout, he had gone into the water. It was a rule you never entered the water except as a last resort. An absolute last resort. The irony, the enormous irony was it had been his last day on paid duty.

After the awful first few days, when Christmas had been forgotten like so much crumpled wrapping paper, information gradually trickled in. His father, one of the few paid employees of the RNLI, had just handed over his shift and was about to go home. A call had come in. Someone had been seen going in the water off a bridge. Almost simultaneously, the phone had also rung with news that volunteer Dougie Ekua's wife had just gone into labour. Kenan had offered to go in his young colleague's place. One more hurrah before he hung up his boots completely, he'd told the other crew. When the lifeboat had got to the location, the casualty had disappeared underneath a pier. Kenan had gone into the murky icy water and came out without his helmet, his head having taken a fatal blow. The man they rescued, thought to have been a suicide attempt, survived.

As Jago stared across the harbour, while Ivy snuffled fishy smells and fragments of bait caught between the cobbles, he thought back to that Christmas, a year ago.

The presents had lain abandoned under the tree for days until he and Avril felt they had to make some kind of effort for a bewildered Merryn. He and Rose had already split up by then, with the divorce about to go through, so he'd gone back to live at home. As he drove through the wet streets in the days afterwards, the happily blinking lights hung on porches and roofs mocked him with their gaiety. He'd taken his father's presents away and stored them in his room, donating them to a charity shop a few weeks later. He and Avril had held it together as Merryn had opened hers a few days later, but Avril had had to disappear into her bedroom soon after. He'd turned the television up loud to cover the sound of her wailing. It had been an ancient episode of *The Two Ronnies* and it formed the backdrop to the game he and his sister had played. Later, when both were in bed, he'd got properly drunk on his father's favourite whisky and disappeared into welcome oblivion.

The year that followed had been a blur; filled with making plans, putting the house on the market, deciding where to move to, ruthlessly stripping out any belongings of Kenan's. They'd deliberately not given themselves time to think, or the space to grieve, and now it was coming back to haunt them. He saw it sometimes in Avril's unexpected panic at things she used to take in her stride, he saw it in Merryn's endless questioning and her desperation to cling on to anyone who offered her even the slightest show of affection or friendship. Had they done the right thing to uproot and move to somewhere so different? Time would tell.

Wrenching his thoughts away from his father, he watched, moodily, as a woman on the prom opened up her beach hut and began decorating it with Christmas stuff. Even from here he could see she had an enormous box and was taking out baubles and a string of lights. How was it he was living in a town where the beach huts were decorated? It was mad. The beach hut owner was joined by a neighbour who began festooning the open door of his with red tinsel. Then they sat on a couple of deckchairs and shared a flask. While Lullbury Bay was proving to be friendly, it was also eccentric. And it seemed determined to lighten his mood this morning. Maybe it was a place they could make new memories, re-invent themselves? He looked longingly back at the RNLI station. No, he couldn't volunteer. He'd promised his mother he wouldn't. Not ever again. She'd lost a husband, she didn't need to risk losing a son.

CHAPTER 11

'SANTA CLAUS IS COMING TO TOWN' – BRUCE SPRINGSTEEN

Wednesday 15th December

The town heaved with good-natured crowds thronging the high street. The shops were open late with light spilling onto the pavements attracting people to gaze on the Christmas displays, their faces aglow with excitement and cold. Vendors were selling fluorescent sticks, candy floss, cheap felt Santa hats, and burgers. Lullbury Bay was out in force to welcome Father Christmas and to celebrate the town's Christmas lights being switched on.

The main road had been closed off to traffic which was just as well as the narrow pavements couldn't accommodate the crowds. Being able to wander into the main road sent children giddy with the freedom.

Honor pulled her woolly hat down over her ears and wrapped her sparkly red scarf around her neck more tightly. When she breathed out, her breath misted in front of her before spiralling up and disappearing into the clear starlit night. Her toes, in her suede boots, had lost all feeling, but she wouldn't have missed this evening for anything. It was the time the little town came alive with all the lights and decorations and Christmas really began. And she loved it.

It was cold. Unusually so. They'd even had a thick frost that morning. The children's excitement had tipped over at the pitiful amount of white stuff in the playground which they'd tried to scrape together enough for snowballs. They hardly ever had snow at the seaside, although they'd had a good covering a couple of years ago. She stamped her feet to recover some feeling and smiled at a parent from school who walked past.

'Honor!'

Turning, she saw her friend Tamara run up. Hugging her, she exclaimed, 'You're back! When did you get back into town?'

'Last night. Sailed around the Med and that's me finished until Christmas Eve.'

Tamara was a singer on cruise ships. Always dressed immaculately, tonight she had her blonde hair covered by an enormous faux-fur hat and was wearing a red coat with faux-fur collar and cuffs. She wore bright-red lipstick and had a nose to match.

Honor linked her arm. 'So you're around for a few days then?'

Tamara nodded. 'But only until Christmas Eve. Then I've got a job on a cruise ship for Christmas and New Year. Heading to Norway. It'll be fun,' she added, when she saw her friend's face drop. 'Look, I'm not like you, I don't have family to drive home to for Christmas. It's just me so if I can get paid work and have a good time too, what's the biggie?' They began to walk down the hill.

'I'm not going back to Worcester this Christmas,' Honor said. 'Mum and Dad are off on their round-the-world holiday for their fortieth wedding anniversary and Blythe is off to her in-laws. With her baby due in January, she's not up to hosting this year.'

She felt Tamara squeeze her arm. 'Aw, hon, what are you going to do?'

'It's not too bad,' she replied, trying to sound brave. She loved

Christmas with her family. She loved Christmas full stop. 'I'm going up for a couple of days when I finish term before they go. We'll just have our Christmas early, that's all.'

'At least you'll get to see them.'

'Yes, and it'll be fun. And I get to catch up with myself on the day itself. I'm normally so zonked by the time term ends, all I want is my bed.'

'And a hot man, babe!'

'Nothing like that on the horizon unfortunately.'

A small child ran across the road. 'Miss Martin, Miss Martin!'

'Hello, Merryn. Are you excited about the lights switch on?'

'I can't wait,' the little girl exclaimed, jumping up and down. 'I love all the little trees hung on the walls above the shops. They're going to be lit up too and the lights hung across the street. It's going to be ace-erooney!'

Honor laughed, enjoying her enthusiasm. 'It is. And are you going to wait for Father Christmas too? He's coming down the hill on his sleigh apparently.'

'He's not the real one,' Merryn said, scornfully.

'You know every time you say something like that an angel loses its wings,' Tamara said, receiving a dig in the ribs from Honor.

Merryn stared at her, obviously unsure how to take the glamorous woman in red wearing a big furry hat.

'I should know,' Tamara added. 'I'm one of Santa's little helpers.'

Honor dug her in the ribs again. 'Who are you with, Merryn?' she asked, to change the subject. 'Mum?'

'No, she's gone off to do something. She wouldn't tell us what. She was very mistress-y.'

'Mistress-y?'

'Big secret,' she said.

'Oh,' Honor twigged. 'Mysterious.'

'Probably gone to buy my present.' Merryn glared at Tamara.

'I get one from Father Christmas, of course, the *real* one, but I get my main one from Mum.'

'Ah there you are.' Jago jogged up to them. 'Don't run off, Mer, I couldn't see you anywhere. Oh hi!'

'Hello, Jago. Good to see you again. This is my friend Tamara. She's a singer on cruise ships.'

'Are you?' Jago looked interested. Honor didn't blame him. Tamara was drop-dead gorgeous. 'What sort of music do you sing?'

Tamara shrugged. 'Everything really. I'd really like to get into a girl group. I adore the Puppini Sisters.'

'Oh yeah. I saw them at Ronnie Scott's a while back. I love all that close harmony stuff. Are you both walking down to the tree in the square for the light switching on ceremony? I was planning on standing at the top of the steps overlooking the corner of the prom, we should get a great view of Santa when he comes. Come on, munchkin,' he said to Merryn, 'and no, you can't have a glow stick. I'll treat you to a burger instead. Look, there's not much of a queue at the moment, here's a fiver. Knock yourself out.' He handed over a note and Merryn ran to the stall.

As they passed the alleyway leading to The Ship, he added, 'What I wouldn't give for an excuse to get in there and warm myself by the fire. I had a really good time the other night, Honor. I'd love to do it again sometime.'

Honor felt her face heat and sensed Tamara's eyes on her. 'Yes maybe.' Her throat closed. Partly in panic, partly with longing. She most definitely couldn't have a meal with him again. At least not without his wife and child coming along.

'You've got to love this town,' he continued. 'When we walked past the beach huts on the prom earlier, they were all open and being decorated. Fairy lights, baubles, the lot. One even had a mini train track inside. What's all that about?'

Honor managed a laugh. Thank goodness the conversation had

moved on from their cosy evening in the pub. 'They're getting ready for the competition. The RNLI put on some carols by the lifeboat station and there's a competition for the best-decorated beach hut. Then they all get closed up again until the spring. It's mad, I agree. Some owners really go to town. One year someone set up a fireside with stockings above it and someone playing Father Christmas. He was one of those mime artists, you know, the ones who stay absolutely still and people think they're a statue until they move to a different pose? Frightened the life out of some teenagers when they went past as he called out, "I hope you've been good this year!"'

'Now that I would have liked to see. Do you join in with the carols?'

'Of course. It's another Lullbury Bay tradition. And I like to support the RNLI. I know Jamie, one of the crew. He's Lucie Wiscombe's husband. Lucie from the estate agents, that is. She's a good pal of mine.'

Jago nodded. 'I had a chat with Jamie outside the station. And Wiscombe? I met a Dave Wiscombe over at the Art School when I was looking into renting some space.'

'That's Lucie's uncle. The Wiscombes are a big local family in town. I've taught at least three.' She was distracted as someone called out her name and she waved back at them.

'Another ex-pupil?'

'Alice Ruddick. A girl in my first class at school here. I taught her in Year Six. She's at university but you'll see her working at the café during her holidays.'

'Can it be difficult working and living in the same community?'

Only when you have the hots for one of the parents. 'Erm, occasionally but, when you see a girl like Alice blossom into the clever, confident young woman she is, then it has its rewards.'

Jago looked at her for a second. 'I can imagine,' he said, admiringly.

'Jago, Jags!' yelled Merryn from the burger stall. 'Come and have a burger. Two for six pounds so I need more money.'

'Duty calls.' He raised one sardonic brow. 'She's obviously been paying attention in numeracy! Can I get either of you anything? I'm assuming these burgers are safe to eat?'

'Nothing for me, thanks, although the smell of fried onions is tempting. And yes, they're great burgers. From Sid's Farm Shop. Organic beef,' Honor added, as if to seal the argument.

'Can I tempt you, Tamara?'

'Not with a burger, no,' she said coquettishly, only to receive another elbow in the ribs from Honor.

He joined Merryn at the burger van and tried to stop her squeezing the entire bottle of tomato sauce onto her roll.

Tamara turned to Honor. 'One. Will you stop poking me in the ribs, it's painful! Two. Who is that gorgeous man who was eating you up as if you were the burger slathered in fried onions and slapped between a bread roll?' She fanned herself. 'Jago. What a name. He looks as if he's just stepped off a pirate ship. All those dark curls and lean muscles.'

'Honestly, Tamara, you can't tell he's got lean muscles, he's got a bloomin' Barbour on.'

'Oh, I can *so* tell. And those cheekbones and those long fingers. What does he do? Who is he? And what were you doing snuggling up in The Ship with him?' She took Honor's arm again. 'Spill the beans on the new talent in town, hon.'

'He's called Jago Pengethley. He's a glass artist, he's just moved into Christmas Tree Cottage on Harbour Hill. He's Merryn's dad who is in my class and, most importantly, he's extremely happily married to Merryn's mother. Oh, and we bumped into one another the other evening and grabbed something to eat. It was all perfectly innocent.' If she said it enough, even she'd believe it. But there was nothing innocent in how she was beginning to feel about Jago Pengethley.

'Oh.' Tamara was deflated for a second. But only for a second.

'Are you *sure* he's happily married? I didn't get that vibe from him at all. And, if he's Merryn's dad, why does she call him by his first name?'

'I'm absolutely positive he's very happily married. I've seen him and Avril together. She's lovely and they looked a very happy family unit.'

'But why does the kid call him Jago?'

Honor shrugged. 'Some children do call their parents by their Christian name. Now, come on, before my toes get frostbite, let's go and find a good place to see Santa.'

CHAPTER 12

'CHRISTMAS LIGHTS' – COLDPLAY

Jago and Merryn joined them at their spot at the top of the steps which overlooked the beginning of the prom, but which had a raised view up the high street. Surrounding them, and below them in the square gathered around the huge Christmas tree, was a huge crowd of people and the anticipation was at fever pitch. It looked as if most of the town had turned out. People had come through a long couple of years, with only greyness and illness in view. They needed the childish thrill that was the age-old lighting against the darkest time of year. The excitement was palpable. So was the cold.

Somehow Honor ended up standing next to Jago. She was glad. His bulk cut her off from the biting wind whipping off the sea behind them.

'Can you see?' she heard him yell to Merryn. The sound system had gone into overdrive. 'I Wish it Could be Christmas Everyday' played so loud it was distorted. Honor winced and shrugged ever further into her coat. She didn't think she'd ever feel her ears ever again. Stamping her feet, she regretted her choice of suede boots; she always forgot they weren't very warm, and buried her icy nose in her scarf.

Jago bent and said against her ear, warming it with his breath, 'It's freezing, isn't it? Wish they'd hurry up and switch on the lights.' He looked above him, at the three tiny Christmas trees fixed above Seasalt's shop window. 'It might not be much of a heat source, but we could do with all we can get!'

She grinned. 'Think we might have to endure the mayor's speech first.' She was so cold her voice trembled.

He shook his head. 'Can't hear you.'

She stood on tiptoe and repeated what she'd said.

'Come here,' he indicated. He positioned Merryn on one side and Honor on the other, slightly to the front of him. They huddled together, sharing body warmth and it helped a little. She liked it. She'd been looking after herself for so long, she'd forgotten how nice it was to be protected by a man, even if was only from the cold. The knowledge she was beginning to like Jago, *really* like him, made her shiver again, only this time not because of the chilly weather. She muttered admonishments to herself and hardened her resolve. It just couldn't happen between them, for all sorts of reasons. Even if the feelings were mutual, she was no home wrecker – how could she do that to a nice woman like Avril and little Merryn? Besides, it would be career suicide. In a close-knit community like Lullbury Bay, she had to keep her reputation intact. It was hard enough teaching and living in the same place as it was; the lines became blurred all too often. Any hint of scandal and she'd be forced to move, and she didn't want to do that. Her roots were here and she loved her little adopted seaside town.

At last, there was movement amongst the officials standing at the base of the tree. The sound system cut out and the town crier, looking like a highwayman, in a coat with broad caped shoulders, breeches, boots and tricorn hat shook his hand bell. The crowd cheered.

'Fancy costume,' Honor heard Jago say drily, and she giggled. She put her arms around Merryn who cuddled into her. At last the mayor, in a similar but much warmer-looking full-length coat, his chain of office gleaming in the streetlights, began his address. It went on a while and Honor sensed the crowd getting restless. Eventually, he announced, 'Boys and girls, ladies and gents, the countdown starts now. Ten, nine, eight…' the count roared to its conclusion as the crowd joined in and yelled, 'Three, two, ONE!'

All around them was flooded with light. Each little tree on the walls of the shops flashed with gold and white lights and the main Christmas tree had lights wound all around it with a lit star on top. Icicles of white shimmered in diagonal lines from one side of the high street to another, interspersed with huge silver stars and gold lights filling in the space between.

The crowd gasped then cheered, looking up and admiring the display. 'Here Comes Santa' blasted out of the sound system to announce the arrival of the great man on his sleigh.

'Are those *real* reindeer?' Honor asked as she screwed up her eyes to look up to the top of the hill. 'And is that Tom Catesby leading them? How wonderful.' Tom did indeed look wonderful. Wearing a leather jerkin over a white pullover, with his jeans tucked into knee-length boots, he looked like a cross between a blacksmith and Prince Charming.

Merryn jumped up and down in excitement. 'It *is* Tom! And that's Elsie and Morag,' she explained importantly. 'I met them at the animal sanctuary. Did you know reindeer have really thick coats to keep them warm and they can't see or hear very well but they've got an amazing sense of smell? And they can run really fast, faster than Urain Broke.'

'Usain Bolt,' Jago corrected gently, tweaking her hair.

'And they eat leaves and,' she frowned trying to remember, 'licky stuff.'

'Lichen,' he helped out. 'Not like Usain Bolt then.'

'And did you know male reindeer's antlers fall off in the winter so the reindeer pulling Santa's sleigh are all girls.'

'Quite right too,' Tamara said. 'And if the three wise men had been women, they'd have taken a catering pack of Pampers and a casserole to the Nativity.'

Merryn ignored her. She was on a roll. 'And they click as they walk. It's something in their feet.'

Honor caught Jago's eyes and they laughed. 'What can I say?' she apologised. 'We did a mini animal research project this week.'

They watched as Tom strode down the hill leading the reindeer who, thankfully, seemed unfazed by the jostling crowds and the racket from the sound system. Santa was joined on the sleigh by elves in jaunty green hats and stripey tights, throwing sweets to the children. As the sleigh neared the Christmas tree, Santa looked up and waved, and Jago, Tamara and Honor, feeling like idiots but carried along by the atmosphere, waved back. One elf stood tall and threw a bag of sweets at Jago which he caught skilfully.

'Is that elf wearing stilettoes?' Honor observed.

'One sexy-looking elf,' Jago grinned.

'Got to be Ellie then,' Tamara replied, referring to Tom's sister, known for her short skirts and sky-high heels which were almost as sharp as her business sense. 'Only Ellie would have the nerve to team a naff Christmas elf cozzie with five-inch heels.'

Jago shared out the sweets and they stood, chewing, admiring the just switched-on lights.

'Is it me,' Tamara said slowly, looking up at the lights strung high across the street, 'or do those gold lights look just a bit like y-fronts?'

Honor peered closer. In between each silver star a pattern was made from the gold lights filling in the space. 'They do,' she gasped, beginning to giggle. 'Or maybe hot pants Kylie-style?' A distinct underwear-shaped image had been created, three of each, in intervals along the high street. Gold pants with an edging of twinkly white flashing lights. She began to laugh harder. 'What were they thinking?'

'What's so funny?' Jago asked.

Honor couldn't speak for laughing so pointed.

'What's going on, Miss Martin?'

'I'm sorry, Merryn, Tamara and I are being very silly. It's just that the gold lights look like–'

Jago saw the joke and joined in. 'Like knickers.'

'Knickers!' Merryn exclaimed. 'You've said a rude word, Jago!'

'Won't be anything like the rude word the mayor says when he realises,' Tamara said which started them all off laughing even harder.

CHAPTER 13

'FROSTY THE SNOWMAN' – COCTEAU TWINS

Thursday 16th December

The following night, Tamara persuaded Honor to go out for Christmas drinks.

'Come on, it'll be fun,' she said. 'Get you in the Christmas spirit. Lucie and Jamie are coming too and they're always up for a laugh.'

They all sat in The Old Anchor, the pub on the harbour, sipping cheap cider and eating crisps. What Tamara hadn't mentioned was her boyfriend Chris was coming along too. Even though she was fond of Tamara, the girl irritated her sometimes. In her opinion Tam sometimes wasn't nice enough to Chris. With Tamara being away so often their relationship was casual and Honor thought Chris was being strung along. She strongly suspected Tamara had a man in every port, as the saying went, and Chris was a straightforward sort of a guy who deserved better. A part-time relationship such as theirs wouldn't suit her, but she supposed it was none of her business and Chris seemed happy enough with the arrangement. Lucie and Jamie, on the other hand, beneath all the banter, had a rock-solid relationship.

Studying the two couples Honor tried, and failed, not to feel like too much of a gooseberry. She'd promised herself the next man in her life would be The One. And, if he wasn't, then she wouldn't bother. She sighed a little. *If only she could meet him.*

The pub was crowded but they'd managed to squeeze around a table at the far side of the pool table, a soundtrack of Christmas classic pop blaring out as a background.

'These are disgusting,' Jamie said, throwing down his bag of turkey-flavoured crisps as 'All I Want for Christmas is You' blasted out.

'I'll have them then.' Lucie snatched them up.

'Your appetite for junk food never fails to impress me.'

'I know, babe. That's why you love me.'

'We need to get *you* a man, Honor,' Tamara said, apropos to nothing but uncannily reading her thoughts. The cider was obviously hitting her. 'What about him at the bar?'

They all turned to look at a man waiting to be served.

Honor pulled a face. 'Looks nice but too much like my ex.'

'Is he still working in Italy?' Tamara asked.

'Yup.'

'And that's why you split up, wasn't it?'

'Yeah. Sort of.' Honor stared into her cider wishing Tamara would drop it. She'd met Gino at teacher training college, and they'd become a couple instantly. When he'd found a teaching job in Italy, they decided to try a long-distance relationship. It had worked for a while, but perhaps inevitably, they'd drifted apart. She glanced again at the man Tamara had pointed out. Medium height, dark-haired, nicely dressed. He did indeed look a little like Gino. A picture of Jago sprang up in her imagination. Tall, loose-limbed with those pale green eyes that bore into you and stripped your soul bare. She deliberately emptied her mind and took a long draught of alcohol. She mustn't go there.

'I met a nice man the other morning,' Jamie said, noting Honor's shuttered expression and changing the subject slightly.

'Walked past as I was opening up the lifeboat station. Had a dog. Lovely black and white spaniel. Walked a bit funny.'

'What, the dog or the man? Are you trying to set Honor up with a man who can't walk properly?' Lucie chided.

'Oi,' Chris put in. 'It shouldn't be the butt of jokes.'

'I'm really sorry, Chris,' Lucie apologised. 'Didn't think. Me and my big mouth.' She peered in her glass. 'What strength is this stuff? It's gone straight to my head.'

'And mine,' Tamara slurred. She ripped open another bag of crisps and shared them out. 'Have some carbs to soak it up.'

'His name was Jago,' Jamie continued, ignoring them. 'Seemed a good guy.'

'I know Jago,' Honor said. So much for not dwelling on him! 'He's a parent of one of the new children in my class. And he's happily married to Avril.'

'Avril?' Lucie said. 'There's an Avril just joined the knitting group. Ellie sold Christmas Tree Cottage to her.'

'You, knitting?' Tamara marvelled.

'Research for my book actually,' Lucie said airily. 'It's really hard.'

'What, the knitting or the research?'

'Both! But at least I enjoy the research. The knitting on the other hand... You should see some of the group, though. You can hardly see their needles for the blur they make, they're so fast.'

'What are you knitting?'

'I'm *trying* to knit a scarf. Trying to start simple, I'm knitting luggins here a scarf, but I've only managed about five centimetres and that was with someone else casting on for me. It'll be *next* Christmas before I finish at this rate.'

'Let's hope you have better luck with the book,' Tamara giggled. 'I don't know how you fit it all in. Working at the estate agents, doing your degree.'

As well as being an aspiring novelist, Lucie also worked part time at the town's estate agency and was doing an English Literature degree.

'Well,' she said gloomily. 'I have long nights to fill when Jamie here is volunteering, or out on a shout.'

'And, Jamie, I *definitely* don't know how you do *that*,' Tamara said with a shudder. 'Especially going out at night. It must be so scary.'

'Not as scary as for the people we rescue,' Jamie said drily.

'Point taken.'

'Is Aggie involved? In the Knit and Natter group, I mean,' Honor asked. Aggie was Lullbury Bay's most notorious pensioner, a huge character and heavily involved in most aspects of community life. She was also a proud pagan and rumoured to be a white witch.

Lucie pointed her nearly empty pint glass at her. 'Aggie,' she said meaningfully, 'has taken advantage of a cheap flight from Exeter. She's gone to Tenerife for a Silver Swingers' Holiday.'

Chris spluttered into his pint and Tamara slapped him on the back.

'And that's research for a book too. One of her books on life as a wrinkly in the twenty-first century.'

'Ugh.' Chris pulled a face. 'That's got me reaching for the mind bleach.'

'They're actually really good,' Lucie protested.

'I agree, Lu,' Honor added. 'Well written and practical.'

'Poor old Austin,' Chris said, referring to Aggie's long-suffering husband. He finished his drink.

'Oh, I don't know. I read the chapters Aggie wrote about a healthy senior sex life. I'd say Austin was a very lucky man,' Jamie declared sagely, and they all laughed.

'But back to setting up Honor here with a man,' Tamara persisted.

'Oh, Tamara, give it a rest, will you. I'm happy being single. And you know you can rule Jago Pengethley out.'

Jamie frowned. 'Now where do I know that name from? Pengethley? I'm sure I've read about a Pengethley.' He gave up. 'No, can't remember. Anyone for another pint?'

Everyone said yes and Chris offered to help carry them.

Once the men had left the table, Honor said mournfully, 'Mind you, it's just my luck Jago's taken.'

'Why's that?' Lucie asked.

'He's so lovely with Merryn, his daughter.' She sighed, aware she wasn't totally sober and letting her tongue slip. 'Really caring. He's just the sort of man I'd like to get serious about.'

'Yeah, not to mention he's a real cutie,' Tamara put in. 'He was at the lights switch on,' she explained to Lucie. 'We hung out a bit. Have you seen the lights? They look like–'

'A right load of pants!' Lucie finished. 'I know! It's hysterical.'

'But, Honor, you don't want to get all serious, girlfriend,' Tamara added. 'Just have some fun.'

'Like you and Chris?' Lucie pointed out. 'Or are you getting more serious? Are you spending Christmas together?'

'No, I'm working and he's going to his family in Cornwall.'

'See, I couldn't be doing with that. Me and Jamie have been together since we were at school. My family are all over Lullbury Bay like the measles and his all live nearby too. I love our big noisy chaotic Christmases.'

'Well, you know me,' Tamara said, with a closed down expression. 'I don't do families. Fell out with my lot years ago. While you're all stuffing your face with badly cooked turkey and dry mince pies and arguing over the remote, I'll be cruising round the fjords sipping Manhattans the barman has slipped me for free. And I certainly won't be pining over possible husbands and babies.'

Lucie winced. 'Now, you've got a point there. Babies. Who'd have one?' She shuddered. 'They've a nasty habit of growing up into spotty sweaty teenagers.' She picked up an empty crisp packet and peered into it hopefully.

Honor laughed. 'What's Eli done now,' she asked, referring to Lucie's younger brother.

'He's only gone and got himself a girlfriend. You know he works up at Tom's animal sanctuary? That's where he met her. Only she's at some swanky-wanky private school in Exeter and he's working all the hours he can in order to buy her a present. He's set his heart on this silver bracelet.'

'Aw, that's sweet,' Honor said. 'It sounds as if he's really maturing. He was always a nice boy when he was in my class. Bit easily led though.'

'Tell me about it,' Lucie replied. 'You and Tom Catesby are two of the few people who believed in Eli. Tom gave him a chance when he got into trouble a few years ago. Remember?'

Honor nodded.

'I mean he only got pulled into some petty vandalism but it caused the town a few sleepless nights.' There had been a spate of car vandalism off and on over a few months. It turned out Eli had been led into it by his gang of friends. Instead of punishment, Tom had taken him on to work at his animal sanctuary. 'Tom Catesby taught him responsibilities and the meaning of hard work. Eli's still a pain but I suppose he's not quite so annoying these days.'

'Tom's a nice man.'

'Gorgeous-looking too, in a quirky kind of way,' Tamara added. 'And single,' she added, meaningfully.

'And only interested if you have four legs, hooves, feathers or a beak. Plus, you'd have to get past Ellie's vetting process. She's very protective of her older brother.' Honor drained her glass. 'I wouldn't fancy taking her on, I'd have a five-inch Louboutin heel in my back.'

Lucie giggled. 'I wouldn't fight Ellie for him either and I should know, I work for her. Glamorous and career-driven manager of the estate agents that she is, I wouldn't cross her.' She sighed soppily. 'You'll just have to find someone as gorg as

Maisie's husband. He's so good for her though, really brought out her softer side. She was all café, café, café before she met him. Or Austin. He and Aggie are so in love it hurts to see them. OAP romance, eh? You can't beat it!'

'What is it with this town? Do they spray love potion in the air or something?' Honor glared at her glass and, realising it was empty, pushed it to one side. 'And all for everyone else,' she added, sounding self-pitying even to herself. 'And thanks, but I don't want to have to wait until I get my teacher's pension before I find love.' Oops. Time to slow down with the cider.

'You'll meet someone when it's the right time.' Tamara patted her hand. 'What's Avril like, Lucie?'

'She's nice. Little and skinny, quiet.'

'How old?'

'I dunno. Old. In her forties maybe.'

'Everyone's old to you, Lu,' Tamara laughed. 'Funny though, I'd say Jago was about thirty-ish. Bit odd.'

'Not really,' Honor pointed out. 'It's been known for men to marry older women.'

'It is strange though,' Lucie continued, 'she never mentioned a husband, only her daughter. And I'm with Jamie, there's deffo something familiar about the name Pengethley.'

'Well, of course there is,' Honor said. 'You sold them a house.'

'Yeah. Suppose. But Ellie dealt with the sale. I didn't have much to do with it. No, I mean something else.' She looked, slightly cross-eyed at her empty packet of crisps. 'Something's nagging at me.' She laughed. 'I'll remember in the middle of the night and sit up and shout it. My mumblings drive Jamie mad.'

'You still living in the flat next to the yacht club?' Tamara asked.

'Yeah. We were going to buy somewhere but I really like living right in the heart of things. It's great to pop down here for a lazy steak and chips and Jamie is near to his beloved lifeboat station. He's right there if he gets called out. It suits us for the moment.

And houses have got so expensive. We'd be paying a lot more in mortgage for some shoebox half the size.'

'And you don't have a horrible downstairs neighbour like mine,' Honor added.

'What's Frank done now?' Lucie asked.

'I got in at eight last night and he banged on his ceiling. When I went down to find out what I'd done, he said I was walking across the floor too loudly!'

'What did you do?'

'I've got some boots with a block heel. Make a racket on the wooden flooring. I put those on and did about a thousand of my steps in them.'

'What did he do then? Knock on his ceiling again?'

'I don't know. I had the telly turned up loud. Oh, I shouldn't, should I?' Honor bit her lip. 'But he's the neighbour from hell. Don't know what's got into him, he wasn't like this when I first moved in. I'd love one of those shoeboxes you mention Lucie but not much chance for me to afford one.'

'Maybe you can marry a rich man like Ellie wants to.' Lucie leaned in and shouted above 'Santa Baby' which was currently playing. 'And did you know Tom is independently wealthy? Maybe Jago is too?'

'Thought we'd ruled Jago out on the grounds he's married,' Honor pouted. 'Not to mention the parent of one of my pupils!'

'Hope on hope ever,' Tamara giggled. 'The way he was looking at you the other night, I think he's got jig-a-jig on his mind. And with you,' she said, as if they were in any doubt about what she meant.

'Tamara!' Lucie and Honor chorused.

Jamie and Chris returned carrying their drinks.

A man staggered into Jamie as he put the tray down. 'Oi, watch it, mate!' The man put up his hand in apology and Jamie sat down. 'Part of me really hates this place at Christmas. Too crowded.'

'I love Christmas. I love everything about it,' Honor said.

Tamara and Lucie rolled their eyes at one another. Honor's love of all things Christmassy was well-known.

'Sorry we were so long,' Chris said. 'Hell of a queue at the bar.' He stopped and eyed them suspiciously. 'I would quote Macbeth,' he added. 'But a, I can't remember any and b, it's bad luck. You three witches look as if you've been scheming the downfall of a man,' he accused.

'What? Us?' Lucie said innocently. 'Would we?'

'Oh yes,' Jamie said as he sipped his new pint. 'Who is it this time?'

'We're still trying to find Honor a man, but they're all taken,' Lucie explained.

'Although there is one single man in town,' Tamara said, grabbing her drink.

'Who?' Honor asked, mystified.

'Eric Snead.'

'Well, you can't say he's not mature,' Lucie pointed out equably.

'Mature?' Honor said, taking a long drink of her cider, feeling it go to her head. 'Have a heart, he's eighty-three!'

They stumbled out of the pub an hour later, the cold hitting them and making the alcohol in their blood rush to their heads.

'This was so not a good idea on a school night,' Honor complained. She stumbled a little on the cobbles in the harbour road.

'You all right, Honor?' Chris came to her and held her by the elbow.

'Ooh, you go ahead,' Tamara called out. 'I need the loo. I'll catch you up.'

They got as far as the open space in front of the yacht club where Jamie and Lucie peeled off to their flat, calling their goodbyes.

'Better wait here until Tamara catches us up,' Chris said. 'You don't mind, do you, Honor? I know it's cold.' He blew out a breath and they watched it mist upward. 'Never known it so cold here.' Icy foam crashed over the low wall separating them from the sea to hammer home the point.

'No, I don't mind. Don't want to desert her.' She peered into the darkness at the postbox at the beginning of the prom. 'What's that?'

'Where?'

'Over there. There's something on top of the pillar box.' She began to make her way over to it but stumbled again.

Chris rescued her, putting his arm around her waist. 'Wish Tamara would hurry up. The sooner we get you home the better.'

'I know. I don't normally drink cider. I can't take it,' Honor moaned. 'And I've got another nativity rehearsal first thing tomorrow morning. What was I thinking? A hundred kids to wrangle and with a hangover.'

'Want to swap?' Chris offered. 'I'm in a meeting at County Hall all morning.'

'We really shouldn't have such responsible jobs. Me a deputy head and you the top money bod at the council.' She shook her head gingerly. 'I just hope I've got some paracetamol at home.'

They'd reached the pillar box. 'What is this? Oh!' Honor clapped her hands together in delight as she realised. 'They're knitted snowmen. Three knitted snowmen on top of the postbox.' She walked around it, giggling. 'How magical,' she said to Chris, her face shining in the reflection from the white sparkly Christmas lights looped along the prom. 'They're fixed on, look.'

They stood admiring it, slightly disbelievingly. Honor let her head rest on his shoulder, feeling sleepy. She slipped downwards and felt Chris's arm tighten around her waist. 'I like their scarves.'

Each snowman was about twenty centimetres high, fat and

padded and stitched onto a white covering which was tied around the top of the postbox. They wore jaunty knitted hats and scarves in sparkly red and green. There were even tiny white lights woven around them to complete the seasonal look.

'It's lovely,' she sighed, her whisper disappearing into the frigid night. 'Bit silly. Very random. But lovely. So Christmassy. What are they called?'

'Snowmen?'

'No silly, the people who do this sort of thing. They do it in secret and sneak out in the middle of the night to put them on.'

'Postbox Toppers? Yarn Bombers?'

'Ninja Knitters!' Honor did a little dance of glee. 'They must be Ninja Knitters to knit that well. You've got to love any group called Ninja Knitters!' They were laughing so hard Honor had to clutch onto Chris to stop herself falling down.

Jago, returning from his late-night dog walk around the harbour, heard the noise and glanced over. His lips thinned as he took in the sight of Honor and a man he didn't know, laughing with their arms around one another. It was ridiculous, he knew, but he'd assumed not only was Honor single but they'd made some kind of connection. A connection he wanted to take further. His heart sinking, he turned on his heel and strode off. Pushing his way through the Christmas revellers spilling out of the pub, he'd never felt lonelier.

CHAPTER 14

'LITTLE DONKEY' – TRAD.

Friday 17th December

Honor never thought it would be ready. They'd snatched time from the curriculum and rehearsed solidly through lunch playtimes, with the choir rehearsing after school. And now, it was the last day of term, and they had a school hall full of excited parents and grandparents waiting expectantly to see their little darlings perform the nativity play. It was never straightforward putting on a play with very small children and she knew any mistakes would be considered charming, but she still wanted it to go as well as possible to reflect the hard work the school had put into it. After this afternoon, term would wrap up in a flurry of tinselly decorations, Christmas cards dripping with glitter and snowflakes cut out from white paper all clutched in chubby hands to be taken home. Honor adored Christmas in a primary school but she was running on empty now and it would be good to have some time to herself. Making sure the two Year Six pupils who were welcoming guests had enough programmes, she did a swift tour of the classrooms to check the children were ready and then, taking a deep breath, went to stand on the stage to get things started.

Lexie Walker, the music teacher, stopped playing 'O Little Town of Bethlehem' and hush descended over the audience.

'Welcome to *The Angel Who Was Late*, our nativity play for this year,' Honor announced. 'The children and teachers have all been working incredibly hard to make this as wonderful as it can be, so I know you'll all enjoy it.' She went on to run through the usual health and safety announcements, trying to not to focus on Avril and Jago who she'd spotted sitting at the end of the second row. 'So, now it's over to the boys and girls and *The Angel Who Was Late!*'

'Oh, Honor, that was lovely!' Avril cried as she approached her afterwards. 'I couldn't believe Merryn had such a big role.'

'Thank you. That means a lot. The boys and girls worked so hard.'

'As you did, I would imagine,' Avril added shrewdly. 'How did you get the little Key Stage One children to dance as so well?' she asked, referring to their performance as stars. 'They looked so cute wearing all black with those huge tinsel stars sewn on. Took me right back to when Merryn was that age. Although she wasn't nearly so graceful.'

Honor rolled her eyes. 'Hours of rehearsal. They made me so proud though. I take it you missed little Jaden picking his nose? What was I thinking of putting him right in the middle of the front row!'

They laughed and accepted the plastic cups of mulled wine being handed out.

Avril took a sip. 'Ooh that's nice.'

'Mrs Arnold, our head teacher, makes it. She likes it on the strong side. Strictly for the adults. The children have got squash and biscuits in their classrooms as a treat.'

Avril looked around the school hall, thronging with staff and parents. The walls had been decorated with scenes from the nativity. One wall depicted very Dorset-looking rolling green hills complete with a flock of cotton wool sheep. Another had a town of white houses made from painted boxes, each with a flickering light glowing within. Even though the full hall lights had been switched back on, the magic the children had created remained. 'I'm so glad we got Merryn in here, she's loving it. It's just the right size for a primary school I think, and I love the old-fashioned building. It's completely traditional. It's lovely having the classrooms radiating off this hall. Feels so cosy.'

'The main part of the school is Victorian,' Honor explained. 'We've a couple of temporary classrooms in the playground until we get funding for an extension, but I'm glad you like it. It's a wonderful place to work; it has a great family feel. I love it and Merryn is making a real contribution to class. She's very bright.'

'I couldn't believe she was on stage so much. Trust her to be the angel who was nearly too late. Late to see the Angel Gabriel, too late to meet the three kings and only just in time to see the baby being born. Talk about typecasting.'

Honor laughed again. 'She hadn't got the main part originally, as she joined school well after we'd begun rehearsing, but poor old Lia broke her ankle skiing at half term so we had to recast. Merryn stepped in. She learned her lines incredibly quickly.'

'Oh, so that's what she was doing up in her room,' Avril said, realisation dawning. 'I thought she was reading out loud to herself.'

'She must have a photographic memory as she nailed the lines within a couple of days.'

'Yes, she probably has.' Avril was about to add Kenan had had a photographic memory so Merryn had probably inherited it, but refused to blight the happy event with grief. Sometimes mourning was about faking it until you made it, but it worked. Her friend Suz was right. There was a lot to be said for putting on a brave face. Kenan would have been so proud to see his little girl shine as she had this evening. But, had he been alive, she reflected, they probably wouldn't be in Lullbury Bay in the first place. They hadn't had much in the way of plans for his retirement. They were going to wait until after Christmas and then think about it. She doubted his plans would have included moving to a little seaside town. He loved London and all it offered. He hadn't missed Cornwall and the sea at all. But it was immaterial now. He'd been robbed of any retirement right on the cusp of it. He should be enjoying having some time to himself after dedicating his life to others. The cruelty and injustice of it all made her swallow sudden tears as they constricted her throat. She was sure Kenan was somewhere looking down on them. Unwilling to give in to emotion, the evening had been beyond touching as it was, she finished her drink.

'Refill?' It was Jago bearing a tray of more mulled wine. Putting it down on a table, he gave Avril a swift, hard hug.

'Yes please,' Avril picked up a cup and concentrated on it. 'Just as well we can all walk home. Where have you been, Jago?'

'Helping Tom get the donkey into its horsebox. I understand it lives at his sanctuary.' He grinned at Honor. 'I can't decide if it was genius or reckless having a live donkey on stage.'

'Mary was immaculately behaved.'

'She was, she didn't even drop the baby Jesus, but I was more worried about the donkey.'

Honor giggled into her wine. 'Mary *is* the donkey.'

'Well, that's just plain confusing, isn't it?' Jago smiled at her, and their eyes met. 'I suppose she has Joseph at home?'

Honor compressed her lips, her vivid blue eyes merry. 'No, sorry to shatter your illusions but he's called Ivor. And I wouldn't have dreamed of having *him* on stage. Far too frisky! Speaking of which, did you hear what happened to Morag and Elsie on Wednesday night?'

'No, what?'

'Tom lost them. He unshackled them, or whatever you call it, unhitched is it, from Santa's sleigh.' Honor's nose wrinkled with the effort of coming up with the right term. 'Someone had the bright idea of blasting out "Step into Christmas" on the Tannoy at top volume at that very moment and off they shot. Galloped along, if that's what reindeer do–'

'I'll have to ask Merryn.'

'Do that. She's bound to know. They galloped along the prom, scattering the crowds.'

Jago began to laugh. 'Oh no, are they still at large?'

Honor giggled. 'No, thank goodness. He caught up with them in the public gardens. They'd crashed through the hedge onto the bowling green and were eating the grass!' Her eyes began to stream with tears. 'The chairman is apoplectic. He takes great pride in the quality of his green. Oh, I know I shouldn't laugh but I can't get the image of poor old Tom chasing them along the promenade.'

'Obviously not Elton John fans. Shame, as Christmas music goes, I always quite liked that one.'

'Me too.' Honor was laughing without abandon now. 'I'm so sorry, Jago, what must you think of me?' she spluttered. 'I'm not usually this cruel. It must be end-of-termitis or something.'

'Was Santa chasing too?'

Honor couldn't speak, she was laughing too much. She nodded, snorting a little.

'Let's just hope he has some energy left for Christmas Eve then,' and Jago collapsed into laughter too.

Avril looked curiously from one to the other. Her interest piqued; she welcomed the distraction from her grief. They were acting as if there were only the two of them in the room. Interesting, she thought to herself. It was about time Jago got himself a nice girl. She'd kept quiet when he was married but had never thought Rose right for him. Jago was too serious sometimes, bore the weight of his responsibilities heavily. She knew he felt responsible for her, and she didn't want that. He was a young man, with his whole life in front of him. He needed someone to inject a bit of fun into his existence and Honor could be just the person to do it. 'I'll just go and collect Merryn,' she said but neither heard; they were still laughing together. It was good to hear Jago laugh like that. She hadn't heard him do it for too long. Sliding away, she left them to it.

'So, what's next on the Lullbury Bay Christmas calendar?' Jago asked once he'd managed to control his laughter.

Honor took out a tissue and blew her nose delicately. 'Oh dear, I haven't laughed that much in ages. I really needed a good giggle.' After mopping at her eyes, she answered, 'Well, for me, it's the end of term. Now the nativity's over, I can't wait. Don't get me wrong, there's something utterly magical about being in a primary school in the run up to Christmas and being knee-deep in tinsel and excitement, but I'm exhausted. I'm the world's biggest fan of Christmas but I need some sleep! What about you, do you like Christmas?'

'Sometimes,' he answered, cagily. 'Maybe I'll learn to love it again this year?'

'I think you should. And I think it might be down to me to teach you how to love a Lullbury Bay Christmas.' She sparkled up at him. She was only half aware of what she was saying. Relief the end of term was here, plus half a cup of Mrs Arnold's strong mulled wine and a fit of the giggles had made her lose any inhibitions. 'Lullbury Bay is the best place to spend it. We've still got the lantern and carnival parade to come and the German Market and loads of other things happening. There's a New Year's Day Dip too if you fancy it. Raises money for the RNLI.'

'The what?'

'You get dressed up in fancy dress and go for a swim in the sea.'

'In December?' he asked, incredulous.

'Nope,' she giggled. What was it about this man? She was on a cloud of something sparkly. 'On January the first.'

'Oh, as it's January, that makes all the difference!'

She watched, fascinated, as his mouth quirked in humour. He had a very lovely mouth. 'Don't look so sceptical,' Honor said, laughter bubbling up again. 'It's huge fun. The Old Anchor puts on hot chocolate and bacon butties afterwards.'

'You probably need more than that if you go swimming in Lullbury Bay in January. Like medical attention.' He grinned, taking the sting out of the words.

'Oh, it's not that bad. I think you should try it.'

'No,' he said, firmly. 'Not for me.'

The larky flirting stopped. Honor felt his mood change and blacken but couldn't understand what had happened. It was as if a grey pall had fallen over him. Then she remembered he was married and unobtainable and her mood sobered too.

'Maybe the lantern making workshop then? It's tomorrow. I'm running it at the Art School. You make a lantern to carry in the carnival parade.'

'Maybe. Do you stay in Lullbury Bay for Christmas?' he asked, changing the subject. 'Or do you head home to family? They're in Worcester, aren't they?'

'Well done for remembering. Sometimes I do. Sometimes they come here. This year, though, my parents are celebrating their fortieth wedding anniversary with a cruise. All around the world, starting from Southampton.'

'Wow. Trip of a lifetime. What are you going to do, though?'

'We're having Christmas early. I'm up there for the day with them and my sister, and then I'll be back here in Lullbury Bay. Quite looking forward to it actually. Some nicely expensive M&S nibbles and heavy use of the remote control.' A frown flickered over her face.

'But?'

'As long as my downstairs neighbour doesn't kick off. I only have to drop a feather and he complains about the noise. It gets a little wearing.'

'Doesn't sound much fun.'

'Oh, he's okay most of the time as I'm out at work all hours but it's hardly relaxing worrying about what he's going to complain about next. Still,' she said, brightly, 'worse things happen at sea.'

Jago remained silent.

Honor watched him as he stared at his feet, scuffing one trainer against the other. He was obviously uncomfortable about something. 'Have you seen the postbox topper down by the Sea Spray Café? Someone has knitted three snowmen and fixed them onto the top of the postbox. It's really sweet. One of those daft things that really cheer you up. I've nick-named them the Ninja Knitters.'

'Good name for them. Think I caught a glimpse of you looking at it last night when I was walking Ivy.'

Honor groaned. 'I was led completely astray. Tamara, you know, who sings on cruises, persuaded me to go to the pub. They were serving the most lethal cider and it went straight to my head. I could hardly stand. Just as well Chris was there to hold me up.'

'Chris?' Jago said quickly.

'Haven't I mentioned him before? He's Tamara's on-off boyfriend. He's an accountant with the council. Really nice guy. Known him for years. He and Tam got me home and into bed. Even left a pint of water and a paracetamol on the bedside table. They're such good friends. It's just I can't tolerate cider. Never could.' She waggled her empty plastic cup. 'And if I have any more of this stuff, I'll be heading the same way.' Another parent called over. 'I must go. Duty calls.' She touched her hand to his sleeve. 'Do try to make it to the lantern making. It's fun and, to be honest, I could do with some help from someone creative. It tends to get a bit hectic.'

He smiled down at her. 'I'll do my best.'

Honor felt her blood quicken and her cheeks blush. She blamed the wine. 'Maybe I'll see you there then. Bye, Jago.'

'Bye, Honor.'

As she walked across the hall, a very specific spot between her shoulder blades felt the heat from his eyes.

CHAPTER 15

'LIGHT OF CHRISTMAS' – TOBYMAC (WITH OWL CITY)

Saturday 18th December

'Hello, man.'

Jago glanced behind him. Apart from Dave Wiscombe, there was no other male present in the hall. He assumed he was the 'man' referred to. 'Hello, boy.'

The little boy sitting in front of him sniggered. 'I'm not a boy. I'm Jaden.'

'Hello then, Jaden. Would you like to make a lantern?'

'Suppose.'

'Well, nothing like a bit of enthusiasm,' Jago muttered to himself and got the required bits and bobs together. He wasn't sure why he was here. He spent his working life making small fiddly things with his hands, it was hardly what he wanted to do on his day off. He could have said he hadn't got a school safeguarding check but it would have been a lie; he'd occasionally run workshops with children and had enhanced clearance. Looking up to see Honor supervising Merryn at the next table, he knew exactly what had drawn him here. What an idiot. He attempted to justify it to himself. He'd had to walk Merryn here anyway. It made sense to stay.

After their conversation at the nativity, he'd watched Honor as she walked away, he couldn't help it. His mood had been all over the place yesterday. He knew his mother was struggling, one look at her face told him. Maybe it was the poignancy of the children acting out an age-old story? Maybe it was because his father wasn't there to see how well Merryn had done. He'd felt it too. Laughter at the silly story of the angel too late to see any of the main events of the nativity turned, too often, to tears he'd choked back. Laughing with Honor over the runaway reindeers had been a tonic. There was something about her that made you want to laugh and smile. She radiated joy. Her pupils must love her. His mood had been further lifted by the knowledge that the good-looking man with the tousled blonde hair was the boyfriend of one of her friends.

He thought he'd shaken off the grief which dogged him. But then the conversation had drifted to the swimming event on New Year's Day and his mind had zigzagged back to his father helpless in the river. He could see his change in mood had puzzled Honor and he'd hated she might think she was the cause. He was trying hard to cling on to the good things which were happening in his life at the moment, and that included Honor Martin, but sometimes his emotions were impossible to control.

When he'd ventured into the main space at the Art School early that morning he'd been astonished. He knew Honor must do things like this most days in her teaching life, but it was a symphony of organisation. There were eight or nine tables each with pre-cut sheets of translucent paper, glue, sticks of willow withies, and scissors. On another table, well away from the messy stuff, were picture books to inspire or just look through in a spare moment. On yet another were sheets of brightly coloured paper, PVA glue and scissors to make a simple cut-out and fold-together lantern, which the children could do independently. The floor under the big Velux windows letting light stream in had been left empty and covered with protective plastic sheeting. Dave, the manager, was setting up a space for those wanting to make something on a bigger scale. Jago had been briefed by Honor that the lantern making workshop would run in two-hour sessions and that all children had been booked in but, she'd told him, be prepared for a few drop-ins even so. Parents, Honor had told him with a smile, didn't often stay for the full session but used the time to pop into town to do some Christmas shopping.

Now, faced with Jaden, Jago felt unaccustomed nerves. He was used to Merryn but she was older, fiercely independent and eager to please. Jaden looked none of those things. 'Jaden, eh? My name's Jago. That's quite similar, isn't it?'

'Suppose.'

Jago plastered an enthusiastic smile on his face. Jaden's mum had deposited him in a hurry, paid the ten-pound fee and shot off without a backward glance. He didn't think the boy was here of his own free will. 'What sort of shape do you want to make?'

'Dunno.'

Jago groaned inwardly. How Honor had the patience to do this sort of thing day in, day out, he had no idea. 'The star-shaped one is good fun.' He held up one he'd made earlier. 'It's quite complicated but I can help you make it. See, we leave a gap here, glue the LED light in so you can reach in and switch the light off and on.' He demonstrated it a couple of times. 'For the parade.'

'Don't know if I'm coming.'

'That's a shame. I'm looking forward to it.'

'It depends.'

Jago didn't like to ask what it depended upon. Something in his gut warned him Jaden may not have the most supportive home life. He smiled sympathetically. 'It doesn't matter if you can't join in the parade. You can use your lantern as a Christmas decoration. It would look great in your bedroom.'

Jaden brightened at the thought. 'Can I do a nottopuss?'

'A nottopuss?'

'Yeah, with lots of testicles.'

'Testicles?' Jago said in alarm. Realisation dawned. 'Oh,' he said, on a long drawn-out breath of relief. 'An octopus with tentacles. Erm, thing is, it has to be a shape with straight sides.'

'Why?'

Jago floundered. 'I'm not sure.' Looking helplessly around he caught Honor's eye.

'Be over in a minute,' she mouthed.

Inspiration struck. 'Tell you what, we can use these diamond-shaped pieces, put them together to make the body of the nottopuss, I mean octopus, and you can go to the other table and cut out some tentacles to glue onto it made out of sugar paper. I'll help you make the frame out of willows and use the glue gun to make it stick together and then we'll leave it to dry before you add them.'

'A gun?' Jaden's eyes widened. He was looking positively animated. 'Can I have a go on the gun?'

'I should say almost certainly not. It has really hot glue coming out of it. Might hurt you if it got on your skin.'

'Pah. I'm tough.'

'I bet you are but Miss Martin told me not to let any children use the glue gun.' Jago pulled a face and was gratified to see Jaden giggle. 'And *I'm* not tough enough to break Miss Martin's rules.'

Jaden shook his head solemnly. He leaned closer. 'You always follow Miss Martin's rules,' he confided. 'She's strict!'

Jago reached for the willow withy sticks and the diamond shapes made out of translucent paper. 'You know, Jaden, that doesn't surprise me one bit.'

By the time Honor had a chance to come over to their table, the body of the lantern was nearly complete.

'Looks great, Jaden,' she exclaimed.

'It's a nottopuss, miss.'

Honor caught Jago's eye, and he saw her suppress a grin. 'So I can see. Over you go to Miss Walker's table now and PVA the paper so it's waterproof. Is it going to have tentacles?'

'Yeah. Going to make 'em outa pink sugar paper.'

'Excellent. I can see you've got it all thought out. Well done. Ah, Mr Pengethley, here's your next victim, I mean pupil. Come along, Lia. What shape lantern do you want to make? Boot-shaped?' Honor gave Jago an evil look. 'I'm sure that's possible. Come and sit down here. Put your crutch under the table so no one trips over it. We don't want any more broken ankles, do we?'

In the staff room during the lunch break, Honor couldn't stop giggling. 'I'm so sorry to laugh,' she spluttered. 'Put it down to end of term hysteria. I couldn't believe it when I saw you with Jaden. Of all our pupils to start the day with!' She hid her glee in her mug of tea.

'Thanks a bunch,' Jago replied. 'I'll have you know, once I'd got used to him, I enjoyed working with him. And he speaks very highly of you. Says you're very strict.'

Fellow teacher, Lexie Walker, sitting next to them laughed. 'If you only knew, Jago. We don't call her Miss Whiplash for nothing.'

Honor's face crimsoned. 'Have another turkey and cranberry sandwich, Lexie, and shut up.'

Lexie, the sandwich suspended mid-air, said, 'What did I say?' She got up. 'More tea anyone?'

'Yes please,' Honor replied. 'I need to refuel before this afternoon's session.' Once Lexie had gone to switch the kettle on, she added, 'Sorry. She forgets Merryn is a pupil. With term finishing yesterday, we're all a bit over-tired.'

Jago shook his head. 'I'm not here as a parent, just as you're not here as a teacher. We're just working together as a team, aren't we?'

'Thanks.' Shooting him a grateful look, she carried on eating. 'You did do well with Jaden though.'

'I gather he's not the easiest of boys?'

Honor nodded. 'Lots of money at home but not enough attention. And that's said in confidence please.'

'I understand.' And he did. Once Jaden had got past the monosyllabic phase, they'd got on well. The boy had nattered away about his favourite football team and that he wanted to be a deep-sea diver when he grew up. He seemed to appreciate having an adult listening to him chatter on.

Jago eased his shoulders back, they were stiff from hunching over sticking paper to withies. 'I can't believe you're here, doing this, when you've only just finished term. Aren't you exhausted? I've only done a morning and I'm knackered.'

'That's why we teachers live on tea. We need the caffeine.' She smiled, her face glowing with happiness. 'I love doing the workshop though. It's become a real tradition. I love the lantern making, the parade. I love anything Christmassy, as you know.' She looked at him intently. 'I'm beginning to sus you don't feel quite the same?'

'I *used* to love Christmas,' Jago said carefully. 'Let's just say I'm,' he paused not wanting to expand on why he might find Christmas difficult this year, and settled on, 'ambivalent now.'

'Then we need to change that.' Honor put an impulsive hand on his. It was rough from dried on PVA glue and crusted with paint but the warmth from the physical contact arrowed straight to his heart. 'I challenge you to learn to love a Lullbury Bay Christmas.' Her blue eyes sparkled.

He couldn't help but stare into them. They were the most astonishing colour, like the most vivid hyacinth, so blue as to be almost purple. 'I like your confidence.'

'You won't be able to help yourself. It's like falling in love.

Even the most curmudgeonly ends up in love with a Lullbury Bay Christmas.'

Or ends up in love he thought.

They gazed at each other, their hands still in contact before hastily snatching them away when Lexie returned with their tea.

CHAPTER 16

'O TANNENBAUM' – GERMAN TRAD.

'Are we all ready?' Honor yelled over the sound system from which was blaring 'Fairytale of New York' – thankfully the edited version. She was standing at the top of Lullbury Bay High Street shivering. It was very cold tonight and, beyond the gold hot-pant Christmas lights, darkness stretched its tendrils out into the alleyways beyond. It was the perfect time for a lantern parade. The perfect time to bring light into the season.

'Mums and dads, are we ready? Children, have you all got your lanterns switched on? Are you in the order I put you in?' Behind them, at a safe distance, she could see the vehicles which would make up the carnival parade. Their headlights dazzled as she looked straight into them, so she squinted at her group. 'Children, please stay with mummy and daddy, or whoever has come with you, and if anyone gets lost, come and find me at the Christmas tree. You'll recognise it. It's the big green thing decorated in white lights.' She was rewarded with a few giggles from those at the front.

Kirstie McColl was replaced with Wizzard's 'I Wish it Could be Christmas Everyday'. Their cue! She switched on the light inside her own star-shaped lantern and held it up. The children at the front held up theirs too and the action rippled back to those furthest away. In all, twenty-five had made it to the parade and pride made tears tickle in her throat. For a second, she allowed herself the indulgence of taking in the sight. Twenty-five little people, all dressed in woolly hats, scarves and warm coats, their mittened hands clutching the product of their hard work at the workshop.

Honor knew what would happen behind them. It was the same floats every year. That was part of the tradition. A slow procession of a variety of vehicles would inch their way down Lullbury Bay's steep main street and then along the promenade. Lullbury Bay folk took great pride in their carnival, especially the Christmas version, and always went all out to disguise the lorries and trucks into something magically Christmas. Amongst many there would be the Comp-Solutions computer company's flatbed lorry, covered in vast swathes of white felt and with three of its employees dressed up as fat snowmen spraying fake snow into the air. The Lullbury Bay community choir would be perched on the back of a truck, all dressed as Victorian carol singers and, of course, Father Christmas would make a welcome return, although he might be leaving his reindeer behind this time.

Surveying her little group of enthusiastic lantern holders, she gulped down the emotion, smiled at them, then turned on her heel, holding her lantern aloft, and led them slowly in the parade.

'That looked fantastic!' Jago gathered Merryn up and gave her a fierce hug. They were standing on the open space outside the yacht club on the seafront. The sight of the children parading had made his heart swell with pride. He had waited at the bottom of the high street before they had turned to walk along the prom all the way along to the harbour and had joined in to walk alongside Merryn and Avril.

'Did you see Miss Martin? She had the best lantern. It was shaped like a star and it lit up the whole night. I pretended I was one of the three kings following it.'

Jago ruffled her hair. 'I did. Look, here's Mum.'

Avril had nipped back to the house to return Merryn's lantern and to check Ivy hadn't eaten Chestnut the hamster. So far, an uneasy peace reigned between them, but the puppy was far too interested in the little brown creature.

'Oh, you've brought Ivy with you,' he said in surprise. 'Do you think she'll cope?'

'Thought it might be good socialisation for her, now the noisy floats have gone,' Avril replied. 'I can always take her home again if she looks nervous. One of the beauties of living right in town.' She shivered. 'I might need to go back anyway to get a warmer hat. My ears are freezing.'

'Maybe hotdogs and churros will warm you up?' Jago looked down at his little sister. 'Fancy going to the German Market?'

'Oh, Jags, churros are Mexican, idiot.'

'Sorry. Forgot. You won't want any then? Especially if they come with chocolate dipping sauce?'

Caught out, Merryn screwed up her face. 'Well, I think they make a lot of chocolate in Germany so it *might* be all right.'

Jago laughed at her reasoning. 'Come on then, let's head to the square.'

'And let's hurry,' Avril said. 'It's a high tide tonight, the waves look as if they might wash over the prom!'

As if to make Avril's point, a huge wave hit the low wall which separated them from the beach and showered them with a fine sea spray. The family shrieked and giggled and skipped away. As they walked back along the promenade in the direction of the town and the cobbled square where the market had been set up, they discussed the carnival parade.

'My favourite was the float with the people dressed up as

Christmas puddings,' Merryn proclaimed. 'They were so funny and round!'

'That reminds me.' Jago felt in his pocket of his Barbour and held up a lolly, its wrapper designed to look like a Christmas pudding. 'They were throwing them at the crowd as they went past.' He handed it to her.

'I'll take that.' Avril intercepted it. 'You've already had too many sweet things. It'll save for tomorrow.' She slid it into her coat pocket.

Brother and sister scowled at one another. 'Mothers!' they chorused and giggled.

'I liked the Majorettes; thought they were very skilled twirling their batons as they danced along. And I loved the snowmen,' Avril said, ignoring her offspring. 'And all that fake snow being sprayed into the air. Made me feel very Christmassy. And the choir perched on the back of that low loader or whatever they call it. They looked fantastic all dressed up in their Victorian gear and belting out "O Come All Ye Faithful".'

'Personally, I'm very glad Father Christmas paid us a return visit,' Jago added. 'Even if he was on the back of a lorry this time and not pulled by reindeer.'

Merryn elbowed him in the hip. 'You just like the girls dressed up as elves,' she accused. 'Sexy!'

'Sexy!' they repeated as one.

Avril tutted. 'It would be nice if sometimes, Jago, Merryn rose to your age and you didn't revert to an eight-year-old.' The only response was more laughter. She addressed the dog. 'Thank goodness I've got you, Ivy. At least I can have a sensible conversation sometimes.'

'And you talk to Chestnut,' Merryn spluttered. 'I've heard you.'

'Is it any surprise when I live with you two?' Avril said with asperity. They reached the end of the promenade where the huge Christmas tree stood. 'Hello, Honor,' she exclaimed as they bumped into her.

'Who's Honor?' Merryn asked, bewildered.

'It's your teacher, Miss Martin,' Jago explained. 'Teachers have first names you know.'

Honor smiled at them. 'How lovely to see you all as a family together, and Ivy too. Hope you enjoyed the Christmas carnival parade.' She addressed Merryn. 'I'm definitely Honor tonight. Term's over, it's Saturday night and it's nearly Christmas.' She held out her hand. 'Pleased to meet you, Miss Merryn Pengethley. I'm Miss Honor Martin.' She made a curtsey.

Merryn took her hand, grinning broadly, and copied the curtsey. *'Methinks it were an easy leap to pluck bright honour from the pale-faced moon,'* she murmured, looking pleased at their stunned response. 'Daddy gave me a book of quotations and I remember I liked that one,' she added as explanation. 'It's Shakespeare you know.'

There was a frozen pause then Jago broke it by joking, 'What can I say,' he spread his hands. 'I think she was left by the fairies. A changeling. I couldn't spout Shakespeare if you held me to ransom.'

Honor took Merryn's arm. 'You, young lady, are always surprising me. Are you all headed into the German Market? May I join you? Tamara and Chris have joined the choir in the pub so I'm all alone.'

'Please do,' Avril said. 'Maybe, Shakespeare quotes notwithstanding, you can save me from what passes as conversation in this family.'

Honor smiled at them all. She glanced at the roaring sea, gleaming inky in the night. 'Come on then, before the high tide washes us away. I need frites with mayo and maybe some *flammkuchen*. That's a sort of a German pizza,' she said to an entranced Merryn.

CHAPTER 17

'STILLE NACHT' – GERMAN TRAD.

The German Market had been set up in Lullbury Bay's cobbled square. Usually a car park, with the entrance through an arch, it was walled on three sides but open to the sea on the fourth. Pretty white lights had been hung along the walls and on the charming wooden cabins, each of which was a lit oasis enticing people in with intoxicating aromas of food and hot spiced wine. The steep roofs had fake snow sprayed on them and dripped with golden lights shimmering against the cold night. Christmas carols played in the background, drowning out the surge of a wild sea out in the bay and the odd squawk of an alarmed gull. In one corner the magnificent tree stood, smothered in white lights and boasting an enormous golden star at its top.

After Jago had treated them all to *wurst* served in paper serviettes and an overexcited Ivy had jumped up and snatched the end of the sausage out of Merryn's roll, making the girl cry, Avril decided to take both home. Leaving Honor and Jago who were standing close together chatting, she dragged a tired but protesting daughter away.

'Can we buy churros first?' Merryn was heard to plead as they disappeared into the night.

Jago smiled after them, then turned to Honor, chewing the last of his *wurst*. 'That was good. What was mine called?'

'*Rostbratwurst* I think the guy said.' Honor frowned. 'I only know a few words of German.'

'Well, whatever it was, it was good. What do you fancy next?' Jago took the serviette off her, their fingers touching briefly, and crumpled the paper up, throwing it in a bin. 'Something sweet? Shall we have a wander around and see what draws us in?'

'Yes let's.' Honor nodded eagerly. He was in his Barbour and had a Beanie squashing his dark curls down. A shadow of stubble decorated his square jaw, making him look even more piratical than usual. She gazed up at him and felt her heart give a treacherous wobble. She was in danger, real danger, of falling for this man. Not only was he amazingly good-looking, funny and intelligent, he was kind and more empathetic than any man she'd ever met before. The way he'd handled the children at the workshop had been heart-warming. It was ridiculous, but her fingers, even at the casual touch when he'd taken the serviette, tingled. Fixing the happy scene of Avril, Merryn and him laughing together when she'd bumped into them on the prom firmly in her mind, she tried to put all thoughts of how lovely Jago was to one side. It was not to be. It couldn't be. Ignoring the siren call to push her hand into his, she walked to the next cabin.

They watched as a woman, dressed in an elaborate pinafore with her hair plaited around her head, slathered hot cheese onto bread, adding onions and pickles. 'It's *raclette*,' she said, in heavily accented but perfect English. 'Would you like to try some?' She put a couple of morsels on a plate and held it out.

Honor took some and groaned. 'So good. Thank you.'

'You're welcome.' The woman smiled and turned to serve another customer.

The scent of spices drew them to another cabin. A man ladled *gluhwein* into little white porcelain mugs. He dropped a sugar cube into one and lit it, the flames bursting into a blue flame in the cold. 'It is *feuerzangenbowle*,' he explained. 'The sugar is soaked in rum. It is very good,' he added, unnecessarily.

Jago turned to Honor and raised his brows in query.

'Yes please. I'd love to try some.'

'Two please.'

'*Zwei?*' The man nodded sharply. 'Of course!'

They went to stand by the Christmas tree to drink it. It was less crowded there. Next to it was a life-sized nativity set on a bed of straw and made out of simple wooden carvings.

'So sweet,' Honor said, sniffing her wine and admiring it. Wafts of delicious hot spice and alcohol rose up with the steam. She sipped a little and choked. 'Oh goodness, that's strong!'

Jago tried his. 'It'll certainly keep the cold out,' he gasped, pulling a face. 'Think I might prefer a pint of Black Ven though.'

Honor looked around, enjoying the crowds and the vibe. 'This is such a good idea. I don't think Lullbury Bay's had a German Market before. It's been a lovely evening, hasn't it? I'm so glad the parade went well.' She stopped, aware the hot wine was making her garrulous. It couldn't possibly be Jago sending her every nerve end crazy, could it?

'You must have been proud of all of the children. They looked amazing walking down the hill holding their lanterns, keeping the dark at bay.'

'And lots of those happy children with their beautifully made lanterns were down to you. Thank you for coming today. It really helped. And I suspect it stopped Jaden kicking off. I saw his mutinous expression when he was dropped off by mum. He so did not want to be there. I think he enjoyed the novelty of having a male teacher for a change. All the Key Stage One teachers are female.'

She drew in a dizzying breath and inhaled the scents of food and alcohol, all underlaid by the sharp pine aroma of the tree next to them. Christmas seemed to be summed up in the lights swaying in the breeze whipping off the sea, people eating and drinking, their faces glowing in the bright light given out by the wooden cabins, and children running about clutching gingerbread and candy floss. 'It's what it's all about, isn't it? Fighting the darkest time of the year, bringing something green into your home. Indulging in something sweet and sugary.' She glanced at the wooden nativity, Joseph a long lean figure standing protectively over Mary and the infant Jesus. 'And, if you're a believer, about a tiny baby coming to save us all. Christian or not, there's something truly magical about this time of year. Sorry, Gino would say that was the alcohol talking. I have to admit it's gone to my head. I can feel my cheeks burning and I've a feeling my nose has turned the same pink in this cold.' She pushed her woolly hat off her fringe and took another sip. Now she'd got used to its potency she was quite enjoying it.

'Who's Gino?'

'A boyfriend. Or was a boyfriend, I should say. We met during teacher training. He went to teach abroad. He's half Italian so when he got a job teaching in Florence he was thrilled.'

'Didn't you want to go with him?'

Honor shook her head. 'I didn't want to live in Italy, no matter how attractive the idea seemed.' She thought back. At the time Gino had accused her of being unadventurous, of putting her need to stay in England over their relationship. It had never occurred to him that he was the one who had put it into jeopardy. She should have recognised his selfishness then. In hindsight, it had been the right decision. She knew she would have been lonely living in a country where she didn't speak the language – and entirely reliant on Gino.

'It can't have been easy, keeping a relationship going I mean. Or did it split you up?'

'It didn't split us up immediately but you're right, it wasn't easy to keep a long-distance relationship going. We tried it for a few years but it didn't work for us.' It had for a while, Honor thought, but had all screeched to a halt when, staying at Gino's apartment in Florence one time, she'd discovered some fancy underwear in a drawer. Fancy underwear that most definitely wasn't hers. It seemed Gino was embracing all things Italian and that included an Italian girlfriend. It had been six years since she'd cut all contact. It had been the only thing to do but part of her still missed him. She swallowed her wine in one, choking a little. 'Could we find something sweet to eat now?' she asked, closing the subject down firmly. 'I need something to soak up all this alcohol.'

They settled on some marshmallows dunked in chocolate and ate them messily. Jago then bought three giant gingerbread hearts iced with pretty patterns. 'One for you,' he handed it over with a flourish, 'and I'll take the other two home.'

'Thank you,' she said, more delighted than she should be, and clutched the biscuit to her. 'Avril and Merryn are very lucky.' A great, self-pitying wave of longing overcame her. He was so lovely.

He grinned, his teeth gleaming white in the light from the gingerbread cabin. 'They are,' he joked.

It was getting late now and the crowds had thinned. The wind blew cruelly over the wall off the sea and Honor shivered. His nearness was unnerving her – for all the wrong reasons.

'You're cold?'

She nodded.

'Perhaps we'd better call it a night then.' Thin clouds parted to reveal a nearly full moon glowing a pale blue in an inky sky. He looked up. 'Honor bright by a pale-faced moon indeed,' he murmured. 'You have a smudge of chocolate on your chin.' He reached out and gently thumbed it off. 'There. Gone.'

Honor gazed up at him, wanting to swim in his sea-green eyes. Just wanting. Her chin rose to meet his mouth…

Inching nearer, he lowered his lips to hers and grazed a kiss so light and sweet, it was as delicate as spun sugar.

'Mr Jago! Mr Jago!' From somewhere behind them a tiny figure detached itself from the *frites* cabin.

Honor backed off instantly. She stared open-mouthed, desire warring with horror.

Jaden threw himself at Jago, wrapping his arms around his waist. 'Did you see me? Did you see me in the parade with my nottopuss? I did great!'

'Thank you for a lovely evening, Jago,' Honor stuttered, 'but I have to go.'

She stumbled over the slippery cobbles, bumping into people as she ran through the market and reached the street and the narrow pavement. Once away from him, angry, frustrated tears coursed down her cheeks, blinding her. It was all so unfair. How could he *do* that when he'd just bought his wife and daughter gingerbread? But she'd hardly pushed him away – she'd willed him on! She'd practically had to stop herself licking her lips in anticipation of his kiss. How could she have let herself kiss a married man? And the father of one of her pupils? And in public too?

Oh, but he was so lovely, so irresistible. Since Gino she'd been careful to keep her feelings in check with any new man she met. And she'd been right to. None of them had been worth her time. And now, she'd met Jago and everything was rushing at her. He was perfect in every way. Except one. She'd had the most wonderful, most romantic evening – but it had been with a married man.

CHAPTER 18

'THE TWELVE DAYS OF CHRISTMAS' – TRAD.

Sunday 19th December

Jago fiddled with the display on the table in his corner of the Craft Fayre, tweaking and re-tweaking until it looked perfect. This was all new to him. Once he'd unpacked robins and stars and other seasonal stuff from his box of Christmas stock, he'd realised he might not have enough. He had tried hard to increase his stock in time for this event but hadn't a clue whether he'd judged it right. He wanted to sell enough so he didn't end up with an embarrassingly full table at the end of the day but also wanted a luxurious looking table that enticed customers over. Pricing had also been an issue. In London, where his large glass panels were sold, the gallery owners decided what to charge and he received a percentage. He had no idea what people would be willing to pay for a light catcher in a Christmas Fayre in a small Dorset town. Too much and they wouldn't buy; too little and he'd be underselling – and undervaluing his hard work. And what hard work it had been! He'd been at his desk all the hours he could spare, pulling some all-nighters too. Ivy had lain by his side, sleeping and occasionally making funny, hiccoughing grumbling noises during her dreams.

Taking inspiration from his new surroundings, heaped up on his table were beach huts, seagulls and one or two specials – of foamy waves with a jaunty yacht incorporated. The wicker baskets to put them in had been Avril's idea and he was grateful. It made his stock look far more organised. As a nod to the season, he'd spray painted a branch white, shoved it in a block of plaster of Paris and hung the Christmas trees, robins and stars from it. They glittered in the flashing lights he'd draped around his table. He'd also made a few dozen crescent moons with semi-precious stones dangling from them; an experiment which had worked out well. They were larger and made a bold statement swinging away. He was pleased how they caught the light. Most of these were the size of his palm and perfect stocking fillers – he hoped – made in his trademark stained-glass style of small pieces of coloured glass soldered together. Simplified shapes that hinted at what was pictured, but effective.

He sat back at last and observed his surroundings. Once again, the main studio of the Art School was being used. In an adjoining room the WI were serving up tea and mince pies and he could already hear the clatter of crockery and cheerful voices as they got ready.

'Nice jumper, my friend,' Dave the manager said.

Jago looked down at the reindeer emblazoned on his chest and grimaced. 'Mum knitted it for me. She thought it might encourage the buyers.' He tugged at an antler which Avril had stuffed with padding so they were 3-D.

Dave laughed. 'Might do as well.'

'It gets worse.' Jago reached under Rudolph's nose and switched it on. The red nose, knitted in red sparkly wool, immediately glowed even brighter.

Dave laughed even more. 'I'm liking your mother's humour. Here,' he handed over a mug of coffee, and three mince pies wrapped in a holly-decorated serviette. 'Grabbed you a few before the hordes descend and they sell out. Might be the only chance you get to eat today. Give one of us a shout if you need a break though. It can be intense once it gets going.'

Noddy Holder yelled from the sound system. 'It's Christmaaaaaaaaaaaas!'

Dave winced. 'Much as I love Slade, that's the third time I've heard "Merry Xmas Everybody". Must be nearly time for the off. Any questions? Got your float sorted? Card machine?' As Jago nodded, he added, 'Ace,' and rushed to the next seller.

As Jago ate, he observed those around him. There was a good selection of produce on offer. Large painted seascapes, a table selling hand-embellished maps of the area in driftwood frames, knitted hats, gloves and scarves all trimmed with fake fur, handmade soap (he promised he'd buy some for Avril), a stall selling pottery with chunky mugs, beautifully carved walking sticks with bone heads, and dog-shaped tree decorations made out of felt. He'd spotted a black-and-white one which bore an uncanny resemblance to Ivy and had asked the seller to put it to one side. Merryn would adore it. There was also Daisy Wiscombe from the florist's selling Christmas greenery out of huge wicker baskets. Holly, ivy and mistletoe frothed out, the berries a lustrous red and white. His mind drifted to when he'd kissed Honor at the German Market the night before. He cursed. He had no idea what he'd done but regretted it bitterly. He'd misread the signals. There hadn't even been any mistletoe around to excuse him. But really, there was no excuse to kiss a woman when she clearly didn't want to be kissed. Frowning, he pictured the scene in his head. But had he misread Honor? They seemed to be getting on increasingly well, getting close even. Certainly close enough for her to confide in him about her ex. And it was hardly a kiss at all, he'd only brushed her lips with his before she'd backed off and fled into the night. He sighed. He knew well enough even a slight kiss wasn't acceptable if the woman didn't want it. And Honor had clearly not wanted it. The trouble was he kept finding himself wanting *her* very much. Very much indeed. Another reason he'd thrown himself into his work; he'd spent the last ten hours working solidly through the night. Trying to blot out the feel of her soft lips and the scent of her drifting up as he'd bent down, he shoved the last half of mince pie in his mouth and slapped his hands together to brush the crumbs off. Remembering his mother always told him the tradition was to wish on the first mince pie of the season, he closed his eyes and, feeling faintly ridiculous, made a wish. Opening them, he was startled to find his first customer was standing in front of his table, looking expectant.

'I'm so sorry. What can I help you with?' he smiled.

Dave had been right. Once the Fayre opened, it was relentless. The room soon filled up. There was a happy buzz of shoppers and Jago's stained glass was selling well. The morning flew by.

'Lots of positive comments coming my way about your stuff, Jago, mate,' Dave said, as he passed by with another mug of coffee. 'One or two mentioned they'd talked to you about larger commissions. You make sure you come and see me in the new year about that space you want.' The sound system died. Dave looked up in relief. 'Thank the ruddy Nora for that. I mean, don't get me wrong, as I said, I love a bit of Slade but even I tire of the same tune after the fourteenth time. Must be time for the girls to sing.' He turned to Jago. 'It's a few from the local community choir. Have you heard them?'

Jago shook his head.

'Then you're in for a treat. Ah, here they come.'

It was Tamara and four other women. All were dressed in figure-hugging red dresses, with snowy white faux-fur edging the sleeves and hem. They took their positions in the middle of the room, standing in formation with their backs to one another.

Tamara held up her hand and a few in the crowd nudged one another, hushed and turned to listen. 'Welcome Lullbury Bay

Christmas Craft Fayre, it's so good to see so many of you are here supporting it. We haven't sung in the town for a while so we're thrilled to be here. We'll kick off with "Santa Baby".'

Jago could see how well Tamara would go down on the cruise circuit; she was the consummate professional and confidence personified.

They sang a cappella and swayed in unison in a series of sexy dance moves. 'Santa Baby' was followed with 'Rockin' Around the Christmas Tree' and 'I saw Mommy Kissing Santa Claus', finishing with 'We Wish You a Merry Christmas' to resounding cheers.

'They're good, aren't they?' a dark-haired woman with a little boy in tow said. 'Hi,' she added brightly. 'I'm Maisie. I own the café on the front.' She reached over a hand, and they shook.

'Jago Pengethley.'

'What a fabulous name! I was an Onions before I married. Can't say I miss it. Although maybe it was a good name for a café owner!'

'Did you think about keeping it?' Jago smiled at her.

She pulled a face. 'Onions are best kept for casseroles. Besides, my husband was already double-barrelled.' Laughing, she added, 'You can only have so much of a good thing.' Her little boy tugged on her hand. 'Oh yes, we'd like to buy two of your robins please.' She picked the child up and rested him on a hip. 'Would you like to hand Jago the money, Joshie?'

Jago took it and gave the little boy a warm smile at which he turned and buried his head in Maisie's shoulder.

'Going through a shy phase,' Maisie explained. 'Could you pop the robins in my bag?' She turned so Jago could slip the tissue paper-wrapped parcels in a large tote hanging off her shoulder. 'Wonderful. They'll look gorgeous hanging on the tree. We've got a whopper this year. Right, young man, next stall to buy a felt version of Stan. That's our spaniel,' she explained. Looking down at Jago's wares, she said thoughtfully, 'You know, if you ever made any glass cupcakes, we'd love to sell them in the café. I'm sure they'd go like–'

'Hotcakes,' they said as one.

Jago liked this woman; she seemed friendly and straightforward. 'I'd love to. Give me some time to experiment with a few shapes. It doesn't always work out.' He gestured to the piece depicting waves and a yacht bobbing on top. 'These were a happy experiment, but it can be tricky with rounded shapes.'

'Wonderful. Pop into the café. If I'm not there, speak to Tracy who's the manager. Think we'd like a few to dangle in the windows. They'd look so pretty.' Joshie flung a pudgy arm around his mother's neck and whispered something urgently in her ear. 'Yes, darling, we're going to get a miniature Stan now. Say bye to Jago.'

'Bye, Joshie.' Jago waved and thoughtfully watched them go. He could remember Merryn being very similar at that age. One minute mischievous, the next clingy and shy. He liked children. He'd found Merryn great fun when she'd been tiny, he still did. At first, he'd been shocked at the idea of his parents having another child so long after having him but, to his surprise, he'd loved having a baby around. He'd enjoyed the work he'd done in schools too and the children's enthusiasm had, in turn, buoyed him on to plough that enthusiasm into his own art. With a grin he remembered how rewarding getting Jaden to talk at the lantern workshop had been. Something inside him twisted, a sudden realisation. He was thirty-five. He was ready to have children of his own. He wanted to settle down with someone and create his own family. And he was beginning to realise he'd like to settle in Lullbury Bay. He'd never felt that way with Rose, neither of them had. They'd both been too busy getting their careers established to even think of starting a family. They'd worked hard and played hard. Anything more grown-up lay in the distance. They thought they'd had plenty of time. But Jago now knew time could be cut brutally short. Life could unscrew in a second and change irrevocably. His father had been looking forward to retirement. But he'd never made it. Jago had learned a bitter lesson through his father dying, he was no longer complacent about having his life stretching out endlessly in front of him. And he didn't want to waste a precious minute of it.

CHAPTER 19

'BLUE CHRISTMAS' – ELVIS PRESLEY

Honor went over to congratulate Tamara and the choir members. 'That was fantastic,' she said, kissing Tamara on the cheek. 'I don't know how you do those close harmonies and remember the words as well as those dance moves. I'd be hopeless.' She turned to the man standing beside her. 'Have you met Ben Townham? He teaches Blenny Class at school. Year Five,' she explained further.

Ben shook everyone's hand. 'Great to meet you all.' He smiled affably. 'It was all very impressive. I really enjoyed it. We must book you to come and do some singing workshops in school, that's if you'd be happy to.' He winked at Honor. 'But we might have to tone down some of those seriously sexy dance moves.' They all laughed. 'I'm just going to check out the candle store,' he added. 'I'll catch up with you in a mo, Honor.'

She nodded. 'Fine.'

Tamara waited until the other members of the choir drifted off in his wake before sidling closer. 'You've kept him quiet. And there we were trying to get you set up with a man and you had one in your pocket all along!'

'Oh give it up, Tam. He's a teaching colleague from school. Besides which, I'm his line manager. Can't go there.'

'Shame.' Tamara stared at Ben as he examined the scented candles, picking them up and laughing with the seller. 'He's lush. All that mucky-blonde hair. Reminds me of that actor from Fifty Shades.'

'Jamie Dornan?' Honor considered the idea. 'Yes, I suppose he does a bit. He'd hate the comparison though. He's a nice bloke, very modest. The kids love him.'

Tamara pulled a lascivious face. 'I bet they do. If I had a teacher that good-looking teaching me at school maybe I would've paid more attention!' She called to her co-singers. 'Right then, ladies, shall we grab a tea and a mince pie? Think we've earned one. See you later, babes.'

'See you, Tamara.' Honor joined Ben at the scented candles table. 'Spending all your money?' she asked jokingly.

He held one to her nose. 'This one is Christmas in a candle. Have a sniff.'

She obliged. 'Oh, it's lovely. Just like a Christmas tree. I was expecting something sweet but it's pine and something else–'

'Eucalyptus and a hint of orange,' the seller explained. 'Makes the room fresh and invigorating.'

'I'll take two if I may,' Ben said, and they watched as the seller wrapped them in pretty tissue paper. He took them, paid, and handed one to Honor. 'I know we did Secret Santa at school, but I wanted to get you something to thank you for all the support you've given me this term. Year Five hasn't been the easiest and I've really appreciated all your mentoring.'

Honor was touched. 'Oh, Ben, you really didn't have to. It's my job. I enjoy the mentoring part of being deputy. And, honestly, you hardly needed any. It's a class that just needs a certain handling and some behavioural strategies put in place. But thank you for the candle, I love it.' She clutched it to her, smelling its sharp tangy scent even through the wrapping. It would be perfect lit on Christmas Day. 'What do you want to have a look at next?' she asked, giving him a warm smile.

'I'm heading towards those stained-glass hanging things. Mum would love the moon with the crystals hanging off it.'

Honor followed as he battled through the crowds to Jago's table. Smile vanishing, her heart sank. She knew he had a stall here but she'd wanted avoid him. It was lucky term had ended; it would have been impossible to avoid him or Avril when they collected Merryn from school. The kiss at the German Market last night should have never happened. Complications of this sort were exactly why she was so circumspect about mixing her private life with her professional. But there was another reason too – it was Gino all over again. Gino having cheated on her had done unimaginable harm to her self-esteem and it had taken a long, long time to build it back up. She was determined the next man she was involved with would be worth the emotional investment. And, even though every hormone and cell in her body was on fire for it to be Jago, it just couldn't happen. She refused to do that to Avril and Merryn. With a pang, she realised the situation could make her the other woman and, after the heartbreak caused by Gino, she refused to hurt another woman the same way.

A loudly distorted 'Last Christmas' burst out of the Tannoy, now the choir had finished singing. The poignant lyrics weren't lost on her. Trailing despondently in Ben's wake, she got to Jago's stall to find the two men deep in discussion over the exquisite piece held in Ben's hand. As if it wasn't bad enough, not only was Jago the perfect father and husband (kissing other women notwithstanding) who was kind to animals and children, but he was also massively talented. Honor thought it couldn't be any more unfair. Gazing at Ben, she wondered why, all professional considerations aside, she couldn't fall for a nice, uncomplicated man like him?

'What do you think, Honor? Do you think my mum would

like this?' He turned to her, his grey eyes alive with enthusiasm, and held out the crescent moon made from frosted silvery glass. He trickled the semi-precious stones which glitteringly hung from it through his fingers.

It was stunning. Much larger than the other pieces on the stall, it caught the light in a magical way, as if it were alive. Honor's heart thumped. Jago was a talented artist. It was delicate and ethereal and caught the essence of the moon in a deceptively simple way. The moon itself shone with a light that seemed to come from inside and the glimmering stones which dangled could easily be the moon's reflection on the sea; she'd often seen it make those shimmering, shifting patterns over the bay. For some reason, the sight of Jago's artwork made her emotional. Her words choked in her throat. 'It's... it's beautiful. I'm sure she'd love it. Anyone would.' She couldn't quite meet Jago's eyes and longed to get away.

'I'll wrap it up for you,' he said. 'Would you like it in a gift bag too?'

'Yes please,' Ben said. 'It'll make it extra special and I'm hopeless at wrapping presents. Thanks so much, Jago is it? I'm Ben Townham by the way, a teacher at St Winifred's. I teach with Honor here. I think I might have seen you at our nativity.'

The men shook hands. 'Jago Pengethley. Nice to meet you. And yes, I came to watch the nativity. Enjoyed it very much.'

Honor saw Jago glance intently from Ben to herself and, ridiculously, felt her face flame.

He handed over the neatly presented gift. 'How are you, Honor?' he asked in measured tones.

'Oh, you know, catching up with myself. Getting ready for Christmas. Busy,' she added, lamely. She felt herself blushing even harder.

'Will I see you at the RNLI carols event? I've heard it's good.'

'It's an absolute blast,' Ben interrupted. 'There's a good sing-along led by the choir, mulled wine, the best-decorated beach hut competition. Oh,' he turned to Honor and grinned. 'We mustn't forget the dog fancy dress. That promises to be a laugh. Can I pay contactless? Brill.'

While he paid, Honor concentrated on staring at the shiny glass robins on Jago's table. She'd love one but couldn't marshal her feelings enough for the transaction. Clutching the scented candle to her, she came over all hot. Maybe it was because she had on her jacket and hat. Pulling it off she shook out her hair and lifted it off her neck to cool down. Over the sound system George Michael was singing about giving his heart away. She had a horrible feeling she had too. What a mess.

'We'll see you at the RNLI carols then?' Ben said chirpily.

'Might well do,' Jago answered.

Honor didn't dare glance at his face to see how he'd taken Ben's casual bracketing of them. She sucked in a breath. What did it matter what Jago Pengethley thought? He was a married man, she was free and single. What did it matter if he misunderstood the situation between her and Ben?

'Bye, Jago,' Ben said. 'Thanks for the moon. I know Mum will be knocked out by it. I've taken one of your business cards too so if she wants another piece, she knows where to come.'

'Thank you for buying.'

'See you, Jago.' Honor still couldn't meet his eyes. This was awful.

'Bye, Honor.'

Was it her imagination or had she heard wistfulness in his voice?

Jago watched them go. Ben was bending down and talking animatedly to Honor. The jealousy had caught him off-guard. It speared in his gut, a visceral pain, turning his stomach over in a gut-wrenching spasm. He'd got it bad.

But how? After all, he and Honor hardly knew one another. They'd met only a few times, and most of those had been in the company of his family. The hour or so he'd spent with her at German Market sparkled in his memory like the moon he'd just sold to Ben. It seemed ridiculous to have developed feelings so quickly but he had. He picked over the conversation they'd had about her ex, the one who lived in Italy. Had she mentioned being involved with anyone else? Had she given him the impression she was single? He'd assumed so, otherwise he wouldn't have kissed her. Maybe he'd got it all wrong and she was with this Ben guy? Maybe that was why she'd fled. But why hadn't she explained?

He wondered what would have happened had Jaden not interrupted them. The boy had gripped him around the waist so hard he'd had trouble detaching himself. Jaden's mother had staggered up to them too, clearly full of *glühwein,* and yanked her son to her, glaring accusingly. She dived into a foul-mouthed rant and it was only when he explained he'd worked with Jaden at the lantern workshop and wasn't a random man taking advantage of her son that she'd mellowed. Then, drunkenly and embarrassingly, she began to flirt. By the time it was sorted and he'd escaped, Honor had disappeared into the night.

Maybe he'd gone in too soon, too strong with Honor? And ruined it all. But he'd been sure they were building a friendship, one that had the possibility of a relationship dangling invitingly on the horizon. He liked her. He liked her love of her community, and the care and kindness she showed Merryn. He even liked her love of all things Christmas, although this year he couldn't bring himself to share it. He really liked her. God, he might even be getting in deeper. And now it looked as if she was with someone. All the warmth Honor had previously shown towards him had disappeared. While he'd wrapped Ben's moon, she'd hardly uttered two words to him. As he thrust a frustrated hand through his hair, he caught the Rudolph nose on his jumper and the wretched thing glowed red. Perhaps she'd gone off him because he was wearing a ridiculous sweater?

He busied himself rearranging the stock on his table. There were quite a few gaps and a lot more white cloth showing where he'd sold pieces. As he did so, he surreptitiously watched as Ben slung a casual arm around Honor's shoulders. They were standing next to the wicker baskets containing the evergreens and laughing. Ben picked up a branch of mistletoe, appearing to make a joke.

'Don't kiss her,' Jago found himself muttering. 'Don't you dare kiss her!' To his relief, Honor took the mistletoe and put it back in the basket.

Of course it made sense Honor would be attracted to a teacher. They'd have so much in common, would share an understanding of the job, share the stresses and the same holidays. One of his mates back in London had gone out with a teacher. Their never-ending arguments about why she couldn't drop everything and go for a four-day weekend to Madrid in the middle of term had consumed a memorable evening in the pub. Equally, his friend hated the heat of the Med in August and refused to go. He could see why teachers often went out – and married other teachers.

Marriage. He groaned inwardly. He'd tried it and it hadn't worked out. Looking back, he knew why. He and Rose had had an instant and hot physical attraction – the sex had been mind-blowing – but once that had waned, they had little in common. He inhabited the world of artists and craftspeople; she was in the hard world of retail management. He half suspected they'd rushed into living together as a way of sharing the rent in order to live in a better part of the city. Then they'd slid, unthinking, into marriage and a mortgage. They liked each other; they still did. He was lucky the divorce had been amicable, and they were friends. He knew, though, his black moods and destructive behaviour after his father died had tested the friendship they'd strived for post-divorce. Rose hadn't been able to get him through those awful days and, as an ex-wife, had no obligation to. But they'd been friends before becoming a couple and, just before the family moved from London, had become so again. Was he ready for another relationship? He wasn't sure but he'd like to find out. He'd like to find out if there was the promise of a future with Honor.

But it looked as if he'd blown it. Idiot! He'd rushed it with Honor, just as he'd rushed it with Rose. Would he ever learn? His father had always said he acted first and thought second. And now he was having to live in a small town and risk bumping into Honor and whoever she was with. It seemed a peculiarly cruel form of torture. So much for his wish on the first mince pie of the season!

CHAPTER 20

'WE THREE KINGS OF ORIENT ARE' – TRAD.

Monday 20th December

Jago couldn't concentrate. Staring down at his work desk in his attic and at the cupcake design he just couldn't seem to get quite right, he threw his pencil down. On his sketchbook, alongside the cake patterns, he'd doodled hearts and lips. No analysis needed there, he thought, grimly. Going to the Velux window, he opened it and stood on the tiny balcony. The weather was in league with his mood. A heavy sky hung sullenly down but the cold air began to revive him. Gulls wheeled and called mournfully, some catching an air current and lifting off into the distance. Part of him wished he could do the same. He studied their shape and the way their aerodynamic bodies effortlessly conquered the air. When he and Merryn had grabbed a bag of chips the other afternoon and had sat on the harbour wall to eat them, they'd been surrounded by gulls, strutting about, stiff-legged, greedily alert for any food scraps. The contrast between how they were on land and in the sky fascinated him. He fetched his sketchbook and made some rapid notes for future reference.

A drizzly rain began to fall, more low sea mist than anything but, in the far distance over the sea, a lighter sky was being chased inland. With any luck it would pass. Closing up the window, he sat back at his desk but still couldn't settle. With Avril at her Knit and Natter Group again and Merryn on a playdate with Holly, a quiet, empty house should mean he could concentrate and get down to some work, but he wasn't feeling it. His enthusiasm for his craft, which had returned spectacularly in preparation for the Craft Fayre, had deserted him again. Ivy whined at his side so, flicking shut the cover on his sketchbook, he made his decision.

Instead of walking along the seafront, he climbed the steep hill leading from the harbour and cut across the public gardens in the direction of the church in the old town. Its squat Norman tower sat serene and high above the jumble of houses. It must have seen its fair share of troubled souls wander past. Jago wondered if he was one of them.

As he walked up the wide pathway to the church door, Ivy stopped in her tracks and began to growl low in her throat. At the top stood three bollards, he supposed to prevent any vehicles getting around the side of the building. He vaguely remembered them from when he visited before. However, the bollards had then stood naked and proud. Now they were covered in knitted costumes. Giving Ivy a reassuring stroke and distracting her with a biscuit, he ventured nearer. The Ninja Knitters had been at it again, the bollards had been yarn-bombed. Humour ate through his low mood, and he began to chuckle. The three bollards had been dressed as the three kings in all their glory, complete with gifts of gold, frankincense and myrrh. All knitted, of course. They were distinctively individual, with one having a long grey beard and one with a shock of black curly hair. All wore sumptuous, knitted cloaks in jewel colours.

'They're great, aren't they?' The vicar came out of the church. 'I'm becoming very fond of them.'

'Hi, Verity. They are. Magnificent. The detail is astonishing.'

Jago bent closer to have a better look. 'Such skill. Look at the gold knitted braiding on this one.'

'It's an amazing art form. Someone must be very talented.'

He straightened. 'You mean you don't know who put them there?'

'Not a scoobie. I'm assuming it's the same people who dressed the postbox down by the Sea Spray café.'

Ivy still wasn't sure. She growled again.

'Oh dear,' Verity said. 'Someone's not keen.' She stared up at the rain, which despite Jago's optimism of earlier, was worsening. She pulled a face. 'If only this was snow. Might feel more seasonal. Look, I'm just about to grab a coffee, do you want one? Got some choccie biccies somewhere too. Unless you want to pop in and say hi to Winnie? The church is open.'

Jago hesitated. Part of him wanted to sit in quiet contemplation in front of St Winifred's stained-glass window. He shivered, feeling the damp trickle down the back of his neck. He'd prefer snow too.

'No? Come on into the house then, until the worst of the rain passes over.'

He indicated Ivy. 'As long as you don't mind the wet dog smell.'

'Well now, isn't she one of God's creatures?' Verity laughed. 'Come on, give me a chance to put my feet up. It's been a mad morning. Always is at this time of year.'

He followed her back down the path and then along a narrow alley he'd not noticed before and waited until she unlocked a door in the side of a building.

'Now, don't judge, my kitchen is a right mess, but I know where everything is and I make a mean mug of coffee so it's worth having to shove a pile of ecclesiastical bumf off a chair. Oh, and there's an Aga too, so you can dry your jacket and warm your behind.'

She led him down a long gloomy passageway and into a

square, high-ceilinged kitchen dominated by an ancient-looking cream Aga at one end. It was pumping out a welcome heat.

'Sit yourself down, I'll put the kettle on. Here, give me your coat. I'm lucky to have a vicarage so near my church. The C of E have shipped a lot of us into new builds miles away from our parish. Then they can sell the original vicarage off at an unholy profit, of course.' She laughed. 'Not that they'd get much for this crumbling pile.' She slipped off her coat to reveal a sweatshirt emblazoned with: *God is Good but the Vicar is Better!*

While she draped their jackets on the back of a chair, turning it to the Aga to dry, Jago hid his amusement at her sweatshirt by looking around. There were Christmas cards on every available surface, including the shelf above the Aga, and bushy strident-coloured strands of tinsel hung across the ceiling. The vast scrubbed pine table was heaped high with letters and magazines and several handleless mugs serving as pen pots, and in the middle of the mess stood a carved wooden nativity, a smaller version of the one at the German Market. The Belfast sink was full of unwashed crockery and there was a rime of dust on most surfaces. Despite the neglect, it was a welcoming and cosy space. He moved a folder and sat down in an old-fashioned, high-backed chair next to the Aga and watched, amused, as Ivy sniffed around and then settled with a sigh against it, stretching out so as much of her back as possible was in contact with the heat.

'Ah, see she's made herself at home. Always amazes me how dogs instinctively know to head for Agnetha.'

'Agnetha?'

'Agnetha the Aga. Big ABBA fan,' Verity said, as if that explained everything. She filled the kettle and plonked it on the hotplate. 'Won't be long. Chiquitita'll let us know when she's ready by screaming.'

'Chiquitita?' He hazarded a guess. 'The kettle?'

'Yup.' Verity pulled up another chair, eased off her boots and tucked her toes under the rail of the Aga. 'Ooh, it gets so cold in that church,' she complained and pulled the sleeves of her jumper over her hands.

Jago was trying not to laugh. It seemed rude.

'What? Doesn't everyone name their household appliances? Don't answer! If they don't, then they should. And ABBA comes second only to God in my eyes. With the Bishop trailing in third.' She shivered and wiggled her toes. 'Bliss. Think they're just about defrosting now. How's things then, Jago?' She peered at him. 'You look less lean somehow. Must be the Lullbury Bay sea air.'

Jago filled her in on the Craft Fayre, how he'd temporarily rediscovered his work ethic and was planning on renting a space at the Art School in order to make bigger installation art. 'I had quite a few people express their interest at the Fayre,' he went on. 'It's something I used to do more of in London but wasn't sure of the market down here.'

Chiquitita obligingly whistled to say she'd boiled and Verity leaped up, making Ivy start. 'Well, that all sounds very exciting. A very positive move.' She grabbed a cafetiere and spooned some coffee into it, added a jug of cream and some mugs and biscuits to a tray, and plonked it all on the table where it sat precariously on a not quite level pile of papers. Ivy sat up, her nose quivering at the scent of coffee and biscuits. Returning to the spot by the Aga, Verity asked, 'And who's this little love?'

'Ivy. Tom at the animal sanctuary rescued her and we took her on. Merryn's always wanted a dog so she's ecstatic. Christmas Tree Cottage is awash with wildlife at the moment as we're looking after Chestnut the school hamster too.'

'And how do they get on?' Verity giggled.

'Great if in separate rooms. Otherwise, Ivy has her nose pressed against the bars of the cage.'

'Oops. And it wouldn't do for her to eat the class hamster.' She reached round and pushed the plunger down on the coffee pot. 'Cream with yours?'

'Please.' He accepted the mug of coffee and sipped. Verity was right, she did make it well.

'And how's Merryn getting on?'

'She's good. Having the dog has helped, although her promise to walk her has waned now the weather's gone wet and cold. It's been left to me.'

'And how have you all been coping? You said your father died about this time of year.'

'Well remembered. You don't forget much, do you?'

'Not about people. Try me on paying the gas bill or taking a parcel to the post office and that's a different story.' She grimaced.

'I think Merryn is doing well, although I'm not sure what will happen on Christmas Eve. It's when Dad died.'

'I'm so sorry,' Verity said, obviously shocked. 'A death is hard at the best of times, but Christmas and all the reminders are almost impossible to avoid. It must be very hard.'

'She's full of her new bestie Holly. The Carmichaels have a big house on the edge of town, and they have horses and dachshund puppies.'

'What a friend to have. Horses *and* puppies.'

Jago laughed. 'They're great buddies. We've done just about everything Christmassy Lullbury Bay can throw at us, so she's been kept busy. She had a starring role in the school nativity, and she's begun quoting Shakespeare.'

'Oh my!'

'Exactly. Mum and I don't know how she does it, but she can reel off great long quotes. Dad gave her a dictionary of quotations for her birthday.' Jago shot Verity a look. 'It was his last present to her. She nagged him relentlessly for one and I think she's been memorising it now school's finished for the term. Not sure how much she understands but her memory is pretty impressive.'

'I'll say. It's a talent and a half.' Verity met his look. 'Perhaps it's a link to him?' she suggested kindly.

'Maybe. Although, if you'd known my dad, he wouldn't strike you as a Shakespeare fan, because he wasn't.'

'Must be the physical book then. It's a connection to him.' Verity sipped her coffee thoughtfully. 'Has she had any counselling?'

'Some. It was organised through her school but it ended up being counterproductive.'

'How so?'

'Mum and I weren't happy about how the school handled it. Merryn became known as the girl whose father had,' he put his mug down and used his fingers to make speech marks, '"died in tragic circumstances". There was a lot of stuff in the media when it happened and we felt the school wasn't very discreet in how they dealt with it. When she returned in the January term there was the beginning of some bullying. Merryn's always been a little different anyway. Her notoriety was something else they could pick on. The school had an enormous intake and Merryn was getting lost in it all. It was another reason we wanted to relocate.'

'I see. Well, St Winifred's has an excellent reputation for pastoral care and it's small enough to have a family feel. Is she happier there?'

'Seems to be so far. We'd been getting outbursts of anger, sullenness. She even lost her appetite,' Jago laughed a little, 'which isn't like Merryn at all. She's still clingy and she still wants to get into Mum's bed sometimes, but she's happier. More like herself.' He paused and blew out a breath. 'She doesn't talk about Dad though, which worries me.'

'Maybe it will happen in time.'

'Yeah. Hope so. It might be our fault. We try to talk about Dad at home but we made the decision not to make a huge deal of being bereaved when we came here. We didn't want to tell anyone. It meant Merryn, and us too, could have a fresh start.'

'I see. But, Jago, her school records will catch up with her at some point and everyone will find out then. The teachers at school are very discreet though. They'll take their lead from you and your mother.' Verity reached round and offered Jago a biscuit. 'I'm not sure how all the record-keeping is done these days. I'm surprised it's not all online.' She frowned. 'I seem to remember when I taught and a child joined the class, I'd get a big card folder of stuff. Examples of work, test results, any notes of things I should be aware of, that sort of thing. I suppose it's possible it's still done that way.'

Jago crunched into his biscuit. 'I've no idea, but we were surprised St Winifred's hasn't been in touch about Dad dying. So, maybe you're right, the paperwork hasn't reached Dorset yet. And we haven't said anything. At least it's meant Merryn could start a new school and just be her, not the child who lost her father in a terrible tragedy.'

'I think it might be wise to tell school at some point, so they know how best to support her and, if you do want some grief counselling for her, there's a super group which meets in Dorchester. It's a charity which gets children who have lost parents together. Sometimes only children who have been through the same thing are the ones who understand properly.'

'Thanks Verity. I'll mention it to Mum. Maybe get something organised in the new year. It's too near Christmas to do anything before then.'

'And your mother? How's she doing?'

'She has her moments. Seems to spend all her time with the Knit and Natter group.'

'No bad thing. They're good-hearted people and you can do a lot of therapeutic talking in the company of a group of women knitting.' She leaned forward and looked at him intently. 'And you, Jago, how are *you*?'

CHAPTER 21

'LITTLE THINGS' – ABBA

Jago gulped the rest of his coffee and accepted a refill. 'I'm fine,' he said carefully.

'Mmm.'

'Not buying it?'

Verity smiled kindly. 'Not really. You said you'd mostly got your work back on track which is wonderful. You're obviously walking Ivy so you're getting some physical exercise and fresh air which, again, is a marvellous and restorative thing.'

'But?'

'But I sense an underlying restlessness.'

'Not surprising considering the year we've all had.'

'True. Forgive me, I don't mean to pry.'

Jago had the feeling she was going to anyway.

'When we bumped into each other in front of good old Winnie that time, I knew you were unhappy, obviously bereaved, lost in a way. Some of that's gone but there's something else now.'

Jago blew out a heavy breath.

'You don't have to talk to me.' She spread her hands. 'I mean, you don't have to talk to anyone, but I've found it helps.'

'I'm not one of your parishioners, Verity.'

'Oh, but you are.'

'I don't go to church.'

'You're still one of my parishioners.'

He sat back and sighed. 'You don't give up, do you?'

'Wouldn't be doing my job if I did,' she said, not quite apologetically. 'Would you prefer it if I found you a man to talk to?'

Jago shifted irritably. 'No. If I were to talk to anyone it would be to you.'

'I'm flattered.'

'Don't be,' he said, with a reluctant laugh. 'There's not much of an alternative.'

'You come in here,' she tutted melodramatically. 'Drink my coffee, eat my biscuits,' she held out the plate, 'have another by the way, they're very good. You hog my Aga and then say that.'

'I like talking to you,' he said helplessly. 'It's the–'

'What?'

'This is going to sound so immature, but it's the God thing.'

'This?' Verity pointed at her clerical collar. She reached round to the back of her neck and unclipped it. Tossing it onto the table, she added, 'There. Gone. Better?'

'Slightly.' He had the grace to be embarrassed.

'So, what is it?'

He shrugged and stared moodily into his mug. 'I think we've made the right decision to come here. Merryn seems happy, or happier than she was. Mum's coping and beginning to find a life for herself. She's even talking about finding a job.'

'Oh!' Verity sat up suddenly. 'They're looking for someone at Bee's Books. Bee is lovely to work for. Have to say a job in a bookshop with a café in it is my idea of heaven. You have to try their waffles.' She giggled. 'Well, apart from my actual idea of heaven, if you get my drift.'

Jago smiled. 'I'll mention it to her. She was at John Lewis before so it might appeal.'

Verity made a face. 'Not quite in the same league but our little bookshop has the advantage of being local at least. But, back to you. Your dilemma. Not work-related, is it?'

'No.' Jago shook his head. 'I thought I'd rediscovered my mojo. Or I had until this morning. I've been working like a demon.' He glanced at her, groaning inwardly. He really had no idea how to talk to a vicar. 'Sorry.'

'What for? If I believe in God, it makes sense for me to believe in demons. And, trust me, I've seen enough people with demons inside them. But that's not your issue, is it? You say Lullbury Bay has been a good decision for you?'

'It has. It is. The problem I've got is every time I walk Ivy around the harbour, I have to pass the lifeboat station.'

'And it's a problem because?'

'I want to volunteer. Every fibre of my being wants to go in and offer my services as crew.'

Verity put her mug on the table behind her. Then she leaned forward and gave him her full attention. 'And that's a worthy ambition. They always need crew. What's the problem?'

'I told my mother I wouldn't crew for the RNLI ever again. I promised her.'

'You've crewed before?'

Jago nodded. 'In London. Out of Tower Lifeboat Station. It was the station my father worked at. He was the Lifeboat Operations Manager.'

'I see.'

Jago wasn't sure she did. 'The Tower Station is organised differently to the Lullbury Bay one where it's manned by volunteers,' he explained. 'It's so busy there are full-time, paid crew on duty 24/7, 365 days a year. They're supplemented by a voluntary crew. I volunteered when I could, and Dad was in charge of the whole shebang.'

'My goodness, what a responsible job to hold.'

'It was.' A smile played about Jago's lips as he remembered

how much his father had loved his job, how he had devoted his life to service in the RNLI. 'But Dad lived for the RNLI.' As he said it, he was aware of the bitter irony.

'And your mother doesn't want you to volunteer again?'

'She doesn't want to lose me like she lost Dad.'

'Ah, of course, I remember you saying. Completely understandable. Would it help if you told me how it happened?'

Jago put his mug down on the quarry-tiled floor. He stared hard at the Aga nameplate on the front of the stove. It was written in curly writing and was slightly tarnished. One or two of his London friends had an Aga on their wish lists but it was something he'd never understood. Now, stretching his hands out to its warmth and comfort he grudgingly admitted to seeing the appeal. He forced his focus away from the cosy kitchen to memories of the previous Christmas. 'It was Christmas Eve,' he began haltingly. 'We were all at home. Me, Mum and Merryn. I'd moved back in as the flat I'd shared with Rose was sold and I was deciding what to do next. Merryn had made Mum buy a second tree.' He smiled at the memory. 'She'd wanted a small one for her bedroom, one with roots so we could plant it in the garden afterwards. We were decorating it and bickering because we couldn't untangle the old set of lights we'd found in the attic. Dad was still at the station. He wasn't on call though, as head of the station he wouldn't be asked to crew. He was just about to clock off and go home, to start Christmas, when one of the other crew members got a call from his wife saying she'd just gone into labour. It was their first, so Dad stayed on. An emergency call had just come through and there wasn't much time to make a decision. He persuaded the new station manager to let him do one last shout but as a volunteer.' Jago looked up at Verity. 'It was Dad's last day at work, you see. He was retiring that day.'

'Oh, Jago! That's so sad but what a good gesture.'

'He was a good man.' Jago shifted, the grief piercing him. 'A great dad too. He'd narrowly missed me being born but he was at

Merryn's and always said no father should miss the birth of his child. So he told Dougie to get himself up to St Thomas's. Apparently, he even shoved a handful of notes at him for a taxi. Said they'd wet the baby's head when it was all over.' He stared hard at the Aga sign, blinking rapidly. 'Only they never did because by the time Dougie's little girl had been born, Dad was lying dead in the same hospital. One life in, another out. I suppose there's a certain symmetry.' He felt Verity take his hand and soaked up the comfort it offered.

'What happened?'

'They got called out on this shout. Bloke spotted in the water. Possible suicide. Someone had seen him jump off a bridge. Nothing that unusual, especially at that time of year. Trouble was the current had dragged him to where it was impossible to get the lifeboat or the police boat to him. They got as near as they could and spotted him clinging to a wooden pier near The Prospect of Whitby.' At Verity's blank expression, he added, 'It's a pub right on the river. The guy was right under the back of the pier and refusing to budge but they couldn't get either boat near enough to pull him into it. Dad made the decision to go into the water.'

Verity hissed in a sharp breath.

'I know, right?' Jago gave a little scoffing laugh. 'We used to tease him about getting on and being too old to hack a proper shout, that he was only up to a desk job at his age.' He looked down and bit his lip hard. 'Maybe if we hadn't teased, he wouldn't have decided to go in.'

Verity tightened her grip on his hand. 'I'm sure he did what he thought was the right thing to do and your teasing had nothing to do with it.'

Jago hardly heard her. Joking with his father about his age was one of the many things he wished he could go back and change. 'It's rare to get in the water, you see. It's an absolute last resort. There are all sorts in that river. You have to battle against the cold, the tide, whatever is under your feet trying to trap you. It's dangerous. And my dad knew all this.'

'Then he was an exceptionally brave man.'

'Yes. He was brave.' Jago looked down clenching his jaw to hold back the tears. 'It was the last brave thing he did in a long career serving the RNLI. He had on a line, had a float. Got to the guy and grabbed hold, calmed him down. He even persuaded him to get into the lifeboat. But as they were getting Dad in, the bloke they'd rescued kicked off again. In all the confusion, Dad slipped back. They think he must have hit his head on something. Like I said, the river is treacherous. You don't know what's in there. Maybe being in the cold water for so long made him lose concentration or something. He went under…' Jago's voice faltered. 'He went under and they lost him for a few minutes in the dark. They got him back on the boat and did what they could, but he died in hospital. Fatal blow to the head, irreparable brain injury.' He dashed a hand across his eyes.

A silence fell over the kitchen.

'I'm so very sorry, Jago.' Verity continued to clutch his hand. She waited for him to recover enough to continue speaking.

Jago shook off her hold and cleared his throat, straightening his shoulders. He'd thought he'd passed the tears stage in his grief, but it obviously wasn't the case. He sucked in a deep, shuddering breath. 'I was told later the guy they rescued went on to make a full recovery, so that's something.'

'Yes, that *is* something. Your father did something wonderful that day. He gave his life so someone else might live.'

'Yeah, if you look at it that way.' Jago wasn't convinced. Still angry at the man the crew had rescued and who had robbed him of his father, he'd rather it had all never happened. Brightening a little, he added, 'Dougie named his baby girl Kendra. It was the closest to Kenan he could get that his wife agreed on.'

'That's very touching. A little light, some joy in a terrible time.'

Verity looked at him intently. 'And it must have been a terrible time.'

'It was. We were all waiting at home for Dad to return. Mer had painted a Happy Retirement banner. Then we got the phone call. We spent the rest of the night in the hospital. They let Mum and me in to say goodbye. We had to gown up, you know, wear all the protective gear? We looked like aliens.' He shook his head. 'It was an alien, out of this world experience. Weird. Rose sat with Merryn, which was good of her. I've never seen a little girl so bewildered. And then we got back to the house. In the panic mum had left all the lights on. The Christmas tree was all lit up in the corner, with the presents underneath, waiting to be opened. Mum put Merryn to bed and we all sat up watching the night turn to Christmas Day, drinking tea. We could hear next door's kids screeching in excitement as they started their day. And all we had was this frozen, grey feeling. Unreal. Numb. As if it was all happening to someone else and Dad would walk in, laugh at us and ask why we were all sitting around looking as if someone had died.' He shook his head again, as if to shake off the trauma he knew would stay with him for the rest of his life. He attempted a laugh. 'And he'd always ask if there was any tea in the pot. I miss him so much.' He bent over, the pain too much, and buried his face in his hands.

'Of course you do.' Verity gently rubbed his shoulder.

'I'm trying to do Christmas.' He thought he sounded almost petulant, like a little lost boy. Perhaps he was. 'I'm trying to enjoy all the lights, the trees, the music. I'm trying for Mum and Merryn, especially for Merryn. She deserves a Christmas after last year. But it's as if I'm numb inside. I'm saying all the right things, putting on a grin at the silly gold hot-pants lights, those daft yarn bombers and most of the time I can, but it's not reaching down where it should.'

'Jago, my child, it's early days. It's not even been a year yet. And all the little things, the rituals we put in place at this time of the year, it's going to make it all so much harder. I think if you're getting up, showering, eating, working, and looking after your family, then you're doing about as well as you can. You're doing far better than most people in the same circumstances. But, as much as you feel you have to put a brave face on, make sure you allow yourself to grieve too. I still don't think you've let yourself do that and you can't move on until you do.'

He sat back up and nodded.

Verity got up to make fresh coffee. If it was to allow him some time, some space, then he was grateful. He felt wrung out with emotion. It had been good to talk to her. While she clattered about the kitchen, he sat in silence, staring at Ivy who had rolled onto her back, stretched out and perfectly content. The pain he felt when telling Verity about his father had been intense. She had been the first person outside the family to whom he'd told the full story. But now he had, he sensed an easing, as if he'd been stuck in a tunnel where the agony and darkness had gripped him, refusing to let him leave. He'd somehow managed to pass through now and was out the other side and, although bruised and tender, he felt lighter, cleansed. Perhaps there was something in this spirituality of Verity's? Or maybe it was simply the relief of offloading.

She sat back down. 'And so you decided to move away. More coffee?'

He accepted another mug. 'Yup. Everyone thought we were mad. We didn't know anyone in Lullbury Bay.'

'Maybe that was the appeal?'

'I think it was.' He drank some coffee, feeling it course through his body: hot and strong, and rejuvenating. 'Mum considered returning to Cornwall. We're from Fowey originally. But I think she wanted a new start. Somewhere she could reinvent herself. Going back to Cornwall seemed too much like going backwards.'

'What about you? Didn't you consider staying in London?'

Jago sucked his lower lip. 'I did, but my marriage was over, I'd drifted from my friends. Maybe I wanted to reinvent myself too.' He eased out a kink in his neck. 'There's a lot to be said for a fresh start.'

'There is. But now you've found yourself living in a seaside town with a very active lifeboat station and you're drawn to volunteering. What are you going to do?'

'I don't know. I promised Mum,' his brow furrowed, 'but it's a good thing to do, to help others, isn't it? It might even be a way to honour my father's memory. Ah, Verity, what would *you* do?'

She smiled gently and, holding her mug to her face, blew on it to cool her coffee. 'I can't solve this for you, Jago. As a vicar I ought to tell you to keep your promise. As a mum I can perfectly understand why your mother asked you never to volunteer again.'

'But?' He looked at her hopefully, desperate for the suggestion that it would be all right for him to renege on his promise.

'But,' she admitted, 'I can also see how it's eating you up, not being able to volunteer. And I can see why you'd want to. I don't suppose there's any way you'd consider a shore-based role? In fundraising or serving in the shop?'

Jago's expression made his answer clear.

'No, I thought not. Then my only suggestion and perhaps the way forward, however painful and difficult, is to discuss it with your mother.'

He was lost in thought for a second. The last thing he wanted to do was to upset or challenge his mother. He knew her request that he not volunteer came from the best and most heart-felt place. On the other hand, surely he had the right, as an adult, to serve his community as best he could? Or was he being pompous? But he longed to volunteer, *burned* to do so. He wanted to follow in his father's footsteps. 'I'm going to have to, aren't I?' Pulling a face, he added, 'But it's not going to be easy. I don't want to hurt her.'

'You never know, you might find that if she knows how it's been tearing you apart, she won't want to hurt *you*. But until you sit down together and talk it through, you'll never know. Do you think that's a plan?'

'It's got to be worth trying, hasn't it?'

'I think so.' Verity frowned. 'But it's not the only thing that's been bothering you, is it? Is there something else on your mind?'

Jago screwed up his face. 'It's a woman,' he said almost apologetically.

CHAPTER 22

'KISS ME IT'S CHRISTMAS' – LEONA LEWIS (FEAT. NE-YO)

'A woman, eh?' Verity said. 'Should be easier to solve. Tell me more.'

'Not necessarily.'

She settled the cushion behind her back more comfortably. 'Oh, I've missed this. My two are heading for marriage and boringly happy. Sorry.' She grimaced. 'Not terribly tactful.'

'I was married. Until quite recently. I suppose it's not something you approve of? Divorce?'

Verity gave him a keen look. 'I want people to be happy and lead good lives. However it comes about and whoever they're with. I'm a vicar but I'm a vicar in a modern, messy world. I take a pragmatic approach to relationships.' She wiggled against the cushion. 'What *am* I sitting on?' Reaching behind her she brought out a small black Bible. Staring at it, she said, 'Now, how on earth did that get there?'

'Don't tell me, it's called Bjorn.'

Verity narrowed her eyes at him. 'Betsey if you don't mind. And she's my favourite copy.' She waggled it at him. 'It's a good book but the devil did it in the end.' Putting it on the table behind her, she gave him a mischievous look. 'Look, I know it's early, but

156

do you fancy a drop of something in the coffee? I mean, it *is* Christmas.' Without waiting for an answer, she got up again and hunted through a larder cupboard at the other end of the kitchen, bringing out a bottle of whisky with a flourish. 'Looky-here. A present from lovely Mr Snead.' She returned to the Aga and poured a measure into each of their mugs. 'He's a nice man. Has a super allotment. Grows all his own fruit and veg. His tomatoes actually taste of tomato. Rumour has it he has a gin still in his shed, but sadly I've never been the recipient of a bottle of that.' She eyed the Famous Grouse. 'Maybe this is better in coffee though?'

Jago laughed, took a gulp of whisky-flavoured coffee and spluttered; it was strong. Verity topped it up with another generous measure. She was an extraordinary woman, he decided. Warm, funny, ever so slightly eccentric and good. Yes, that was it. She was a good woman. Without being preachy or judgemental, she radiated joy and goodness. He swallowed another mouthful of coffee, feeling the whisky make his head fuzzy.

All the movement had disturbed Ivy who leaped to her feet and began to prowl around the kitchen.

'Think she might need to go out,' Jago said meaningfully.

Verity cottoned on. 'Ah. Half a sec.' She rummaged around on the messy table and unearthed an enormous brass key. Holding it up, she said, 'Isn't he a thing of beauty? They don't make things like him anymore. He's called Benny,' she added.

'Of course.' This time Jago didn't bother to hide his smile.

'This way.' Verity led them back to the narrow passageway but in the opposite direction this time. Opening a door, she ushered them out into a courtyard which had steps leading up to a lawn. On either side the bare branches of dog wood bushes dripped with a brooding wetness, but Jago hardly noticed. He followed Ivy up onto the lawn and stopped dead. The back garden of the vicarage faced the sea, with the beach far below. Lullbury Bay opened up in front of him, with the sweep of Charmouth and the ginger biscuit-coloured cliffs to his left. To his right the sea stretched silver grey, beyond the curling harbour wall, and blending into a low sky which sank into the water. The rain had passed over now and clearer light had come in with the tide. A watery pale sun filtered through the clouds and gleamed a wide passage on the flat sea. Gulls wheeled and mewed against the watery light. Ivy scratched about, finding the perfect spot on the lawn, but Jago ignored her. He was entranced by the view. It was calm, beautiful and utterly soothing. He sucked in a deep, cleansing breath and absorbed pure ozone.

'It's wonderful, isn't it?' Verity murmured at his side. 'Such a gift. Sometimes, if I'm having trouble finding God to have a good old natter to and I can't find Him in church, I come here. This view always helps me believe again. It's such a privilege to have it.'

Jago knew he needed to capture it. Taking his phone out of his back pocket, he asked, 'Do you mind?'

'Of course not. I'll leave you for a minute. Come and find me when you're ready.'

Jago didn't know if it was the unaccustomed whisky drinking so early in the day, or the lightness in his heart after his talk with Verity, but the view filled him with a joyful serenity. He'd lost his father, and nothing would ever bring him back. No man would ever take his place, but he was beginning, just beginning, to find acceptance in the fact and take joy in the blessing he'd had his wonderful father for thirty-four years. The grief was still there but it wasn't as raw and angry as it had been. He'd never stop grieving for his father, but it was no longer wrenching at his gut and wrecking his head.

A woman strode along the beach below wearing a red-and-white Santa hat. A dachshund in a jaunty matching coat trotted alongside, its stubby legs moving at surprising speed. Maybe it was Holly's mother, Merryn's new schoolfriend. The sight made him smile. He felt himself thaw a little, his insides unclench. He couldn't stop Christmas happening. It was a great tidal wave of tinsel and tedious pop music which overwhelmed everyone and everything. And maybe he wouldn't be able to truly love it this year, but he'd accept it was happening. Honor's words at the German Market came back to him. Maybe she was right. It was all about bringing in the light against the darkness in the world. He glanced back at the vicarage. Perhaps Verity was onto something, and it was about an innocent baby. Or perhaps it was to do with family coming together, celebrating with good food, enjoying giving presents, watching the excitement as children opened theirs. Whatever it meant, he promised himself he'd make it the best he could for his mother and Merryn. From the depths of the building behind him, he heard a phone ring. It brought him back, and to the fact he was cold standing out here without his coat.

Ivy, having done what she needed to, was now on high alert staring at the woman on the beach and the dachshund. She stood, tail straight, nose quivering. Jago whistled to her before she began barking and they returned to the kitchen and the warmth of the Aga.

'Ah, there you are,' Verity said, putting down an old-fashioned phone. 'Your coffee's on the warming plate.'

Jago picked up his mug and stood with his back to the stove, leaning against its comfort.

'See. Told you Agnetha was good for that.' Verity sighed. 'I suppose at some point I'll have to move out of here and leave her but this old Victorian wreck of a place and especially this kitchen is such a joy. It's a blessing to be in the heart of the parish. People know right where to find me. Just been on the phone to Nora from Dolphin View, that's the nursing home up on the hill.' She glanced at her wristwatch. 'Not due there until tea-time though so I've still got time. We got distracted. What woman and what problem?'

Jago stayed leaning against the Aga, sipping his coffee

thoughtfully. He'd got chilled through standing outside soaking up the view, but it had been worth it. He knew he would have to capture the essence of it in glass. Perhaps a large stained-glass panel in gull-grey and shimmering silver? Or something smaller and jewel-like. He forced himself back to Verity's question. 'It's Honor.'

'Honor Martin, our delightful teacher at St Winifred's Primary?'

Jago could see her mulling over the thought.

'But that's perfect,' she exclaimed. 'I think you'd be perfect together. She's single, or as far as I know. She split up with her boyfriend some years back, I believe. He was in Italy and didn't appear to want to return to the UK. Mind you,' she shrugged, 'living in Florence, you can see his point. And I believe Honor didn't want to move abroad. She's a bit of a fixture in our little town, is Honor.' She frowned. 'I don't see what the problem is.'

He sat back down, staring into his mug. He wasn't sure he wanted any more coffee so put the mug back on the warming plate on the Aga. 'I was married to Rose for three years. We lived together for a while before.' Glancing up he saw Verity was listening intently. 'We decided to get married on a whim.' He winced. 'We took ourselves off somewhere hot, got married on a beach. It was romantic, impulsive. I upset Mum and Dad as they couldn't get organised in time to get out there and I'll always regret that. We were young and didn't really think about anyone else, we rushed into it. Seemed like a good idea at the time. Looking back, I wonder if I wanted what my parents had. Don't get me wrong, they argued just like any other couple, and I always suspected Mum never truly settled in London, but they were the happiest married couple I'd ever come across. Truly happy. Supportive, happy to compromise, kind to one another and they never lost the ability to laugh together. Maybe it was why I was so keen to run into marriage with Rose. I wanted to replicate my parents' happiness for myself. But, instead of waiting for the right one, I married the first one.

'And it was good at first. We had an amazing extended honeymoon travelling around Thailand and Cambodia, but then came home to the grey reality. I think both of us thought we were in it for life, and we were devastated when we realised it wasn't working out. We lived two very different lives; Rose had to go away and train people and I was off at craft and art fairs. We ended up not seeing enough of one another. Rose met someone.' He bit his lip. 'And the worst of it all was knowing part of me was happy for her. The problem being lockdown happened and we were stuck with one another in a dying relationship, trying to work, trying to stay friends but knowing all the time we'd be best apart. She's living with Mo now and they're happy. We tried really hard to remain friends and had a civilised divorce. I think the one success of our sad, doomed, short marriage was we've managed that.' He laughed shortly. 'I'm even invited to their wedding. I'll go and I'll drink to their health and mean it. Rose is a wonderful person, she just wasn't the right, wonderful person for me.'

'Do you know, it sounds to me as if you've been incredibly grown up in an awful situation.'

'Maybe. Though, it was a situation I shouldn't have got myself into in the first place. I rushed into the relationship, I rushed into a marriage without really thinking it through. It's what I do. I rush things.' He laughed again. 'It's weird as it's in direct contrast to what I do for a living. Crafting with glass is one thing you can't rush. You have to take time, respect the material.'

Verity put her head on one side and smiled sympathetically. 'And I'd be shocking at your sort of thing. All fingers and thumbs. We all have our different talents, don't we? The world would be a boring place if we were all good at the same things.' She sipped her coffee. 'But where does this leave Honor?'

Jago grimaced. 'I think I've messed up.'

Verity settled herself more comfortably. 'Do tell.'

'I've bumped into her quite a few times now, hard not to when she's teaching Merryn and this is a hell of a small town.'

'Oh, it certainly is.'

'I thought we were getting on really well. Thought I was getting the right vibes from her.' He grimaced. 'Then I tried to kiss her.' He shook his head at the memory. 'I was so clumsy. Honestly, Verity, I could have been fourteen and trying out my first pass. Actually, when I *was* fourteen, I had more luck. Don't laugh. It was shocking.'

'Oh dear.' Verity suppressed a chuckle.

'We got interrupted by this boy I'd bonded with at the lantern workshop. I helped out at it earlier in the day,' he explained. 'Jaden.'

'Jaden? Yes I know Jaden. A right wriggler in the assemblies I do in school. Always getting into trouble, but it's never ever quite his fault somehow.'

Jago smiled. Sounds like him. 'Odd kid but interesting, quirky, you know? We got on like a house on fire. In some ways he reminded me of myself at the same age. I wasn't your typical little boy. Hopeless at sport, couldn't even kick a football around in the park.' He spread his hands in front of him, the long fingers stretching out. 'This is where my skill is, in my hands. Once I'd grasped that I didn't mind being left out of the football team, or not picked for cricket. I knew I was clever but in a different way. I'm a lot like Mum in that respect.'

'As I said, we all have our different talents. Were you bullied?' Verity asked curiously.

'No, strangely. I think it was because Dad always had my back. He always told me I'd be good at something, just not something involving a ball and my feet. The one thing he gave me which I treasure the most is confidence. I was always self-confident, and I think the other kids sensed it.' He paused. 'That's what makes me so sad for Merryn. She'll never have that from Dad. She appears confident, overly so sometimes, but it's all brittle, on the surface. There's no substance to it. It's even more apparent since the accident.'

'It could be your gift to her,' Verity suggested gently. 'Give her the confidence your father bestowed on you, to her.'

'Yes, you're right.' Jago nodded. He thought for a moment, running the idea through his head. 'I'll make sure I do. And she's such a clever kid, she could go on to do anything.'

'From the little I've seen of your sister, I think the same. But back to Honor. What happened after the interrupted kiss? Where were you when all this happened?'

'At the German Market.'

'So you were in public?'

'Yeah. Jaden's mum misinterpreted the situation between me and him and by the time I'd prised the kid off me and explained, Honor had gone.' He blew out a frustrated breath. 'I'm certain there was something developing between us. Trust me, Verity, I wouldn't have kissed her if there hadn't.'

'Well, it might have been a case of it being the wrong place,' she said thoughtfully. 'Honor has a position in the town. She's a teacher and, old-fashioned as it sounds, the community still expects its teachers to maintain a certain level of dignity when it comes to their personal life.'

Jago scuffed his boots together. 'I hadn't thought of it like that.'

'Have you seen her since?'

'Yes. At the Craft Fayre.' He winced. 'It was all a bit awkward.'

'Did you talk to her?'

'No, not really. She was with some bloke from her school. Ben? I wondered if there was something going on between them. They looked very cosy.'

'Ben Townham? No, I don't think so.' Verity stopped to consider the idea. 'Or at least if there is she's been incredibly discreet about it. Oh, Jago, you've got an awful lot of talking to do, haven't you? You need to talk volunteering as crew with your mother and you really must talk to Honor. Clear the air. Find out where you stand with both women.'

Jago's mouth twisted.

'That's if you want to move things on.'

'Point taken. I'm worried I've rushed things with Honor, just as I did with Rose. It's just that–'

'What?'

'It feels so right with Honor. In a way it doesn't feel as if I'm rushing things at all. I really think,' he corrected himself, 'I *thought*, it was perfect. It felt exciting and I'm really attracted to her but it's more than that. I could actually see myself building a good life with Honor, here, in Lullbury Bay.'

'But?'

'What if it ends up just like me and Rose?'

'Oh, Jago.' Verity stood up. 'You are a deeply lovely man. Hugely sensitive and, dare I say it, prone to over-analysing things. Go and find Honor and say all these things to her. She can react one of two ways. She'll either accept your explanation and you can stay friends. Or–'

'Or?' He gazed up at her, trying to conceal the desperate hope he felt.

'She'll leap into your arms!'

CHAPTER 23

'IT DOESN'T OFTEN SNOW AT CHRISTMAS' – PET SHOP BOYS

Jago walked back down the steep hill towards the promenade and strolled along it, taking his time. He needed to clear his head and he needed to do some thinking. A lot of thinking. To his amusement he saw the Ninja Knitters had attacked the prom too. Great swathes of knitted garlands, red and sparkly, had been wound round the railings which ran the length of it. Hung from them were baubles, tiny robins, trees and miniature Father Christmases – all knitted of course. He stopped and admired them and saw tiny fairy lights had been tucked through too. At night it would sparkle. Merryn would love it. Stopping to take a photo on his phone he couldn't help but grin. It seemed to sum up the town; hard-working, creative, community-minded and completely eccentric.

An older man with an equally aged German Shepherd paused beside him. 'Gladdens the heart, doesn't it? Silly bit of nonsense but cheerful. You walking to the harbour? Mind if we walk along with you?'

Jago did mind, it interrupted his thinking time, but he didn't want to seem rude. 'Not at all,' he answered, putting Ivy on his left side as a precaution. 'But would you mind if we kept the dogs well apart. Ivy here is a rescue and nervous.' Even as he said it, it sounded ridiculous. The old dog didn't look as if it would bother anything.

As they walked the man introduced himself as Austin and the dog as Gretel. 'On her last legs now, poor old girl.' He chortled. 'Bit like me, but we soldier on.' He tapped his nose. 'Secret to a long life, gentle exercise, a bit of what you fancy and the love of a good woman.'

Jago laughed and introduced himself.

'Ah yes,' Austin said. 'The new folk who have moved into Christmas Tree Cottage. On God-Almighty Hill.'

'God-Almighty Hill?' Jago shook his head. 'No, it's on Harbour Hill. The road that leads up the cliff out of the harbour.'

Austin chuckled. 'Harbour Hill is what's written on the map, young man, and maybe on the road sign, but we locals know it as God-Almighty Hill. On account of it being so steep, you're so puffed out by the time you've walked to the top, all you can do is wheeze out, *"God Almighty!"*'

Jago decided he loved this town.

'Lovely name for a house I've always thought. Christmas Tree Cottage. Not so much a cottage though since the last owners extended it.'

'Do you know why it's named that? From its position, I thought it would be called something like Harbour View or Sea Vista.'

'No idea,' Austin replied cheerfully. 'Perhaps the first folk who lived there loved Christmas so much they wanted to be reminded of it all year long.'

Jago remained silent. He was trying hard to fall back in love with Christmas. Maybe he would at some point in the future, but he wasn't sure he'd manage it this year. Not completely. He looked up at the sky. The day was fading fast, he must have stayed at Verity's longer than he'd thought. It was growing even colder, with a penetrating wind slicing off a grey sea. 'Do you think it'll snow?'

Austin sucked his teeth. 'Doesn't often snow in Lullbury Bay but when it does it can come down with a vengeance. Last time we had it was a couple of years ago. And then we had a bucketful. Even covered the beach, and that only happens once in a lifetime.' He chortled. 'Everyone was snowed in as the roads were so bad. Steep hills in this part of Dorset, see.' They'd reached the open space outside the yacht club by now and the wind gusted through the gap between the building and the café next to it. Austin stopped and pointed over the low wall and out to a stone-grey sea. 'You can't imagine the beach covered in white, can you? Doesn't seem right somehow. Looked all odd, I can tell you, but magical it was. I'm fond of a bit of snow, as it's rare down here. Snowed the day I married my first wife in the chapel *and* when I married my Aggie. What are the chances, eh?' Austin smiled, his face creasing into well-worn lines, lost in his reminiscence. 'But we got married in the registrar's office on account of Aggie being pagan. She don't hold no truck with church folk.'

Neither had Jago until recently. Snow on one wedding day sounded romantic, let alone on two. No wonder the old man was so fond of it. 'Sounds perfect. Snow on your wedding day, that is. Although I suppose it depends if the guests can get to it. When was this?' Jago asked, expecting Austin to tell him it was back in the sixties.

'Only a couple of years ago. Aggie and I got married and it was the happiest day of my life, even with everything folk said. Gossiped about us something rotten, they did. Said she was after my money. They don't know the half of it; she's got more stashed away than the whole town put together! Ah yes, happy day, that was.' He reached down to ruffle his dog's feathery ears. 'I waited a long time for my second wife to come along and our courtship wasn't without its problems, I can tell you, but that day was one I'll never forget. I can heartily recommend married life. You have to compromise, of course, and I've done more than my fair share with my Ag but it's all been worth it. She's a little cracker is my Aggie.' He straightened. 'You married, young Jago?'

'I'm not.' Jago didn't know what to make of the old man. It felt surreal talking relationships standing in the dark and cold, with sea foam flecking in off the sea with the wind. But then, there had been something surreal about the whole day.

'Then, take my advice, find yourself a good woman.' Austin shivered. 'If nothing else, she'll keep you warm.'

'Well, I've someone in mind,' Jago answered, liking the man more and more. There was something about him which reminded him of his father. 'Sort of.'

Austin pointed a finger. 'Then get a shifty on. You never know what's round the corner in this life, or how long you've got. Doesn't pay to fiddle-faddle about, as my Aggie would say. Grab any opportunity which comes your way, and I don't just mean with women. We're only here the once and we don't know for how long.'

'You don't know how true that is,' Jago replied feelingly, a resolve beginning to form.

'Granddad?' A slight figure ran out of the café, her long apron flapping in the breeze. 'What are you doing standing around in this cold? Come on into the café. We're not too busy, just the Knit and Natter Group. I'll make you a Hot Chocolate Special and get you some of Tracy's Christmas shortbread, fresh batch just out of the oven.' She bent down and ruffled Gretel's ears. 'A doggie biscuit for you, too.' Straightening, she smiled at Jago.

'This is Jago Pengethley, new in town,' Austin explained. 'Jago, this is my granddaughter, Alice. She works in the café when she's not at university.'

'We've met already. Hi, Alice. Hope you're not quite as busy as you were when I came in with Tom.'

'Thankfully not.' She grinned and then bent to croon at Ivy. 'And who's this little darling?'

'Ivy. We adopted her from Tom as it happens. He'd taken her in at the sanctuary. She might say hello if you're calm but she's still quite nervous of strangers.'

Alice felt in the front pocket of her white apron. 'Dog biscuit?'

'Worth a try.'

She crouched down by the dog. After shying away, Ivy caught the scent of the treat, nose twitching. Alice held it in her palm and the dog decided to take it. She stood up, having given Gretel a biscuit too. 'Nice to meet you again, Jago, and lovely to meet little Ivy.' Taking her grandfather's arm, she scolded him. 'Now come on, Granddad, it's icy out here and you're frozen.' As they made their way in the direction of the Sea Spray Café, she looked over her shoulder. 'Can we tempt you too? I make a mean hot choc.' She grinned, her dangly earrings bobbing back and forth.

Jago gazed at the brightly lit steamed-up windows of the café. As a shower of spray hit his neck like tiny needles, he could see how it got its name. He could smell the coffee and cake wafting over deliciously and was seriously tempted. 'Not this time. I have something I have to do.' He stood watching as they disappeared into the warm fug of the café. It seemed everyone either knew one another in this town or were related. The sight of young Alice looking after her grandfather so tenderly filled him with hope for the world. Hearing Ivy whimper and press herself shivering against his legs, he turned away. It might be the whisky in his blood giving him Dutch courage and he knew he was going against Verity's advice to talk to Avril first, but he needed to do it. As Austin said, there was no time to fiddle-faddle about. He only had this one life, and it was his responsibility not to waste any of it. He owed his father that. Walking at a pace, before allowing himself to change his mind – and to warm himself and Ivy up, he strode in the direction of the brightly lit lifeboat station.

CHAPTER 24

'COZY LITTLE CHRISTMAS' – KATY PERRY

Avril looked up as Alice steered an older man and a shaggy German Shepherd to a seat at a table in a warm corner, well away from the Knit and Natterers. She noticed one or two of the group wave, so assumed he must be local. Concentrating back on her knitting needles she navigated a tricky part of the pattern, frowning at it through her reading specs. Having conquered it, she sighed, put her knitting down and finished her cooling coffee.

'Thank you for the flowers, Brenda,' she said to the woman who was sitting next to her. Of everyone in the group, Brenda was the one she'd become closest to. Brenda had dropped off a bunch of pale pink tulips the evening before. Along with Tracy, she was beginning to count the two women as close friends – and was starting to feel slightly less new in town.

'Oh you're welcome, my lovely. They're only a cheap bunch from the florists I picked up when I did my shopping but it's always cheery to have flowers around at this time of the year. And I was down in town anyway.' She dropped her voice. 'Putting the garlands out on the railings.'

'You were lucky not to get spotted.'

'In that we were! We hid in the shelters on the front and nipped out in between the late-night dog walkers. Luckily, it was so cold there were few folk about. I felt like I was doing something downright naughty. Such a giggle.'

'I had a quick look this morning. It looks fantastic and the lights will be really pretty when it goes dark. The holly leaves came out well. I was a bit worried I hadn't got those quite right.'

'They're just the ticket, Avril, don't you worry.' Brenda chuckled. 'I do think it's fun, although it won't be long before we're rumbled.'

'I don't suppose it'll take an Einstein to link a knitting group with the yarn-bombing.'

'Is that what they're calling it?'

'Well, Merryn and Jago are calling us the Ninja Knitters. Not that they know I'm part of it all, mind you.'

Brenda put her needles down and began to giggle. She laughed until tears came. Then she whispered it to the rest of the group and they joined in with the laughter. 'Oh, I love it. Never thought I'd be a ninja anything. Oh, that's fair made my day.' Picking up her knitting, she resumed. 'And how is Merryn getting on?'

Avril considered the question. Her youngest child seemed to be okay. 'She's settled really well at the school. Had a lead role in the nativity. Her new teacher knows how to challenge her and trust me, it's not easy with Merryn. I never know what she's going to come up with next. Do you know she's taken to quoting Shakespeare? She doesn't know what half the words mean, of course, but she's learned some off by heart.'

'Golly, she must have a wonderful memory. Mine gets worse all the time.' Brenda sighed and put her knitting down to drink tea. 'I can remember lots about my childhood but ask me what I had for lunch yesterday and I simply couldn't tell you.' She grinned at Avril. 'What's started that all off? Does she want to act?'

'She might. She certainly enjoyed all the attention she got from being on stage in the nativity, but I'm not sure. One minute she wants to run an animal sanctuary like Tom's up at Lullbury Bay Farm, then this morning she declared she has her heart set on being a vet. So, who knows? Jago and I think the Shakespeare quotes thing might be because she had a book of quotations bought for her by my husband for her seventh birthday. It's a link with him, I suppose. She badgered and badgered him for one, no idea why. Another of her whims. She's got a butterfly mind, has my Merryn. Has bursts of enthusiasm for things which are all-consuming but brief.'

'Well, she's very young.'

'Yes, not nine until February.' Avril thought back to when she'd found out she was pregnant. 'It was a bit of a shock falling pregnant at forty-six.'

'Oh my lovely, I expect it was.' Brenda shuddered. 'I'd gone through the change and out the other end by that age. How did you cope?'

'That's what I thought it was. The menopause.' Avril giggled. 'Never occurred to me I might be pregnant.' She finished her coffee remembering how she'd gone off it completely whilst pregnant with both Merryn and Jago. 'I should have realised as soon as I couldn't bear the smell of coffee.'

'And you do like your coffee.'

'This is very true.'

'What was the pregnancy like? I mean, at that age.' Brenda had stopped knitting and was listening intently.

'I had to take it easy. They're always worried about gestational diabetes and blood pressure with geriatric mothers.'

'Is that what they called you?' Brenda was indignant. 'The cheek.'

Avril chuckled. 'Oh, trust me, there were much younger women than me termed geriatric.' She smiled, remembering Kenan's shock and then delight at the news. 'I dropped to working two days a week. I was office-based so that wasn't the problem. It was the commute in that was!'

'I can imagine.'

'But I was fit and healthy and the midwives looked after me well. Think I was a bit of a fascinating case for them.'

Brenda frowned, her nose wrinkling up on her immaculately made-up face. 'There was someone famous who got pregnant when she was quite old.' She shook her head, making her long earrings dance. 'Who was it? A while ago now.'

'Do you mean Cherie Blair?'

'That's the badger! I remember all the to-do in the newspapers. Didn't they claim the baby was conceived at Balmoral when they were staying with the queen?'

'Probably. Can't say that was our excuse. Kenan was so obsessed with work, we were lucky to get a weekend in Brighton!' Avril picked up her knitting needles again but held them mid-air, thinking. 'Brenda, the Blair thing must be over twenty years ago now. That Balmoral baby must be an adult.'

'Hang on, you've got me all agog now. It'll prey on my mind until I find out.' Brenda got out her phone. 'I'll google it.' There was silence while she scrolled. 'Ah, here we go. 1999. So the baby would be, what, twenty?'

'Twenty-four. Goodness. Is 1999 twenty-four years ago?'

'Don't even think about it. It's too depressing. I was in Bromley and dreaming of an escape to Lullbury Bay.'

'Which you did.'

'Which I most certainly did!'

Avril smiled at her friend. 'And I'm so glad our paths have crossed.'

'Me too, my lovely. I can honestly say you've been a wonderful addition to our little town.'

Tears collected thickly at the back of Avril's throat. Friendship was important. She'd always valued her friends but making one as dear as Brenda at this stage of her life had come as a delightful surprise. Brenda had been the first person in Lullbury Bay to whom she'd mentioned Kenan's death. She placed a hand on Brenda's and was moved to see tears in her new friend's eyes too.

Brenda cleared her throat as if to say that was enough sentimental nonsense. 'So, your Merryn. Eight going on nine, eh?'

'Eight going on thirty-five, more like. I sometimes think she's more mature than Jago. And full of beans.'

'How wonderful to be that age and so full of zest and enthusiasm. If she likes acting, you know, maybe you should think about enrolling her in the youth group? It meets at the Art School. It's well thought of. It's called the Lullbury Bay Rising Acting Talent Society.' Brenda winced. 'Bit unfortunate. The acronym is LUBRATS.'

They giggled.

'Mike Love is behind it, and he directs theatre in London and the States. He's quite famous. He's patron of the theatre over in Berecombe. That's Devon way.'

'Thanks, Brenda, I'll check it out. She might need something to get her through the next few months. She's fine now but it's coming up to the first anniversary of Kenan's death. It's not going to be easy and I simply don't know how she's going to react.'

Brenda put her knitting down again and regarded her with concern. 'And the first anniversary for you.' She put a hand on Avril's arm. 'I'm so sorry. It's going to be hard for you too.'

Avril choked back the tears again. Any laughter had gone. 'Thank you,' she replied eventually. Giving herself a shake, she added, 'But it's done me so much good coming here, meeting this group. Meeting you and Tracy. I'm beginning to feel more like my old self.'

'Good to hear.' She patted Avril's hand. 'And remember, I'm only at the end of the phone line. Any time. Just ring me. Especially if things get difficult at Christmas.'

'That's lovely of you, Brenda, but surely you'll be busy with your family?'

'Have a heart, we're off to my youngest for the day. Two grandchildren and an unruly Boxer dog. Fun but chaos. I'll welcome an opportunity to slip away, sip a quiet sherry and answer my mobile.'

'Then thank you.'

'What are your plans for Christmas Day?'

'Jago, Merryn, little Ivy, a turkey that's too big which we'll be eating well into March, and lots of presents to open. I'm keeping it as traditional as possible. We didn't have any of that last year. I've got some making up to do.'

'Sounds perfect. But don't forget to put aside a quiet moment to remember your Kenan.'

'I never forget him. He's always there, but I know what you mean.'

Brenda clasped a hand across her mouth. 'I'm so sorry. How tactless of me. Of course you never forget him.'

'Don't worry.' Avril managed a smile. 'I'd rather you mention his name and risk being tactless than ignore the situation completely. I like to talk about him. We had a very long and mostly happy marriage. I have two incredible children and lots of wonderful memories and that's all down to him. My Kenan.' Her eyes sparkled with unshed tears but she was proud to keep her voice steady. To talk about him without breaking down was a recent development in her road of grief.

The women smiled at one another in understanding.

'It's an unusual name, Kenan,' Brenda said, after a pause during which they gathered their emotion.

'Isn't it just? I've no idea what his parents were thinking. They always did have pretensions. Mind you, they levelled the same accusation at me when I named Jago.'

'Do you get on with your in-laws?'

'Oh yes,' Avril said, blithely. 'Especially as I don't live in the same town.'

'Always helps, I've found.' Brenda giggled.

'It was another reason not to move back to Fowey. Here, I'm in striking distance should they need me but not so near they can pop in unannounced. Every day.' Avril stopped, then gasped. 'Oh, that makes me sound dreadful, doesn't it? I mean, I lost a husband, but they lost a son. I should be more charitable. Of course I love them but I needed the space to breathe my own air. Lullbury Bay's provided that.'

'Totally understandable and not dreadful at all, my lovely. Pragmatic. Have you much family in Cornwall?'

'As well as Kenan's parents, I still have mine plus a brother- and sister-in-law, a few cousins. We'll maybe see New Year in with them.'

'A new year and a new start. For you and the children.'

'Well, I can hardly class Jago as a child.'

'They're always your children. He's a talented boy by all accounts. I hear Maisie Lloyd-Owen was very taken with his glass when she saw it at the Craft Fayre. As well as some bits for the café here, she's thinking of commissioning him to make a window for her cottage.'

Avril twisted to catch Tracy's eye. She was desperate for another coffee, she seemed to live on it these days. 'I'd be delighted if she does. He's making all these small items, but the bigger commissions are where the money's to be made. I wish he'd do more but he seems to have lost his way lately. He used to exhibit in galleries in London. He was quite sought after.'

'I imagine he's adjusting too.'

Avril sighed. 'He is. He's been my rock, but he seems to think he's responsible for me.'

'Perfectly understandable.'

'But, Brenda, he's my son not my husband. I'm quite grown-up enough to look after myself. I wish he'd get out there, find himself a nice girl, settle down, give me a couple of grandchildren. I don't need him fussing over me all the time.'

'Have you told him?'

Avril pulled a face. 'I don't want to hurt his feelings. He's a sensitive boy.'

Tracy came over and pulled up a chair. 'Going well today, ladies?' She peered over Avril's shoulder. 'What are you knitting there?'

'It's a crown for one of the three kings. We're planning a nativity scene for the little garden opposite the church. It'll be life-sized. It needs to be finished before the Nine Carols Service.'

'Never fails to amaze me how those flat scraps of knitting and crochet get turned into something three dimensional. A life-sized nativity, eh? That'll take some setting up.'

'We'll have to do it in the dead of night, I suppose. No letting on, Tracy,' Avril warned.

'My lips are sealed.' Tracy made a dramatic twisting gesture with her fingers against her lips and giggled. She waved her pad. 'Any orders, ladies? I take it you want a coffee, Avril?' She wrote down the rest of the orders and then leaned in. 'Word on the Lullbury Bay prom is Bee in the bookshop is looking to hire. You know, Bee's Books on the high street. You fancy working in a bookshop, Av? Perks of the job being fairly close proximity to me and my lush cakes and sarnies. Just a hop and a sprint along the front. Won't have far to go for lunch and a goss.'

'Now, there's an idea,' Brenda said.

'I was going to look for a job but had put it off until the new year,' Avril said thoughtfully.

'Bee's looking for someone part-time for the moment. And, let's face it, the commute down Harbour Hill from your place isn't exactly onerous. Along the prom with a sea view, or you could cut through the gardens. Still have the sea view! She's lovely, is Bee, no sting despite her name and she'd probably be happy with you working around Merryn's school hours.'

'Sounds ideal to me,' Brenda put in. 'Weren't you in that sort of thing before?'

'I worked for John Lewis but I was office-based rather than on the shop floor.'

'This would be a doddle after working for John Lewis,' Tracy put in.

'Or, knowing Lullbury Bay's good and godly, absolute hell,' Brenda said. 'And you'd be busy once the tourists return.'

'Fair enough. Any customer-facing job isn't a picnic,' Tracy admitted.

'But, I could try it out to see if I liked it?' Avril said slowly, the idea beginning to appeal. 'And if Bee would have me.'

'Of course she'll have you.' Tracy put an arm around Avril's shoulders. 'She's over in the bookshop now. Why don't you pop along the prom and discuss it with her?'

'I might, Tracy. Do you know, I might just do that!'

CHAPTER 25

'IT'S BEGINNING TO LOOK A LOT LIKE CHRISTMAS' – MICHAEL BUBLÉ

Tuesday 21st December

Honor popped into the bookshop on the afternoon of the RNLI carols event. She needed to get a few last-minute Christmas presents and thought some holiday reading for her mum would be perfect. She was surprised to see who was serving behind the till.

'Avril, what are you doing working in here?'

'Hello, Honor. How lovely to see you. I'm having a trial run to see if I'm up to the job. If Bee thinks I'm up to muster, I start properly tomorrow.'

Bee, the bookshop manager, staggered past, laden with a pile of hardbacks. She collapsed onto a chair, her coltish legs splayed out in front. Blowing her fringe out of her eyes she made her violet eyes go huge. 'Trust me, I'm never letting her go. She's already sorted the children's corner and it looks a million times better.'

Honor looked around. She loved this place and popped in all the time. Bee often hosted children's events so Honor would bring her class in. The bookshop was a quirky convert from a

179

couple of shops and was situated perfectly on the high street. Some time ago, the premises adjoining the book shop had been converted into a community-run café and social hub and knocked through. It was possible to buy a book and then sit and read accompanied by some really good coffee and one of the café's delicious waffles. Honor's all-time favourite pastime was to get engrossed in a fat best-selling paperback while scoffing a waffle topped with melted chocolate, pecan nuts and whipped cream. If she was lucky, she scored a table against the window at the back which overlooked the bay and the endless shifting sea. As it was four o'clock and dusky-dim, now all that could be glimpsed was the festive flashing white lights strung all along the prom and gently swaying in the breeze. The red lights decorating The Old Anchor could be spotted at the far end, on the harbour. Dimpsey was the local word for this time of day, and it summed up the soft light just before night fell perfectly. Turning away from the view of the pub, she shuddered a little, remembering her adventures with cider in there. It hadn't ended well and she had sworn herself off cider for life. Or at least until another night in the pub with her friends.

Bee always decorated the bookshop according to season; her Hallowe'en displays were legendary, and now she'd really gone to town with all things Christmassy. Festooning Bee's Books at the moment was white netting hung low from the ceiling, with thousands of tiny white lights threaded through. It made the place feel magical. On tables, at intervals in between the bookcases, small white Christmas trees had been set up and decorated with the same lights. A larger, real spruce stood in the middle with a red upholstered chair, a glowing stove, a pile of recommended seasonal books, and a glass bowl heaped with sweets wrapped in glittering paper, with a sign saying to help yourself. A cosy reading area with leather sofas, comfy cushions and throws with a Nordic theme was half hidden behind an arch with greenery and hung with yet more tiny twinkling white lights. Frank Sinatra classic Christmas songs played quietly in the background against the happy hum of contented booklovers browsing to their heart's content.

'That's fabulous, Avril,' Honor said, returning her attention to the woman behind the till. 'I can't think of a nicer place to work than a bookshop at Christmas, and it's looking gorgeous in here at the moment.' Seeing two customers waiting to pay, she added, 'I'll let you go. Looks like you're busy.'

Bee returned, looking puffed out. 'I meant it when I said I wasn't letting Avril go. She's been marvellous.' She dusted down her hands and asked, 'What can I help you with, Honor?'

'Holiday reading for my mum. Paperbacks please as she's got to cram them into her suitcase.'

'Well, I hate to say it, seeing as I sell print books for a living, but she might be better to load up her Kindle.'

'It's a cruise, so there's no weight limit. There's a library on board apparently, but Mum wants a few to keep her going until she gets the hang of things. They've never cruised before.'

'Exciting! What does she like to read?'

'She likes most things, historical romance, a cosy crime.'

'This way then.' Bee led her to the side of the shop next to the leather sofas. 'You can have a browse through our General Fiction section. Romance is on these two bookcases, crime's on another and anything we can't categorise is listed alphabetically on the third. I'll leave you to it but give one of us a shout if you need any help. If you buy a pile, which I most sincerely hope you do, and you're on the way to the carols at the lifeboat station, Avril will stash them behind the desk for you. We're open late tonight so you can pick them up on the way home. The Sea Spray is, too. Doing a nice range of takeaway soup and turkey rolls, I think. Your pal Lucie is in charge, with some help from little Merryn who is selling home-made mince pies, and all proceeds go to the RNLI.'

'Thanks, Bee.' Honor was fond of the woman, who was of a

similar age to herself. She'd like to be better friends and was always inviting her out for a drink or a trip to the cinema, but Bee was welded permanently to her shop. In the same way Tom was dedicated to his animal sanctuary, Bee was besotted with books. Honor turned to peruse the bookshelves. She loved books, her to-be-read pile at home was enormous but she accepted that, along with her mother's presents, she'd sneak in an extra couple for herself.

Twenty minutes later, she carried ten fat paperbacks to the till and joined the queue to pay. She noticed, for the first time, that Ivy, the Pengethley's spaniel, was curled up in a dog bed by the desk. The dog raised her head and looked intently at the shop's door. The sight cheered Honor inexplicably. She liked living in a town where the bookshop tolerated dogs and gave away sweets. A second later, she started as a rush of icy sea air blew in. The shop door opened and then shut. Looking around, she saw it was Jago. Ivy whined in a loving greeting and Honor felt like joining in.

'Hi, Honor.' His hair was squashed down under the beanie and he had the collar of his jacket turned up. His nose was tinged pink and he looked frozen but alight with a glow of happiness she'd not seen in him before. 'Icy out there.'

'Hi, Jago. It is,' she agreed. 'I'm heading down to the harbour for something hot from the café after I've paid for this lot.'

'I've just come from there. Wanted to check in on Merryn. See how she's doing.'

'And how is she doing?'

He grinned. 'She's having a ball. Not letting anyone in or out of the café unless they've bought at least three mince pies. She had a cooking frenzy last night. You should have seen the state of the kitchen. Flour everywhere.'

'It's a good thing she's doing and you're very trusting to let her do it.'

'Lucie's keeping a close eye out. They've hit it off.'

'I didn't realise you knew Lucie that well?'

Jago paused and Honor could swear he looked embarrassed. 'Well, she sold us the house and I've got to know Jamie on my early morning dog walks round the harbour and where Jamie goes...'

'So does Lucie,' she finished for him, and they laughed. They shuffled forward in the queue. Honor sucked in a deep breath. 'I've been meaning to talk to you.'

He stared deep into her eyes. 'Me too.'

'After that night at the German Market, I wanted to explain...'

'So do I...'

The door to the shop opened again with another blast of frigid air.

'Jago!' Jamie shouted urgently, looking around. 'Jago, are you in here?'

Jago turned to face him. 'Hey, man. What can I do for you?'

'Ah good. Lucie said you were heading up this way.' He greeted Honor briefly and then addressed Jago. 'You know you offered to help tonight?'

Jago flicked a quick glance towards Honor. 'I did.'

Jamie grinned. 'I've got just the job for you, but I need you to come now.'

'But I was just talking to Honor.'

'No time I'm afraid. I need you like yesterday. Sorry, Honor. I have to drag him away.'

Jago shot an apologetic look at Honor. He blew out a regretful breath. 'I'm so sorry but I have to go. Can we, do you think, catch up later?'

She nodded, frustrated.

'Come on, Jago, no time to waste.' Jamie thew a horrified glance Honor's way. 'Sorry. That didn't come out as I meant. It's just I've got a bit of an emergency on.'

'No problem, Jamie,' she smiled at him. She knew he was too nice a man to casually insult. It must be a real emergency.

'Honor, I hate to ask but could you do me a favour?' Jago said beseechingly. He nodded in the direction of Avril. 'Can you pass on the message that I've checked on Merryn and she's fine and selling like a finalist on *The Apprentice*. That's what I came in to say.' He clicked his tongue at Ivy and she slipped to his side. 'Say I'm taking the dog out too, would you mind?'

'Will do.'

He mouthed, 'Sorry,' gave her an apologetic look and left.

Honor watched as the two men hurried away and out into the night, followed by the faithful black-and-white spaniel. She bit her lip and sighed. It was all she could do not to join them. The need to follow devotedly at Jago's heels, just like Ivy, shocked her inner feminist. 'Get a grip, Honor,' she murmured to herself. Hoping she'd get the chance to clear the air with him before she went away, she turned to Avril, piled the books on the desk and foraged in her bag for her credit card.

CHAPTER 26

'I SAW MOMMY KISSING SANTA CLAUS' – THE JACKSON 5

Honor asked if she could leave her books at the desk.

'Of course you can,' Avril replied. 'I'm finishing at seven but don't worry, Bee will still be here.' She leaned nearer. 'If you ask me, she works too hard.'

'I know! I keep telling her. She's lucky to have you. I hope the job works out.'

'I think it might. I've really enjoyed today, even though it's been so busy. Before I came on the till, I was recommending hardback reads for presents. It was great fun. It's lovely to be busy and feel appreciated again.'

Honor thought it an odd comment but didn't pursue it as there was a queue behind her waiting to pay. She passed on Jago's message and said she'd see them all at the carol singing.

'I'll be there. See you later, my lovely. Now, who's next please?'

As Honor buttoned up her coat and fished out her gloves before going out into the cold, she smiled fondly at the sight of Avril serving at the till. The woman looked to be having a ball. She frowned. It was sad she didn't feel appreciated. Whenever she'd come across the Pengethley family, they'd seemed a closely-knit, loving trio. Maybe there was trouble in the marriage? She hoped not. The unsettling image of Jago kissing her at the German Market rose in her mind giving her a hot flush of guilt. He had always given off such strong flirty vibes. Maybe he was like that with all women and that was the source of Avril's dissatisfaction? He'd been extra friendly to Tamara too, but Honor had put it down to the woman's glamour. Tam drew men to her like a siren. Pulling on her woolly hat and dismissing the horrible idea of Jago being a serial philanderer, she opened the door and went out into the crowded street.

The lifeboat station was situated at the beginning of the harbour and had a steep slipway leading into the water. The tide was in and the red-and-green flashing lights decorating the lifeboat building reflected sparkles in the dense, black water. As well as being decorated, both station and slipway were lit and ready for business. Just because it was Christmas didn't mean there wouldn't be a team on standby for a shout. At one side was a small shop which usually sold RNLI merchandise but tonight it had been converted into Santa's Grotto. Red paper blocked out the windows, there was a beautifully decorated Christmas tree to one side of the entrance and Welly Dog Major and Minor, the station's mascots made from yellow welly boots, stood to attention, complete with Santa hats and cheery red jackets. Two elves stood talking to the parents and children in the queue. Honor recognised the curves of the one nearest to her in a second.

'Hi, Tamara,' she said on a giggle. 'Nice costume but aren't you cold?'

The elf whirled round. 'Hi, Honor! It's great, isn't it? Ellie couldn't make it and Lucie's up at the café so me and Maisie are doing the honours.' She did a twirl and then stuck her behind out and twerked. Straightening, she added, 'I borrowed it from the depths of the community theatre's costume department. Not sure what sort of panto they had in mind but it's so sexy I think I'll keep it.' The green velvet dress flared out over her hips barely concealing bright red knickers worn over sparkly green tights. Tamara wore a jaunty hat perched on her blonde hair and a pair of fetching suede ankle boots on her feet. Her only concession to the chilly night was a white fake fur mini cape. She was, as usual, immaculately made up with a slash of vivid red lipstick and flicky eyeliner.

'You look great,' Honor answered truthfully. 'How's it going?'

'Been really busy now we've got a Santa Claus. Eric Snead, who was supposed to do it, came down with flu, poor thing, so we had to get a replacement at the last minute.' She said it loudly and one or two parents looked alarmed and shuffled their children away, covering their ears. 'I mean, we had to ring the North Pole and ask Santa to get a shifty on if he was going to give out all these presents tonight.' She put a hand over her mouth. 'Whoops. Nearly gave the game away there. Better go, the natives are getting restless. I've been leading impromptu sing-alongs to take everyone's minds off the cold.'

She went back to the queue and bellowed, 'Right, who's ready for another singsong? What about Rudolph the Red-nosed reindeer? What colour nose did he have?' She cupped a mittened hand to her ear. 'Was it red?'

The children yelled back, 'Red!'

'I didn't hear that and all the elves back at the North Pole working hard on getting your presents wrapped are so far away, they need bigger voices. What colour nose did Rudolph have?'

'RED!'

'That's better. Your bestest voices then, all together, Rudolph the Red...'

Honor, smiling, turned away. Tamara had missed her vocation; she should have gone into teaching. To kill time before the carols began, she pushed through the crowds and strolled along to the beach huts to admire their decorations. She wandered past one with a miniature train set puffing round and one with a bed, stockings hanging over the fireplace and a jolly

Father Christmas face peering in through a fake window. As she got further along the row it became more crowded with people, so she decided to turn back. The sharp wind whipping off the sea and a beach hut full of weird blow-up Santas, trees and snowmen, had her hurrying to the café in search of something hot to drink.

Lucie, Tracy and Merryn were obviously having a breather and sitting at the table in the window drinking hot chocolate. Lucie was also tucking into an enormous slice of rich fruit cake.

'Miss Martin, Miss Martin!' Merryn shouted. 'I mean, Honor.' She got up, ran to her and threw her arms around her waist. 'I sold all the mince pies!'

'Good going, Merryn.'

'This one,' said Tracy as she hauled herself to her feet, 'is a one-woman selling machine. She could sell snow to Eskimos. We're about to close up but I can do you a hot choc.'

'Ooh yes please, if it's not too much bother.'

'No bother at all, maid. Sit yourself down.' Tracy disappeared into the kitchen.

Honor sat down. 'It's looking lovely in here.' It was. A real Christmas tree stood in one corner, so tall its top was bent against the ceiling, making the fairy in her gold fluffy outfit lean perilously. Great swathes of silver and blue tinsel covered the ceiling and there was a mass of twinkling lights. 'I like these.' She picked up a giant troll. Or it was possibly a gnome, Honor couldn't tell. Consisting of an oversized hat reaching down to a stumpy body, the only facial features were a pink nose and a huge beard frothing down its front. One stood in the middle of each table.

'They're great, aren't they?' Lucie said. 'Courtesy of the Knit and Natter group. Speaking of which, have you seen the latest?'

'Latest what?'

Lucie winked and polished off the last of her cake. 'The latest knitted graffiti.' She looked extremely pleased with herself and Honor couldn't work out why.

'Knitted graffiti?' she asked, puzzled. 'Oh, you mean the Ninja Knitters? That's what I call them.'

Lucie spluttered. 'Such a great name for them. Ninja Knitters. Brilliant. Love it.'

Honor began to sip the hot chocolate Tracy had brought over. 'Thanks, Tracy, I need this.'

'You're welcome. It's on the house. I've cashed up and I'm so zonked I can't be bothered to open the till again.'

Honor clasped her hands around the hot mug and shivered. 'It's so cold out there tonight. I think it might even snow.'

'Snow?' Merryn said excitedly. 'We hardly ever had snow in London!'

'Sorry to disappoint you, my lovely, but we don't often get it by the sea either,' Tracy said to her, 'but when we do, we really do. It's a fair sight to see snow on the beach. All very odd. I can remember one year when I was a kid in Cornwall going on the beach in all the snow. Building snowmen right by the sea was great fun. We gave them seashell eyes. Now, come on, young lady, you can help me fill up the sugar dispensers ready for tomorrow.'

'What, the ones shaped like little pink scallop shells?'

'The very ones. And then we have to count out some serviettes. How good at counting are you?'

'I'm nearly nine. I'm not a baby,' Merryn answered scornfully.

Tracy chuckled and led her away, saying, 'I never for a moment imagined you were.'

Honor fixed Lucie with her fiercest year six on a triple-wet-play-day look. 'What have the Ninjas done now then? And why are you looking so cagey and pleased with yourself about the group? Oh,' she said, on a long breath. 'Of course. The Knit and Natterers are the Ninjas and you're part of the group.'

'Well, I only went a couple of times. Couldn't squeeze any more visits in.' She leaned forward. 'But don't tell anyone.'

'Oh come on, Lu. It's easy to guess. I'm surprised the Lullbury Bay Echo hasn't run an exposé already. You know how it likes to sniff out a story. Why all the secrecy anyway?'

'Just makes it all the more fun, I suppose. And that's what it's all about. A bit of silly fun to cheer people up.'

'So, as well as the postbox topper here and the garlands along the prom, which look fabulous by the way, what's new?'

Lucie's eyes went huge. 'One of the beach huts has been made into Santa's workshop, complete with Father Christmas in his shirtsleeves and braces, Mrs C, toys, wrapped presents and a bunch of elves. All knitted. There's even snow on the roof. It's brilliantly bonkers.'

'I've just been to have a quick look at the beach huts,' Honor said, puzzled. 'I didn't see that one.'

'It's the very last one, right at the end.'

'Ah. I gave up before then. Decided there were too many people about and I was frozen.'

'Did you see the one with all the blow-up stuff in it?' Lucie pulled a face. 'Gave me the right wiggins when they all blew about in the wind.'

'Ooh, me too. I'll go back and have a look at the Ninjas' beach hut. It sounds hilarious and I hope it wins.'

'It had better. The ladies put in an awful lot of work on it.'

'Why do they do it?' Honor asked curiously.

'No idea. One or two of them are obsessed. They sneak out in the middle of the night to put the postbox covers on so it's a surprise. It's team work too. Each person knits a part and then it's all sewn together. Clare Cheney, you know, from Cheney Garden Centre over Bereford way, does nothing but crochet the bases which get stretched over the top of the postbox. She says it's easier for her to concentrate on that as she lives in Italy for part of the year and can't make all the meetings. They're a great group, I know Mum loves going. Just wish I had more time.'

'You've got a lot on, Lucie.'

'Tell me about it,' she said, moodily. 'I'm going to have to make a decision soon. If I really want to concentrate on my degree and do well, I think I'll have to give up working at the estate agents. I can't do both at the same time.' She pulled a face. 'It's just as well our landlord hasn't put the rent up. Money's going to be short.'

'What does Jamie think?'

'Jamie wants me to be happy, bless him. He's so supportive. I couldn't do any of this without him. And, to think, I nearly blew it with him.'

'I remember.' Lucie and Jamie had split up, having been going out since school. They'd parted ways more times than Honor could remember but this break-up had been for nearly a year. She and Lucie had become close during that time. Luckily, Jamie and Lucie had reconciled after Honor had sat them both down and given the pair a good talking to, forcing them to see sense. 'You two are made for one another,' Honor said kindly. 'Anyone can see that. Speaking of which where is he?'

'Oh, didn't you hear? He had a Santa Claus crisis.'

'Tamara mentioned Eric Snead was poorly. Poor man, I like Eric. Jamie's not had to do it himself, has he?'

Lucie laughed. 'He couldn't. For one thing, he's too shy, plus he's in overall charge tonight so he needs to be available. No, he got the lovely Jago to do it. Going down a storm apparently, especially with the yummy mummies. They were all shoving their little munchkins off his knee and demanding Christmas kisses for themselves under a sprig of mistletoe!'

Honor spluttered into her cocoa. 'I wish I'd known when I was talking to Tamara earlier. I would have paid my fiver just to witness that.'

'I know what you mean. If it wasn't for Jamie, I'd definitely have Jago Pengethley in my stocking!'

CHAPTER 27

'DECK THE HALLS' – TRAD.

The women walked the short distance to the lifeboat station for the carol singing, with Merryn bouncing along beside them. When the girl spotted Avril, who was holding Ivy by the lead and talking with Ciara Carmichael and her daughter Holly, she squealed and dragged Tracy over to join them. Honor was disappointed to see Father Christmas had shut up shop and the RNLI 'grotto' was now a temporary kitchen from which the mulled wine was being handed out. She would have loved to have seen Jago in his full Father Christmas regalia.

Tamara was marshalling the community choir to stand by the Christmas tree and lead the carols. Still dressed as a sexy elf and now being a bossy one too, she was passing out song sheets to anyone willing to risk the cold long enough to take their hands out of their pockets. Maisie, who was dressed more conservatively in her longer and warmer looking elf dress, had joined her husband, who was holding their little boy in his arms. Chris, in a smart overcoat, leather gloves and a pair of giant reindeer antlers, stood next to Brenda who, in turn, was arm in arm with the vicar, Verity. They all waved. Both Brenda and Verity looked frozen, despite their woolly hats and bulky coats.

Alice hugged her grandfather to her and shivered in a pair of unseasonal denim cut-offs worn over thick tights. The singing couldn't come a moment too soon. It had gone really cold, with that penetrating damp found by the seaside which gnawed into your bones, no matter how old or young.

Shoving her hands in her coat to keep them warm, Honor said to Lucie, 'It's a good turnout.'

'There must be at least a hundred here,' she agreed. 'Ah, here's my husband.' Giggling, she added, 'Ooh husband! Still haven't got used to calling him that. Sounds far too grown-up for either of us.' She held up her face to Jamie for a kiss. 'You've done ever so well, babe. There are loads here. Let's hope they throw some money in the collecting buckets. Come on, Honor, come and stand with us at the back. We can huddle against the wall of the lifeboat station, out of the wind. Plus, if our mouths are too frozen to sing, Tamara won't pick on us!'

As Verity welcomed everyone and wished them all a Happy Christmas with a reminder of the Nine Carols service at the church on Christmas Eve, Honor looked around for Jago. He was tall so would be easy to spot, but she couldn't see him anywhere. The wind got up and blew the halyards on the dry-moored yachts in the yard behind her. They clinked so hard it was difficult to hear what Verity was saying.

'Oh good,' Lucie said next to her. 'She's reminding everyone to donate generously. Oh, here we go. "'Tis the Season to be Jolly". Got your song sheet, Honor? And we're off. Ooh. Who's that screeching?'

Honor giggled. 'Marion Crawford. She thinks she's Kiri te Kanawa but she can't hit a note.'

'She can't knit either but she told us all Kaffe Fassett pinched one of her patterns.' Trying not to laugh, Lucie gave a loud snort instead.

Jamie elbowed her. 'Come on you two, you're not even singing.'

Honor and Lucie looked at one another. When you thought about it, it was such a silly carol. 'Fa-la-la-la-la, la-la-la-la!' they sang and burst into giggles.

'Oh thank goodness, you're here, Jago,' Jamie said as the man slipped out of the back door of the RNLI shop. 'Can you sort these two out? Think they're on a sugar high. Far too much of Tracy's hot chocolate, if you ask me.'

'Well, she does sneak rum into it,' Lucie explained. 'And I had two.'

'I must try it,' Jago said.

'Here, stand between me and Honor and then you can share a song sheet with her. I'll snuggle up with my beloved.' Lucie turned to Jamie and batted her lashes at him. He tried to look cross but a grin stole through and he kissed her.

Honor was embarrassed. She and Jago had had little to do with one another since the kiss at the German Market and now really wasn't the time to clear the air. She thrust the piece of paper towards him and he held one side of it. They had to stand close together to see the words. 'Sorry I missed you being Father Christmas. I hear you were a hit,' she said, over the sound of the carolling.

His eyebrows rose so high they disappeared into his beanie. He bent to talk into her ear. 'With one section of the population maybe. Not so much with the children. I had one kid slide off my lap when I gave him his present saying it wasn't bicycle-shaped and I was a crap Father Christmas if I thought it was. Then he tried to pull my beard off! Wouldn't have minded but Jamie had stuck it on with some kind of glue.' He rubbed his cheek. 'I am never, *ever* doing it again. Eric Snead must be a saint to do it every year.'

'Oh dear,' Honor said, reining in the giggles. There was an awkward pause. It occurred to her that she might not be the one he wanted to be with. 'Avril's at the front with Merryn if you want to sing with them.'

'Why would I want to?'

Honor frowned. 'I assumed you'd want to celebrate with your wife.'

Jago did a double take. 'With my wife?'

'Yes. Avril,' Honor repeated, louder, as if he was stupid. Maybe the stress of being Father Christmas had got to him. Or maybe he'd been at Tracy's hot chocolate too.

'Avril's not my wife. I don't have one.'

Lucie prodded him. 'Come on, guys. Sing. This is the fun bit.'

'Fa-la-la-la-la, la-la-la- la!' they roared.

'You're not married to Avril?' Honor said, returning to the conversation and blinking at him dazedly. 'Then who is she?'

'Avril's my mum,' he said on a laugh.

'Your *mother*?'

He nodded. 'My mum.'

'Then Merryn is your–'

'Little sister, yes.'

'Not your daughter. You're not married?'

'I'm not married.'

They broke off to half-heartedly sing, 'Fa-la-la-la-la, la-la-la-la!'

Honor stopped singing once the chorus was done. 'You're not married!' She stared at him. At his stubbled, square-jawed chin. At his eyes, mossy-green in the dark. At the glossy curls escaping from his hat. For the first time she noticed he wore a tiny gold hoop in one ear. It made him appear even more piratical. She felt as if she'd never been this close to him before, had never seen him properly. Her breath hitched in her throat. She wanted to gaze and gaze at him, soak in every detail and commit it to memory, to her heart. More than anything she wanted to tug him to her and kiss the life out of him. He wasn't married. She'd got it all wrong. But *how*?

'I mean, I was married. To Rose, not Avril. I'm divorced now.' He looked utterly confused. 'Why did you think I was married?'

'It doesn't matter. Oh, Jago, I'm just glad, so glad, that you're not.' She reached up and cupped his face in her mittened hands. The song sheet fluttered to the ground ignored. 'I'm so glad you're not,' she repeated in a whisper and kissed him with all the love she had.

'Fa-la-la-la-la, la-la-la-la!'

CHAPTER 28

'ALL I WANT FOR CHRISTMAS IS YOU' – MARIAH CAREY

They snuck off, heading away from the crowds, not really heeding where they were going, and found themselves walking along the promenade. Most people were at the carol singing so they had it to themselves – and the starlit night.

'My hands are freezing,' he complained.

'Here. You can share my glove.' She slid his nearest hand into the mitten she was wearing. They entwined fingers and she put both their hands into the pocket of her coat. They had to walk very closely together as a result. 'Better?' she smiled up at him.

'You can't imagine how much better I feel.' They stopped walking and he kissed her tenderly. 'We have a lot of talking to do. A lot of unknotting the misunderstandings,' he said, against her lips.

'I'd rather just kiss you,' she murmured, loving the vibrations the sound made. Behind them, the slow shifting sea shushed gently against an indigo sky.

'So would I, but I'm freezing. It's not romantic to die of frostbite.'

She giggled. 'You won't die of frostbite. I'll keep you warm.'

'I'll hold you to that.' They kissed again, more lingeringly this time and with heat.

'This is certainly warming me up.'

'I really think we ought to admire the decorated beach huts,' she admonished.

'Are the beach huts decorated? I hadn't noticed.'

She pushed him off, albeit reluctantly. 'I could stand here and kiss you all night but we've got talking to do.'

'We have.' He blew out a breath. It misted upwards. 'Shall we go somewhere warm to do that talking?'

Honor nodded. 'Yes let's. The Old Anchor will be rammed with half-frozen carol singers when they've finally finished.' She cocked an ear as singing floated across the sea from the harbour. 'Ah. "O Come All Ye Faithful". Always a favourite. How about we walk up to The Ship?'

He lifted her hand to his mouth and kissed it. 'Perfect. Wasn't that where it all started?' Then he pinched out some wool which had stuck to his lip. 'And the sooner we get there the better.'

They walked along the prom hand in hand, absentmindedly admiring the decorated beach huts but only having eyes for each other until they reached the last one.

'Well, I'm not quite sure what to say,' Jago observed.

'You can't say the Ninja Knitters don't go all out.'

The beach hut was a thing of wonder. A life-sized Father Christmas stood at his work bench examining a toy train. Mrs Christmas stood at the back of the workshop, her arms full of wrapped presents, her hair a snowy-white knitted mass. Five elves were dotted about, wrapping presents and filling stockings. The floor was a vast white knitted blanket spilling out onto the prom and there were even knitted icicles hanging from the 'snow' covered roof.

Jago pulled Honor in for a hug. 'How much work has gone into it?'

'They must have been planning this for months, if not years. It takes ages to knit that much. It's quite something,' she added, on a giggle.

'I can safely say I've never seen anything quite like it before.' He dropped a kiss on her head. 'Hope it wins.'

Honor pointed out a small sign held by one of the elves. 'First Place,' she read. 'And even the sign is knitted! Overly optimistic or well-prepared?'

He laughed. 'We live in a strange but magical town.' As he turned her to him the softest touch landed on his nose.

'Was that a snowflake?' Jago stared hopefully into the dark sky.

They looked up.

'Surely it's too clear for snow? I can see stars.'

'Maybe it was just the one. One snowflake just for us.' He kissed her, his lips cold against her warm mouth. 'A blessing from the universe.'

'Do you think the Ninjas knitted that too?'

Jago laughed and laid his forehead against hers. 'Have you no romance in your soul, woman?'

'Oh, I've plenty of romance,' she replied and reached for his kiss again.

The pub was packed but, once they'd squeezed past the crowd at the bar, they found a quieter back room with a table in a corner next to the wood burner.

Honor looked around. 'Not sure why this one's free but I think we'd better grab it.' By the time Jago had returned from the bar with their drinks, she'd stripped down to her T-shirt. 'Found out why the table's free. It's The Ship's tropical corner. I don't know if it's the contrast with outside or whether that stove is pumping out too much heat but I'm boiling.' She accepted her mulled wine. 'Thank you. It's a good table though, quite secluded.'

He slid in next to her. 'Just what we need. Cheers.' They clinked glasses. 'And, trust me, no opportunity for talking next door. Bruce Springsteen is blasting out.' At her enquiring look, he added, 'Santa Claus is Coming to Town.'

'Ah. That's a good one. I love Christmas music.'

'You just love Christmas full stop, don't you?'

'What's not to like? Cheesy music, the excuse to eat lots of great food, everyone's in a good mood, oh and cards. I love getting Christmas cards!'

He smiled wryly and sipped his pint, grimacing. 'Half-wishing I'd bought a coffee to warm me up.'

Honor smiled. 'Never seen the appeal of beer and I've sworn off cider for life. I'll stick to mulled wine, thank you. Warming and very seasonable. You don't seem as much of a fan. Of Christmas, I mean. I always sense you're going through the motions somehow.'

Jago blew out a breath. 'You're an astute observer. I am, I suppose. I used to love Christmas but something happened to change that. Don't get me wrong, I'm sort of enjoying all the Christmassy stuff going on in Lullbury Bay but mostly it's a way of keeping things upbeat for Mum and Merryn.' He paused, wondering how much to tell her.

Honor put her hand on his. The skin-on-skin contact took her breath away. 'What is it, Jago? What happened?'

'Do you really want to know? It'll put a real downer on the evening. It's not a very Christmassy tale.' He feathered a light finger across her neck, tenderly stroking her hair out of the way. 'I'd rather talk about us.'

'Of course I want to know. I want to get to know you. We seem to have been at cross-purposes so much, I'd like for there to be honesty between us. There'll be plenty of time to talk about us.'

'Okay then.' He turned back to his pint, staring moodily into the glass.

She sat absolutely still, wondering what was coming.

He told her, not sparing any detail. About what had happened on the shout, about the rush to the hospital after the call every RNLI family dreads. The endless waiting around, trying to get information out of a Covid-fatigued skeleton staff overrun and overworked on Christmas Eve. The awful, awful saying goodbye to a husk of a body which had once been his much-loved, vibrant father. Coming back to a house which had only one person missing but which felt like an echoing, empty shell and was no longer home. The utter shock and bewilderment.

'Mum fell apart, not surprisingly. They'd been married for over thirty years. Didn't quite make their thirty-fifth anniversary. Merryn went into herself; it was horrible to witness. I had to keep everyone together, as well as sort out the minefield of all the paperwork.' He shuddered. 'God, that seemed endless. It was just as well, in a way, I'd moved back after splitting up with Rose.'

Honor sucked in a breath, inhaling his hurt. 'It must have been, and probably still is, an awful thing to go through. I'm so sorry, Jago.'

He picked up her hand, turned it and kissed her palm. 'Thank you,' he said, in a voice guttural with emotion. Releasing it, he straightened and took a long draught of beer, making an attempt to control his emotions. 'You can see why I warned you it would bring the mood low,' he said, drily. Clearing his throat, he added, 'By the way, Rose is my ex-wife. Very amicable divorce, we're huge friends and she's getting married next year to a great bloke. I'm very happy for her and she's very much an ex-wife.' He managed a smile. 'I can't wait for you to meet her. She'll love you.'

Honor returned the smile. 'In that case, I'd love to.' She put her hand on his shoulder, moving it up to caress his cheek. There was a slight red mark where the glue had stuck Santa's beard on. She reached forward and kissed it gently. 'And, as to bringing the mood down, I said I wanted to know all about you. No more secrets, no more crossed wires or misunderstandings. I want to know what makes Jago Pengethley tick.'

He looped an arm around her shoulder and brought her close. 'Well, now you know why, every now and again, I might struggle with Christmas, certainly this year and maybe in the future. The trouble is, it's so difficult to avoid.'

As if to underline his point, a chorus of, 'I Wish it Could Be Christmas Everyday', blasted out from the adjoining bar.

Honor felt a sigh reverberate through him and rested her hand on his stomach, feeling the rise and fall of his breathing. He'd been through so much, was still going through so much. But he'd obviously been the one who'd held his little family together. She'd witnessed his tenderness with Avril and Merryn and could understand it from a different perspective now. Her heart swelled with feeling for him. She wanted this man in her life. She wanted it very much.

They sat there for a while, each lost in their thoughts, enjoying the simplicity of being warm and close to one another, breathing the same rhythm.

'Another drink?' he asked eventually. 'Beer's not really hitting the mark tonight, I think I'll get a whisky. What about you?'

She shook her head. 'I'm fine thanks.' She watched him as he stood up. Her feelings had been tender and protective but, as he pulled off his sweatshirt to reveal a T-shirt and she caught a glimpse of dark-haired muscle underneath, she felt a coil of hot lust. He really was a very beautiful man.

When he returned, she'd got herself under control.

'I brought you a drink anyway.' He put another mulled wine down. 'The bar's so busy, it was a rugby scrum to get these in.' Throwing down an assortment of packets of nuts and crisps, he added, 'To soak up the alcohol.' He grinned wickedly, 'After all, haven't you been at the doctored hot chocolate?'

'Oh yes,' she pulled a comical expression. 'I'd forgotten about that. You wait until I see Tracy!'

He sat down and shoved a hand through his curls, making them even more unruly. 'She seems nice. Mum says she's from Cornwall.'

'She's great fun.' Honor screwed up her face. 'I'm still adjusting to thinking of Avril being your *mum*.'

He twisted round to her. 'Why did you think I was married to her?'

She explained about seeing them all in the café on the evening of Merryn's first day. She felt her face heat. 'I've been so unprofessional. I jumped to the obvious conclusion, and I really shouldn't have. And you were so good with Merryn, I always got fatherly vibes off you, not big brother ones.'

He pulled a regretful face. 'I suppose I've stepped into that role and I genuinely enjoy her company. You never know what to expect next from her.'

'That's very true.' Honor paused and thought back over all the conversations she'd had with the Pengethleys. 'Did I miss anything? The file from her old school hasn't come through yet otherwise I would have read up on her background and would know your family dynamics. I usually ring the school the pupil has come from, but I have to confess to not having the time. It all got a bit hectic towards the end of term and the parents or guardians of the child normally tell me what I need to know. As Avril didn't say anything, I made an assumption, another assumption, that there was nothing untoward. Actually,' she said, 'on reflection, with something that vital, you'd expect the other school to let the new one know. It's important that we do.'

'To be honest, it doesn't surprise me they haven't. We weren't very happy with how they handled it. It was an enormous school, with several acting members of senior management staff. They were trying to cope but didn't do us many favours.'

'I still feel awful. I feel I've let Merryn down!'

Jago shook his head. 'Don't feel awful. You certainly haven't let her down. She loves being at St Winifred's and especially in your class. It's perfect for her. You hadn't missed anything. Or at least, you hadn't missed anything we didn't want to tell you. When Mer went back to school after Dad died, she had a really tough time. She's always been a bit different to the other kids, quicksilver smart and a bit eccentric, only now, on top of all that, she was the child whose father had died in sudden and tragic circumstances. She was a magnet for bullies. Any counselling we found for her, and any strategies put in place by the school didn't work, in fact they made things worse.' He took a breath. 'When we moved here, we made the decision not to say anything about what had happened to us, at least for a while, to give us, and mostly Merryn, the chance to find her feet without all that notoriety hanging around her. We just all wanted, craved I suppose, a fresh start. It's why we moved to Lullbury Bay. To each find our way without having tragedy hovering over us.'

Honor thought back to the night in The Old Anchor when she'd met up with her friends. 'It might not be possible for much longer,' she said slowly. 'From what Jamie said, one evening in the pub, I think he's linked you with what happened to your father.'

Jago nodded. 'I had a chat with him about it. Came clean. As he's a volunteer with the RNLI, he's in the circles to know about when there's a loss. It's a tightly knit world and Pengethley is an unusual surname.'

'Jamie's lovely, he'll be as discreet as you want him to be. He won't gossip about you. I can't say the same for some others in this town though. Gossip's a life force for some people.'

'I think we're resigned to the information getting out eventually. We just wanted a little time to ourselves before it did.'

She nodded slowly. 'I understand. And I'm relieved I didn't miss anything. It would be useful to have a chat in the new year about what we can put in place for Merryn, though.' She frowned. 'I'm surprised Merryn herself hasn't once mentioned anything.'

'She's stopped talking about it. Hardly talks about Dad at all.

It's understandable but worrying. I've been having a few chats with Verity Lincoln, you know, the vicar? She mentioned there's a children's grief charity nearby.'

Honor nodded. 'There is. We can refer her. They're excellent. And I think being around other children who have suffered the same loss will help. They do talking therapy too. I'll get onto it first thing in the new term, after talking it through with Avril first, of course.' She bit her lip and blushed. 'I do feel a fool for thinking you and Avril were married though.'

He laughed. 'Shall we tell her? She's got twenty years on me, she'd be enormously flattered.'

'Don't you dare! I'm embarrassed enough about the whole thing in the first place.'

'My lips are sealed.'

'Your lips are irresistible.'

He smiled at her so intently, she thought she'd combust. When he kissed her again, she nearly did.

CHAPTER 29

'BELIEVE' – JOSH GROBAN

They stopped kissing, aware it wasn't the right place or time and sat, forehead to forehead, giggling a little. Jago turned away, gave an embarrassed cough and concentrated on his whisky. 'I feel like a teenager,' he laughed.

Darting a glance at the couple on the other side of the room who, luckily, had been oblivious, Honor pulled herself together and ripped open a couple of bags of crisps to share. She settled on something more matter of fact to discuss. 'There's a big age difference between you and Merryn.'

'There is.' Jago smiled. 'I can see why you thought I was her dad, I'm certainly old enough. Mum and Dad had me well on the way when they got married. We lived in Fowey until I was four.' He screwed up his face. 'I can just about remember it, but it's mixed up with memories of visits to family later. Dad got an opportunity to work full-time with the RNLI in London so we all relocated. It was just us three for a long time and then Mum found out she was expecting Mer. It was a hell of a shock as she was forty-six.'

'Wow. It must have felt like starting all over again for her.'

'Yeah. I haven't really thought about it that way. Mum had

been working for John Lewis in Victoria for years. I suppose she thought she was getting her life back and wham, along comes Merryn. She went part-time after Mer was born but I know it wasn't easy. She'd never really settled to city life, not truly. So, when Dad died, she saw it as an opportunity for a new start. She took redundancy and we came here.'

'You must find it very strange compared to living in London?'

'I do and I don't. I think the sea lives in your soul, there's something about it that draws you back. I was never sure if I was a city boy. I loved aspects of it, but I was never fully committed to city living. I see that now. I'm beginning to love Lullbury Bay. It's quaint and has its share of eccentrics but I can see it offering a good quality of life.'

'And you're not alone. I've had three new pupils join the class this term alone, and all from London. I think the pandemic made people rethink their life choices, re-evaluate. It's great for the school though. Rural schools struggle for numbers, especially in a town that's popular with the retired.'

There was a pause then Honor felt she had to ask the inevitable. 'So, you're divorced?'

'I am. Married Rose too soon, we found out we're not truly compatible too late. Lockdown had us living and working in too close a proximity. Brought things to a head. The divorce was just coming through when Dad died. But I can assure you, I no longer have any feelings for Rose beyond fondness, I'm most definitely not married anymore and have the papers to prove it. Plus, Rose and I have managed to stay friends which is a miracle. Verity said we should be proud we've achieved that.'

'Sounds like Verity has been giving you good advice. She's a nice woman.'

'She's great. She told me I needed to talk things over with you. I've something to apologise for, Honor.'

'What?'

'For rushing you with the kiss at the German Market. I misread the signs.'

'What signs?'

'I thought you liked me.'

'I did. I mean I do. Very much.' Honor felt her face grow hot.

'I should have thought about you being in the public eye and wanting to keep your reputation as a teacher. I shouldn't have kissed you somewhere so public.'

She smiled at him. 'It can be tricky in a small town. Half of my pupils and parents think I disappear up in smoke when I leave school. The other half think I should behave like an angel. But it wasn't that. After all, we've spent most of this evening snogging each other's faces off in very public places.' She giggled.

'Then what was it?'

'At the time I thought you were married to Avril.'

'Ah.' Jago's reply came out on a long, drawn-out breath of understanding.

'I have to apologise too.'

'What for?'

'For stupidly running off. I was so mixed up in my head. I was getting vibes from you that you were interested and even Tamara said you were.'

'Wise woman, Tamara.'

Honor smiled. 'In some ways. So, on the one hand, I sensed you liked me but on the other I saw you as this loving father, and husband to Avril. A woman I've come to like very much. I couldn't believe you were flirting with me when all the time you were married. It was driving me crazy. It was like two warring emotions in my head. I was beginning to like you very much, I thought perhaps it was reciprocated but I refused to get into a situation where I'd be the other woman.'

'Hence your relief when you found out the truth?'

'I can't tell you,' Honor said warmly. 'All the fuzzy muddle in my head cleared. It's been awful.'

'I'm sorry.' Jago dropped a kiss on her temple.

'You've nothing to be sorry for! It was all me. I've been so stupid. I saw you in the Sea Spray Café that night and you looked like the perfect family.'

'When was that?'

'A Monday back in November.'

He thought back. 'Was that Merryn's first day at school?'

Honor nodded. 'I walk home along the prom sometimes as it's more pleasant. Clears the head after a day in school. I quite often pop into Tracy's for something to eat on the way home, so I looked in to see how busy it was and saw you all.'

Jago nodded. 'It was Merryn's first day with you. Mum and I had been fretting all day about how she'd get on, so the relief when she bounced out smiling like a toothpaste ad was enormous. We all got a bit overexcited and over-sugared having had at least two hot chocolates with extra marshmallows, then Mum agreed to us having a dog.' He smiled at the memory. 'Mer was so excited she couldn't speak.'

Honor laughed. 'That would explain it. I think, when I looked in, she was sitting on your lap.'

'I can see why you thought I was her dad.'

'You looked a very close family unit.'

'Which we are,' he agreed.

'Just not the one I thought you were.'

'You should have joined us.'

'I didn't want to interrupt.'

'You'll never interrupt.' He tweaked a coil of her blonde hair. 'Mum's really fond of you, Merryn thinks you're the best thing since sliced bread although, with Merryn we all have to accept our ranking.'

'Which is?' asked Honor, amused.

'Somewhere below Ivy, Chestnut, the Carmichaels' horses and dogs, and pizza.'

Honor giggled again. She felt giddy and it wasn't the alcohol or the heat from the stove, it was being able to bask in Jago's attention.

The couple opposite got up, gathered their coats and left. They were alone.

'And where do I come in *your* ranking?' she asked, unable to resist flirting.

'Perhaps this will answer that.' He kissed her, long and hard and hungrily.

'Oh,' she said weakly. 'That's nice.'

'Nice? I'm outraged. Come here, woman. I'll show you nice.'

When they broke apart, both were shaken by the storm of passion. They stared into each other's eyes, dazed.

'Blimey,' was all Honor managed.

Jago was silent for a moment. 'Blimey indeed.' He backed off, looking shocked. He shook his head wonderingly. 'When I saw you after the advent service, I thought you looked like an angel. You were wearing a white coat and holding some tinsel wings. I'd never seen anyone so beautiful or so pure.'

'I'm no angel, Jago.'

He smiled so tenderly she thought she could bathe in its warmth forever. 'No angel.' He reached forward and kissed her again. 'But something so much better.'

The noise from the bar next door rose to a crescendo as Lenny the landlord called time. The night had flown.

'May I walk you home?'

'You don't need to walk me home, Jago.' She couldn't stop saying his name. It was as if by saying it, it cleaved him to her even more. 'It's only down the hill.'

'I'd like to.'

'Then you may.'

'And does that mean I can kiss you goodnight?'

Honor tilted her head coyly. 'It does.'

CHAPTER 30

'I'VE GOT MY LOVE TO KEEP ME WARM' – LENNY MARTIN

Wednesday 22nd December

They agreed to meet up again the following evening. It was a late-night shopping event in town, a fancy dress dog competition was promised, along with a brass band. It was the only day free before Christmas that Honor had, as she was driving up to Worcester to see her parents early the following morning.

She made sure she kept herself busy, but her mind wasn't really on wrapping the presents she was taking with her, or throwing clothes into her suitcase. She kept thinking back to how Jago's lips felt on hers. She knew he was someone she could get serious about. Happiness helped her glide through the day in a sunny haze. She sang along to the cheesy Christmas songs on Radio Two and even went as far as to post a Christmas card through her surly neighbour's door downstairs. His response, on her return to her flat, was to bang on the ceiling and shout at her to turn the radio down.

But even Frank couldn't spoil Honor's mood. She stood in front of the wardrobe and considered what to wear on the date. It was cold again outside, with the added wind chill of a stiff breeze. It would have to be the white coat, it was smart, warm and besides, Honor felt herself dissolve inside at the thought, Jago said it made her look like an angel. She found a white knitted hat her mother had bought the previous Christmas, but which she'd always been too self-conscious to wear as it had an enormous faux-fur pom-pom, tucked her gloves into her pocket, fished out her bag and locked the flat.

The cold air, as it hit her when she turned the corner into the bottom of the high street, physically took her breath away. She sheltered against the wall of an empty building and pulled her gloves on. The building, once home to a swish restaurant, was now empty and boarded up. It looked rather forlorn and she wished someone would take it on. It held a prime central position in town and blighted the otherwise pretty street. Some wise crack had painted a Christmas tree on one of the boards in an attempt to make it look festive.

'Honor, hi!'

'Hi, Tamara.' She kissed her friend. 'Good to see you before you go away. Happy Christmas.'

'Happy Christmas, babe. I'm on my way up to The Ship, want to join me?'

Honor shook her head. 'I've got a date,' she said, not bothering to hide her glee.

'A date? Wey hey, good for you, babe. Who with?'

'Jago Pengethley.'

Tamara did a double take. 'Not the married man you weren't touching with the proverbial bargepole?'

'Turns out he's not even slightly married. Merryn is his little sister not his daughter and Avril is his *mum*. I made the wrong call.'

Tamara frowned, marring her perfectly made-up face. 'How did that happen then?'

'I jumped in with both feet from a great height and got it all horribly wrong.'

'Doesn't sound like you, Honor. Sounds more like something I'd do. Maybe I'm a bad influence on you! Although, girlfriend, now you come to think about it, it makes a whole load more sense.'

'I know.' Honor bit her lip and looked shamefaced. 'I can only blame end-of-term exhaustion.'

'Well everyone knows you work far too hard.' She gave her a swift hard hug. 'But I'm made up for you. He seems a lovely bloke and is dead sexy.' She shivered. 'Look, I'm going to go, too cold to stand around. I'll see you next month. Text me, you hear? I want all the goss.'

'I will. And looking forward to catching up with you after your cruise gig. Have a fabulous time.' Honor waved as her friend jogged up the hill. It must be cold if Tamara broke into a run. She usually glided everywhere, serene and immaculate.

She turned and bumped into someone male and very solid. Jago's arms came round her. 'Just the person I wanted to see above everyone else.'

'Hi, Jago,' she gazed up at him. The cold air had pinked up his cheeks and highlighted the enviable cheekbones. He smelled heavenly.

'Hi, Honor. It's been too long.' He bent and kissed her.

'It's been *far* too long!' She giggled, kissing him back.

He nuzzled her nose, then backed off and grimaced. 'Could you bear to do me a favour before we start our evening proper? Would you mind?'

Honor, putting her arms around his waist, thought she'd grant him anything. 'What's that?'

'Could you bear to start our date with going to see the Dog Fancy Dress competition? Only Merryn has entered Ivy and she wants us there.'

Honor giggled some more. 'Only if you buy me some roasted chestnuts on the way.'

'Deal.'

They bought the chestnuts from a vendor selling them from a brazier contraption which looked as if it had been constructed from a large tin can, and walked slowly along the prom messily sharing them. The first few were almost too hot to peel, but the wind whipping off the sea soon cooled them.

'Look at my hands,' Honor cried, holding them up for Jago to see, her fingertips were grey with charcoal. The white coat didn't seem such a good idea now.

He took one finger and put it very deliberately into his mouth and sucked, all the time making eye contact.

'I don't think it's legal to feel quite so turned on in public,' she gasped.

He gave a wicked grin, fished out a snowy-clean handkerchief and handed it over. 'Maybe it would be safer, for both of us, for you to use this instead.'

'Very possibly.' She took it and wiped her hands. 'I never had you down as the cotton hankie type.' Handing it back she added, 'You're full of surprises, Jago Pengethley.'

He bent down and kissed her nose gently. 'And you've only just scraped the surface.'

The arrogance took her breath away, or it could have been the gust of wind that wrapped itself around her legs. Her teeth began to chatter. She told herself it was the cold. 'Think we'd better get to the fancy dress competition.'

He backed off, a twinkle in his eye. 'Better had.'

The competition was being held on the prom in one of the huge shelters there. In summer, people rented deckchairs and sat out of the sun relaxing. In winter folk huddled on the benches trying to get out of the vicious wind that sliced off the sea. In the evenings, it was the favourite haunt of teenagers who felt they had nowhere else to go. Now, it was lit up, with Christmassy music playing quietly in the background, and quite a crowd had gathered. Cones marked off a circle which created an arena for the dogs to parade in, with an entrance path from the adjacent shelter. Honor could hear barking from it, so she supposed it was the makeshift holding pen.

As Honor and Jago found a spot to stand in, out of the wind, Austin Ruddick took to the microphone, his German Shepherd clinging to his side. 'Good evening, ladies and gents, boys and girls and four-pawed pals, from me and Gretel. As organiser I welcome you to Lullbury Bay's very first Fancy Dress Competition for our Canine Companions.' He cleared his throat, looking emotional, and Gretel whined to comfort him, putting her nose against his leg. 'It's wonderful to see so very many of you here. I hope, after this, you'll go into town to buy those last-minute presents, treat yourself to one of Gladwin's turkey pasties and enjoy the brass band. And now, speaking of brass bands, as it's right brass-monkey weather tonight, I'll start proceedings without further ado. Rules are simple, folks, dress your dog up in something Christmassy and the representatives from the council here will decide a winner. I'll now hand over to Maisie who owns the very dog-friendly Sea Spray Café and who will introduce each dog and owner.' He passed the mike to Maisie and nodded to his granddaughter Alice who looked to be in charge of music. She pressed a button on the large and battered CD player and Carols from King's changed into 'All I Want for Christmas is a Beatle'. One or two in the crowd tittered.

'Hi, everyone,' Maisie said, her dark hair blowing in the wind. 'Thank you, Alice, can you turn it down a little? Much as I love Dora Bryan, she's a little loud to talk over. All our music tonight has been chosen especially by Austin, so I'm taking absolutely no blame.' There was more laughter. 'Our first entrant is Mitzi the Chihuahua who is owned by the Lawrences from Sandy Shores B&B and is being shown by Michael.' As Michael Lawrence walked Mitzi into the circle and paraded her round, Maisie continued. 'Mitzi has come as The Ghost of Christmas Present. A very clever idea as you can see.'

The Chihuahua preened as if understanding. Michael

Lawrence took her to the middle of the circle where she could be admired by all. The dog wore a pale grey coat with chiffon strips floating from it and which was festooned with glittery red and green wrapped presents. They dangled and caught the light as the chiffon strips flew in the wind. Dog and owner paraded three times and then posed on a low box covered in red velvet in the centre.

'Thank you very much, Michael and Mitzi.' To a ripple of applause, dog and owner left the arena.

'Next, we have Benson, a Great Dane entered by Sid Grant from Grant's Farm Shop and Dairy.' Maisie giggled. 'Magnificent Benson is entered as a Christmas pudding.'

To laughter, built-for-rugby Sid and his equally enormous dog ambled into the ring. Benson, looking about as embarrassed as a dog could, wore a papier mâché globe from which his gangling legs protruded. It was nominally painted a shiny dark brown with a white felt splodge of 'icing' stuck on. A wreath of holly adorned the dog's ears, or it did until Benson shook his huge head and it slipped off to be retrieved by a frustrated Sid. The Great Dane then rolled over and smashed the Christmas pudding. Getting up, it gave a goofy grin, tongue lolling and pulled its owner out of the arena like a steam train.

Everyone roared with laughter. 'That's a Great Dane for you, always the clown,' Maisie said, spluttering with laughter. 'Thank you, Sid and Benson.'

Alice changed the music. 'No one Loves a Fairy when she's Forty' rang out which made the crowd laugh even harder, and one or two ran into the circle to collect the broken shards of Benson's costume.

'I'm not sure what I was expecting,' Jago laughed, 'but it wasn't this.'

'I know.' Honor wiped the mirth from her eyes. She was laughing so much, she was crying. 'It's the first time they've done it, but I hope they make it an annual event.'

'Thank you again, Sid and Benson,' continued Maisie. 'Remember though folks, plum pudding is not to be fed to dogs as it can make them very ill. Please save it for your Christmas afters.'

The next dog was an immaculately behaved Labrador in a Santa outfit who posed perfectly, followed by a terrier dressed as an elf who raced round barking and shot off in the wrong direction, through the crowd and onto the prom, its owner at the end of the extendable lead puffing behind.

Once the crowd quietened, Maisie said, 'Thank you to Toffee and owner Agnes for all that excitement. If we could have the music turned down now, please, Alice, and could I ask you all to be as calm as you can, as next we have a very special entrant.' The strains of 'O Little Town of Bethlehem' could be heard as Carols from Kings played in the background again. 'Please welcome, but do it quietly, Ivy and her young handler, Merryn.' A quiet ripple of applause sounded as a beaming Merryn led Ivy into the ring, the dog's limp hardly noticeable. Avril hovered apprehensively on the sidelines.

Honor felt Jago stiffen at her side. She looked up to see his eyes glisten with proud tears and tucked her hand into his arm.

'Ivy is a special dog,' Maisie whispered, 'as she's a rescue and a very recent one. Merryn has been working hard on training her. I think we'll all agree she's looking splendid as the angel on top of the Christmas tree.'

Someone 'ahhed' in the crowd.

Merryn preened as she led a slightly jittery Ivy around the circle. The dog wore a short white satin coat over her front two legs, with angel's wings and a tinsel halo protruding from her collar. As she turned around, the pièce de résistance could be seen; a Christmas tree complete with baubles attached to her back. All knitted.

Honor gasped. 'Oh, that's so sweet. I take it Avril knitted the costume?'

Jago nodded. 'Mum's really got into her knitting again, or had before she began working in the bookshop. She's so much happier.'

Honor hugged his arm to her. 'I'm glad. She certainly looked in her element when I went in the bookshop yesterday.'

'She loves it, and her Knit and Natter group. She's making friends.' Jago looked at his little sister. 'We all are.'

Ivy only managed a quick lap before beginning to look anxious, so Merryn handed her over to Avril who led her out. The music returned to full volume and Tom brought Tiny the Irish Wolfhound in.

'Seen enough?' Jago asked.

Honor nodded. 'I think I need to move. My feet are frozen. But don't you want to see if Merryn and Ivy win?'

'She's already won in my eyes. Come on, let's hit the town and find some warmth.'

She reached up and kissed his cheek. 'You are an unbelievably nice man, Jago Pengethley.'

CHAPTER 31

'SILVER BELLS' – HARRY CONNICK JNR

They hurried along the prom in the direction of the high street, hardly noticing the twinkling white lights or the knitted Christmas garlands twisted around the railings. They kept their heads down and their hands in their pockets. The wind was getting up.

Once they'd turned the corner into the shelter of the high street, it instantly eased.

Honor blinked, her cheeks stinging. 'That was bracing.'

Jago laughed. 'It was.' He tucked a strand of hair back under her woolly hat. 'What would you like to do now?'

As they hesitated, a clip-clopping sound could be heard echoing against the shopfronts, rising above the buzzy chatter of the late-night shoppers. The high street had, once again, been closed off to traffic and the town was thronging with people wrapped up warm against the cold. As well as the chestnut seller, the burger stall was back, along with one advertising doughnuts and another pulled pork, turkey rolls and falafels. The brass band underneath the Christmas tree started up, playing 'Jingle Bells'. The scents and sounds combined to make it impossibly Christmassy.

The clip-clopping resolved itself into a horse and open-top carriage. It appeared in the narrow gap at the end of the high street which led to the cobbled square. With a jingle of bells it drew up next to Honor and Jago. Painted white, it had two lanterns hung on the front, a red one at the back and was decorated with a mass of silver bells.

'Hello there, Jago. Oh and it's Miss Martin!' It was Ciara Carmichael, a parent from school and mother of Merryn's best friend. She was sitting up in front holding the reins and dressed smartly in an old-fashioned riding habit complete with top hat and whip. 'Fancy a ride? Come on up. Lots of rugs to keep you cosy and any donations to the RNLI. Say hello to Pasco the Pony first.'

Dutifully they went to the pony and rubbed its nose. In response Pasco threw his head up and snorted so they backed off with a giggle.

Jago turned to Honor. 'Shall we? Looks like Pasco might need some exercise.'

'I'd love to.'

He took her hand as she stepped in and helped her up. Sliding in next to her, he pulled the heap of fake fur rugs over them. There wasn't a great deal of room, but it suited them just fine to snuggle in together. Jago found her hand and held it.

'All set?' Ciara shouted over her shoulder.

'All set!'

Ciara clicked her tongue and the carriage moved with a jerk, throwing Jago and Honor back into the seat. Thankfully, it then settled into a rhythmic motion that was quietly soothing. As they climbed the steep high street, crowds of shoppers parted before them and people looked up, waved and smiled.

Honor waved back. 'This is fun. I feel like royalty.'

'You'll always be a princess to me,' Jago joked.

She groaned.

'I'm not surprised the Queen always had a rug on her knees

though,' he continued. 'Now I remember why I don't drive a convertible in the winter.' He pulled his beanie down further over his ears and pulled a face.

Honor kissed his cold cheek. 'My prince!' she exclaimed, teasing his soft city ways.

'Now it was his turn to groan. Shall we stop with the corny jokes now?'

'Yes please.' Honor snuggled further under the rug and laid her head on his shoulder. With warmth stealing through her she felt happy and complete.

They continued up the high street, leaving the bustle and noise behind, and then turned left into the public gardens. It was sheltered here, where the wind off the sea couldn't quite reach. White lights had been strung through the trees, which swayed gently, and the only sound which could be heard was hooves on the tarmac path and the tiny bells jingling on the carriage.

'I've got something for you,' Jago said. 'It's something I made a while ago, not long after I'd moved here, just after the advent service.' He reached into his jacket inside pocket and gave her a tiny box. 'Don't worry,' he said, amused at her expression. 'It's not a ring.'

Honor blushed. She could hardly say that, despite them barely knowing one another, she wouldn't have minded had it been a ring. In fact, she grasped the idea with a pang, she'd like it to be one. 'Bit early for all that,' she mumbled and realised she sounded ungracious. 'Thank you.'

Jago handed over the box, their hands nudging into one another as the pony and trap bumped over the uneven path.

With difficulty, as her hands were shaking and the carriage ride was bumpy, Honor opened the box. Inside was something small wrapped in pale blue tissue paper. She unfolded it and drew out a blue and silver angel on a silver chain. Staring at it, she gasped. 'Oh, Jago, it's beautiful.' It was. Made of glass in the same technique she'd seen his work done in at the Craft Fayre, this pendant was smaller and much more intricate and detailed.

'The first time I saw you I thought you were an angel.'

'I remember you saying. But I'm really not, you know.'

'Angels come in all forms,' he replied, his voice choked. 'I went back and worked on it that night. I've made angels before, but this one is special.'

When she began to undo the clasp to put it on, her fingers were clumsy. 'My hands are too cold,' she lied but it was emotion that was making her tremble.

'Let me.'

She held her hair out of the way while he fastened the pendant around her neck. The light touch of his fingers on her skin made her stomach flip. Putting it into position just above where her breasts met, he bent forward and kissed the sensitive spot on her neck, just under her ear. 'Happy Christmas.'

She turned and met his mouth with her own. 'Happy Christmas, Jago.'

Their lips sort of met but slid off as the carriage jolted again. He laughed quietly and rested his forehead against hers. 'We might have to let the kissing wait until we're safely on terra firma again.' Pulling the rug back over them, he put an arm around her shoulders and hugged her to him.

Honor nestled into him, holding the angel pendant between her fingers. She didn't think she had ever been happier. Pasco took them onto the main road down into the harbour and, to the sound of rhythmic clip-clopping, she laid her head back on Jago's shoulder and enjoyed the view. Sea and sky spread out before them, the water inky black; a clear night and with a full moon. Its reflection carved a shimmering path along the sea. The prom, with its white lights, snaked along to their left. Even the harbour buildings were looped with twinkling Christmas lights. They'd come nearly full circle, almost back to the shelters on the prom.

Ciara dropped them near The Old Anchor pub. Jago got down

first and held out his arms for Honor to jump into. Putting a hearty donation into the collection bucket, they waited as another couple clambered in. Hugging one another close against the cheek-numbing cold whipping off the sea, they waved them off as Pasco trotted along the promenade, his red taillight swinging. As they ran around the corner of the pub, a gust of wind carried them along, blowing them into a large red object tethered to the entrance porch.

'Ooh hello, what's this?' Honor clutched her coat about her as the wind snatched at it and looked up into the face of a knitted Father Christmas, complete with sack of toys. 'Looks like the Ninja Knitters have been at it again.'

Jago didn't reply but, with difficulty, hauled open the pub door and they were carried in by the wind.

They stood for a second getting their breath back.

'Gettin' wild out there,' Claude the landlord said. 'They reckon a storm's comin' in.' He was serenely polishing a glass behind the bar. The pub, with 'When a Child is Born' playing quietly in the background, was completely empty. Even the pool table lay abandoned.

'Where is everyone?' Jago asked.

'In town. Last couple just left. Folk can't be arsed to get themselves down here in this weather. They're all up at this late-night shopping thing.' He sniffed. 'I was just about to close up as a matter of fact.'

'Oh, please don't stay open on account of just us,' Honor said, hoping he would as she didn't relish walking home along the prom until she'd warmed up.

'Nah. Sit yourselves down, my lovely. It's no bother. Wood burner's lit till it isn't. If you don't mind the place to yourselves, I'll go and watch a bit of telly in the bar. What can I get you?'

Jago looked at Honor. 'Two whiskies please, and a beer as well for me. What would you like with your whisky, Honor?'

'Well, I'm not touching the cider in here again.'

Claude laughed. 'It were a good batch that. How about a nice glass of wine?'

Honor wasn't sure about mixing wine and whisky. 'I've got a long drive in the morning, so I'll stick to just wine then.'

'Not a problem. Sit yourselves down and I'll bring them over.'

They chose the sofa in the corner by the wood burner and held out hands to warm. On the mantelpiece above was an array of Christmas cards and three stockings hung down. Johnny Mathis shifted into Judy Garland and, with the gaudy tinsel, flickering lights and Christmas trees dotted about, it felt cosy.

Jago unwound his scarf and took off his jacket. Eyeing the tree nearest to them, he said, 'Ours is being delivered on Christmas Eve. Do you think it's cutting it a bit fine? Mum and I want to replace Merryn's memories of last Christmas Eve with ones of decorating the tree.' He collapsed onto the sofa with a sigh and stretched his long legs out. Taking his hat off, he scrubbed a hand through his curls making them stand up.

'It sounds a lovely idea. You can have some Christmas pop songs on, Ivy jumping around getting in the way and the traditional argument over the knotted lights.'

'Don't remind me,' Jago replied on a laugh. 'Last year we shoved them into a box any old how. God knows what state they're in.'

Claude brought their drinks over along with a plate of mini sausages. 'Help yourselves,' he said cheerfully. 'I cooked 'em up this arvo thinking we might be busy tonight, so they'll only go to waste.' He patted his generous girth. 'Or add to my flab.'

'Ooh thanks, Claude.' Honor took her coat off. 'Hope you've got Santa tied up well out there.'

'Oh don't you worry, we're used to the gales down here on the harbour. Everything gets tied down with a length of polypropylene and a hitch knot.'

'Was it the knitters again?'

Claude laughed. 'Must be. Only thing I know was I got up at

seven for a delivery and there he was, proud as punch and twice as ugly. Customers have liked him though so he can stay till new year unless he decides to cut his anchor loose and fly off to the North Pole. I'll be in the bar if you want anything. Just yell.'

'Thanks again.' When he'd ambled off, Honor wiggled her feet nearer the stove. Her toes were just about thawing. 'Do you know, I thought I was lovely and warm on the carriage ride. In the five minutes it took us to get to the pub, I got frozen through again. Must be that wind.'

'Yup. Never underestimate a wind chill factor. Come here.' He wrapped an arm around her shoulders and kissed the top of her head. 'Where are you off to tomorrow then?'

'I'm driving up to see my family.'

'Oh, of course. Will you be away long?'

'I'll be back on Christmas Eve afternoon in time for the Nine Carols. Are you coming? Verity leads a great service and it's such a traditional start to the season.'

'In that case, I may do. What will you do tomorrow?'

'Oh, presents, a humongous turkey, some family bickering. You know. The usual. Then Mum and Dad are driving down to Southampton on Christmas Eve to board the ship so I'll follow on, see them off and will drive home afterwards.'

'Where are they going?'

'It would be easier to name where they're not going. Lisbon, then to the Greek Isles, Dubai, Singapore, Sydney and then on to Cape Town.'

'Wow. That's some trip.'

'They've been saving like crazy, helped by the fact they haven't been able to go away as much as usual lately. It's a real once in a lifetime experience.'

'Certainly is. And you said you have a sister?'

'Yes, Blythe. She's extremely pregnant with her second so we're having Christmas at Mum and Dad's. I'm in charge of sorting out leftovers, by which I mean I'll be piling enough food into the boot to feed a small battalion for the entirety of January.'

'But what are you doing on the actual day?'

'Eating said leftovers, watching TV and staying in my PJs. It'll be great.'

Jago sat up and stared at her. 'You can't be on your own on Christmas Day!'

'Of course I can. I'm looking forward to it actually. I need some chill time.'

'Oh no.' He shook his head. 'I can't have you eating cold ham and watching the terrible stuff that passes for television on Christmas Day. You must come to us.'

'Oh, Jago, it's really sweet but I couldn't possibly intrude.'

'How would you be intruding?'

'It's your family time.'

He took her hand. 'I want you to become part of my family.'

Her breath hitched at his tender expression. 'And I'm more than happy to be part of your family. I do sort of feel that already. But *this* particular year, won't it be difficult. Wouldn't you rather just be in your own family unit?'

Jago blew out a breath. 'Yeah, I can't lie, Mum and I are dreading it. It *is* going to be difficult. But I think having you there would help. We want to make it as different as possible. Make new traditions, new memories. We're in a new town, a new house, we have Ivy the dog, not to mention Chestnut the hamster. If you were there too, it would be as different to how our Christmases used to be in London as could be. So,' he grinned impishly, 'you'd be doing us a service. In fact, you can't refuse.'

'Oh, why's that?'

'You're honour bound, Honor.'

She groaned. She thought of the day in her flat, tiptoeing around so as not to annoy Frank in the flat below, having to have the television on extra quiet, not being able to sing loudly to the radio in the morning. Despite the obvious tensions that might arise at a Christmas Day with the Pengethleys, it was far more appealing than having to spend the day alone. 'Let's ask your mum first shall we, before I accept. You can't just foist an extra guest to the table.'

He gave her an old-fashioned look. 'Have you seen how much food my mother cooks? You mentioned a small battalion? I raise you a large army!' He passed her wine over. 'Cheers.'

Defeated, she clinked glasses with his. 'Cheers!'

CHAPTER 32

'MERRY CHRISTMAS DARLING' – THE CARPENTERS

Honor and Jago sat watching the flames lick at the glass of the wood burner, not saying much, listening to the Christmas music playing in the background.

Eventually Jago spoke. 'Would you mind telling me about Gino?' he asked.

Honor shifted. 'I'm not sure I want to talk about him on such a romantic evening.'

'No, perhaps not. I'm sorry.' He grimaced. 'You're right. Let's not spoil the mood.'

She eyed him surreptitiously. The lights from the tree were flashing on and off and lending an intermittent red light to his dark hair. She could see strain in the pucker worry lines around his eyes. He was a man who took his responsibilities seriously. One she could trust with everything she was. The music stopped and then started up again with The Carpenters' 'Merry Christmas Darling'. It was one of her favourite songs and now she might have someone to sing it to. He'd certainly be on her mind when she was away from him tomorrow. It was faintly ridiculous how her feelings for him had escalated so rapidly. She'd fought the attraction ever since meeting him and now she knew there was no barrier between them, she really thought she was falling in love with him. So he deserved the truth about Gino and about what had happened. Holding the angel pendant, she twisted to face him.

'There's not an awful lot to tell really. Gino and I began going out when we met at teacher training college. He was good-looking, charming and had this half-Italian vibe going on that I found irresistible. We both got teaching jobs straight after training in the same town. He was secondary languages, I was primary. It all seemed perfect, and I thought he was the one. We even found a flat together.' She faltered. 'I thought we were going to get married. He was my first serious boyfriend you see, so I wasn't all that experienced. After the first term, I could tell he wasn't happy but put it down to probationary nerves. That first year of teaching was pretty gruelling. Nothing they teach you in college properly prepares you for the realities of the job. We limped on past Christmas into Easter, and I put all our arguments down to exhaustion. I thought the long summer break would sort everything out. We'd planned to tour a bit of Europe. Then he announced he was really unhappy teaching in the UK and had been looking for posts in Italy. Before this he'd never mentioned it. I was flabbergasted and hurt, as you can imagine.'

'And angry too, I should think.' Jago frowned.

'Funnily enough I wasn't, not then, but I was deeply sad the future I saw happening between us had evaporated. Not long after his bombshell, he told me he'd secured a teaching post in the international school in Florence.'

'Was there any discussion about how this affected you, whether you could go together?'

'Not a great deal. I think he thought I was unadventurous wanting to stay in England, but I was settled and happy teaching in the school I was at. It was a primary school in a village not far from Worcester; I loved it there. I think I saw us staying together, buying a house, having children at some point.' She gave a hard laugh. 'I think I was rather naïve.'

'No, just trusting.' Jago smoothed back a strand of her hair tenderly.

'To make things worse, he then explained he was going straight off to Italy as soon as the summer term ended. Said he needed to get an apartment sorted, get settled in. He was going to spend some time with family too. He has relatives in Rome,' she added.

'What did you do? All your plans for the summer were shattered.'

'I was a bit of a wuss about it. I mean, I could have travelled around Europe on my own, but it didn't sound much fun. I went home to Worcester and licked my wounds while being looked after by Mum and Dad. Oh, and being laughed at by my big sis who had just got engaged.'

'Sisters, eh?'

'Yeah. When you're female and have a sister it's as much about rivalry as it is about love. Blythe was concerned for me, but she couldn't resist sticking the knife in.'

'What happened next?'

Honor shrugged. 'I went back to teaching at the school in the village. I wasn't as happy there any more though. Gino had got what he wanted, he was insisting we could have a long-distance relationship, but I felt all, oh I don't know, that everything had been thrown up in the air and shattered. I began looking round for jobs somewhere *I* really wanted to live and ended up at St Winifred's.'

'What happened between you and Gino?'

'We actually kept it going for about five years. In a weird way our jobs suited us having a long-term relationship. We had good chunks of time free at Easter and in the summer of course. For a while I enjoyed breaks in Florence. I mean, it's no hardship having to spend time in that city. It left the term time for us to concentrate on teaching.'

'But?'

'But as I became involved in community life here in Lullbury Bay and my workload increased it started becoming more and more difficult to make time to fly to Italy.'

'Didn't Gino ever come to Dorset?'

'Once or twice, but he always said his heart lay in Italy. And, one Easter, I found out it really was.' She sipped her wine, thinking back to that awful day.

'Go on,' he prompted gently.

'Do you really want me to? All this doesn't paint me in a very good light. I mean, what strong independent woman sits around waiting for her boyfriend to make up his mind about her. I should have kicked him into touch years before.'

'But you didn't.'

'No. I suppose part of me hoped there would be some kind of resolution. That I'd decide to live in Italy, or Gino would come back to the UK. Then I got promoted to deputy head and the workload quadrupled and I was quite thankful for the status quo. I threw myself into the job and holidays in Florence. And then, one Easter, I was putting some washing away in Gino's apartment and came across a pair of underpants. All I can say is they weren't M&S white cotton ones and they most definitely weren't mine. When I confronted him, he admitted he'd been seeing another staff member at the school, someone from the office. I suppose it was inevitable in a way. We'd been spending so much time apart. It certainly forced me to take action. Action I should have taken years before. The problem was I still had five days before my flight back and I couldn't afford to rearrange it.'

Jago winced. 'My poor love. What did you do?'

'Slept on the couch. Spent the days walking around. Trust me, I have no desire ever to return to Florence. I spent a lot of time in San Miniato al Monte. It's the church just up from Piazza Michelangelo. I'd sit and listen to the Gregorian chants. There's a cemetery behind it. A real Italian affair, with huge great family mausoleums. I wandered around there and cried a lot. Read the loving epitaphs and wondered why Gino didn't love me like that.'

'Oh, Honor!'

'I know. It was a bit grim. Have to confess to wallowing in all the misery, but I did a lot of thinking too. Decided I'd be more careful in the future about who I gave my heart to and they'd bloody well be deserving of it. Found my inner backbone, attached it to my self-respect and got on with it. Came home, threw myself into the job and that's been my life ever since.'

'But you didn't meet anyone else?'

She shook her head. 'I don't think I really wanted to. Not for a long time. Besides, it's not always easy to meet people here. The town's full of tourists in the summer who go home eventually and in the winter the population is on the older side.' She punched him softly on the arm. 'And then you blew into town.'

'I did.' He smiled. 'And you thought I was married.'

Honor put her empty glass down and hid her face in her hands. 'Don't remind me. What an idiot. Blame it on end-of-term brain fog. It's been an incredibly stressful couple of years in teaching and the autumn term's always knackering.' She lifted her head to gaze at him. 'But, honestly, how could I have made such a mistake!'

'Hey. You're human.' He ran a loving finger down her cheek. 'And don't forget we were sparing with the truth.'

She turned her head and kissed his palm. 'Such a stupid thing to think though. This month's been hell. I've been trying so hard to be cautious with my feelings around men and there you stood, looking drop dead gorgeous and more than a little piratical in that way you have. Not only that but you're a shockingly good artist and, to make it even less fair, you're brilliant with kids.'

'You'd better stop. You'll make me conceited.'

'Honestly though, my head was telling me there was no way I could even think about having a relationship with the married parent of a child in my class and I tried hard to listen to it. Trust me, I tried so hard. My heart, though, was beating to an entirely different drum.'

Jago looked confused. 'Is that a saying?'

'I doubt it. See what a muddled affect you have on my thinking?'

'And you didn't want to be the other woman?'

'I did not. I didn't want to be the one responsible for breaking up what seemed to me to be a very happy marriage. I was the victim of someone having an affair and it's soul-destroying. Besides, I've seen the effects of marital breakdown and divorce on kids in my class all too often. So I steeled my resolve, to absolutely no effect whatsoever I might add, and then promptly ran away when you tried to kiss me.'

Jago gave a short laugh. 'Well, that was understandable, even though it left me puzzled. If it hadn't been for Jaden's mum and her attentions, I would have run after you to apologise or explain.' He shrugged. 'Or maybe kiss you again.' He gave her a wicked look. 'You're very kissable you know.'

'Am I?' she asked, delighted.

'Yes.' He proved it by kissing her lightly. Backing off and looking more serious, he said, 'You do know I'm not going to mess you around, don't you? I would never ever do that to you. I know it'll be hard, when you've gone through what you have, but know this; you can trust me. I promise, hand on heart, my marriage is well and truly over. I like you very much, Honor. No, scrub that, I am extremely attracted to you. I want to see where this thing leads. I think we could have a real future. I want us to have a future.'

'So do I,' she whispered.

They kissed again and it held the promise of more, much more.

CHAPTER 33

'TWO THOUSAND MILES' – THE PRETENDERS

When Jago returned with two fresh drinks, he sat down looking puzzled.

'What's wrong?' Honor asked.

'You and I. Us. Is it going to be a problem for you at school?'

'I shouldn't think so. I'm single, so are you. As long as we're fairly discreet and don't run around naked or have sex on the beach or anything.'

'Ah shame. I was looking forward to that. Although you're probably right. It's a bit cold for that sort of stuff at the moment.'

She grinned, and then pulled a face. 'What about Merryn though? How do you think she'll take it?'

'If I'm honest, I think she'll be thrilled. I know she ranks you highly–'

'Following Ivy, Chestnut the hamster and pizza,' Honor finished. 'I know. I'll have a quiet chat with her next term. See how she feels about it. She's already had a lot to deal with.'

'She has. So has Mum but, to be honest, I think they'll both be delighted.' He paused, obviously struck by a thought. 'Although neither of them is going to be pleased when I tell them my other news.'

'What news?'

He winced. 'I've volunteered for the Lullbury Bay RNLI.'

'But that's great, they need all the willing volunteers they can get!' Then she realised what he meant and gasped. 'Oh, you mean after what happened with your dad?'

'Mum made me promise never to volunteer again. After losing Dad, she didn't want to lose me.'

'But the statistics are low on deaths of crew during a shout, aren't they?' She wrinkled up her nose. 'Or are they? I can't think of there being any loss of men for ages.'

'True. The last one I can think of is the Penlee disaster and that was back in the eighties. That's famous, or should say infamous. Do you know anything about it?'

Honor shook her head. 'Not a great deal. I know it happened in Cornwall.'

'Yes, Mousehole. The lifeboat went out in December 1981. God, that's over forty years ago now! Sixteen people died, eight of them crew from the lifeboat.'

'Oh, that's so awful.' Honor put a hand to her mouth, a stricken look on her face.

'And, while it's true nothing on that scale has happened since, no crew goes out without the fear, the knowledge, that something might happen to make it his or her last shout.'

Honor reached out and held his hand.

'When I was volunteering in London and on the odd occasion Dad went on a shout, they'd never call me in too. Never a good thing to have two family members on one boat.'

They were silent as they absorbed the statement's implication.

'Mum knows the statistical likelihood of me dying on a job is infinitesimal. She's lived her whole life around the RNLI and her childhood was by the sea, she knows to respect the sea and she knows what happens if you don't, but fear and grief aren't logical things.'

'Then why did you volunteer again?' Honor asked gently.

He sucked in a deep breath and stared at their joined hands. 'I don't honestly know. A desire to serve, to do something I'm trained and useful in. I want to give back to the community – you must understand that. Plus, I miss the comradeship, the jokes and banter. It's like a family, you know? Despite promising Mum, it was tearing at my soul. I couldn't not rejoin.'

'And maybe you wanted to honour your father's memory?'

He took in another long breath and eventually answered. 'Yes, that too.'

The Christmas music clicked into The Pretenders' 'Two Thousand Miles' and the music fell, sweeping and melancholy into the empty pub.

'But you haven't told her yet?'

'No, I only signed up the other day. Jamie explained I'll have to do some retraining first. Get familiar with the boat, up my knowledge on this part of the coast and the local danger spots, navigation, that sort of thing. I'll need a refresher First Aid course too.'

'Maybe you can stall telling her until after Christmas? You mentioned it's not going to be an easy time for any of you. Perhaps wait until things are less emotionally fraught?'

'Yes. I think I'll do that.' He gave Honor a worried look. 'And hope no one tells her before I have.'

'It's nearly Christmas Day. Once the Nine Carols service is over, there are no more town events. Everyone retreats back into their own little houses until the New Year Day Swim.'

'The what?'

'I think I've mentioned it to you before. The fancy dress swim in the sea.'

'Oh yes.' He shuddered. 'It sounded so horrendous I'd deliberately forgotten it.'

'Claude here lays on hot food afterwards. It's a very popular event.' She paused. 'Actually, as you're a RNLI volunteer now, you'll be on duty.'

'Why?' Jago asked, looking startled.

'It's one of their major fundraisers and crew are on standby just in case of any problems. Some stand in the sea to double-check no one's gone under. Crew man the buoys which mark the area you're allowed to swim in although, to be honest, it's more a sort of wade in then dash out and shiver affair. There's not a great deal of swimming involved.'

'What time does it start?'

'Depends on the tide, but usually around eleven. It gives people a chance to get over their New Year's Eve hangover.'

Jago flinched. 'I would have thought running into the sea in January would be kill or cure for any hangover.'

'You have a point.'

'Have you done it?'

Honor nodded. 'Every year.'

'Mad fool,' he said, tenderly and tweaked a curl of her hair to take the harshness out of his comment.

'I did a naked calendar for the Young Farmers once too,' she added, matter of factly.

'You did what?'

'A naked calendar.'

'And here's me worrying over upsetting your reputation as a fine and upstanding member of the Lullbury Bay town community.'

'We had a teacher who was married to a farmer and the theme was school subjects mixed with farming themes. It was all very tastefully done. I was Miss Geography and stood in a field of cows.' She giggled. 'They were very nosy as I recall. I was covered by two enormous globes and an atlas. And I wasn't naked at all, I had a light brown bikini on.' She reached for her wine and sipped innocently. 'It was all a big con to be honest, although Ben Townham stripped off before anyone could tell him not to.' She rolled her eyes. 'Such an exhibitionist. He was Mr Food Tech and was in a cider orchard with some strategically placed apples. All this was way before Mrs Arnold, our current head, took over.' She suppressed a grin. 'It's not her sort of thing at all.'

'Can I confess something?'

'What?'

'I thought you and Ben had something going on. When you came to the Craft Fayre together you looked very cosy. I was jealous as hell.'

'Were you?' Honor tried to stave off the smugness and failed.

'Don't look like that. He was all over you.'

She pulled a face. 'If I'm honest, he used to have a bit of a crush on me. All very awkward as, nice and good looking that he is–'

'Okay, don't rub it in.'

'I'm his manager. Now that's something the head would most definitely disapprove of.'

'Why, if you're both single?'

'Conflict of interest I suppose. Doubt if I could manage his career progression objectively if I was going out with him. And there's one other thing.'

'What's that?'

'He's not you.' She was rewarded with a look from Jago so hot it sent lightning bolts down to her toes.

They grinned stupidly at one another for a minute then Jago sat back. 'And are there any of these calendars still in circulation?' He leered jokingly.

'Sorry to disappoint you.' Honor raised her brows in a prim manner. 'They sold out in a week. It's a shame we couldn't do another,' she added. 'They were a good money-spinner, but the current head wouldn't be up for it. As I said, she's a bit of a stickler for maintaining the propriety of the profession. But, Jago, the serious point, which you've missed, is you have until eleven on New Year's Day to tell Avril. Otherwise she's going to find out in the worst possible way.'

'She mentioned the possibility of going to Cornwall for New Year. See the rellies.'

'And if you don't, you're bound to want to watch the swim. You only live fifty yards from the beach. It'll be impossible to avoid.'

'I hear what you're saying. Agreed then. I'll tell her the day after Boxing Day. We should have steered ourselves through Christmas by then.'

Honor frowned. 'Are you sure you want me there on the day?'

'Absolutely.' He slung an arm around her shoulders and pulled her to him. 'Especially if you can track down a copy of that calendar to slip in my stocking.' He nuzzled her hair. 'I'm going to miss you so much when you're away.'

She turned to him, loving the emotion on his face. 'I'll only be gone a day and a half. I'll see you at the church service. Promise?'

'Promise.'

CHAPTER 34

'O COME, ALL YE FAITHFUL' – TRAD.

Christmas Eve

Honor slipped into a pew at the back of the church. She was running late, and the early evening service was about to begin. She sat back and caught her breath as she listened to the organist quietly play 'O Little Town of Bethlehem'. The journey from Southampton had been tedious and long, with Christmas Eve traffic blocking the A35 all the way from Dorchester. Conditions hadn't been good either, with driving sleety rain and gusts of wind buffeting her little car. She was tired and stiff from driving so much in two days, and hadn't even had time to go to her flat first. Despite all her weariness, though, every nerve was standing on end in anticipation of seeing Jago again. It was ridiculous but she'd missed him, despite being busy with the family. It had been the usual cheerful chaos and she'd loved every minute, but the pull south and to Jago had been physical. She'd had to fight hard to rein in her impatience as the traffic slowed to an inevitable crawl around Bridport.

Peering over heads, she could see Avril and Merryn sitting near the front, but there was no sign of Jago. Perhaps he was running late too. She looked around St Winifred's admiring the Christmas tree dressed in subtle white lights and the huge arrangements of poinsettias on either side of the altar. She'd already spotted the three wise men who stood guard outside and who had remained relatively undisturbed despite revellers getting frisky on the way home from the pub. Whatever damage done had been repaired by the knitting fairies. The new addition of the life-sized knitted nativity scene in the garden opposite the church had caused quite a stir in the town too. There was something magical about it as it sat under a specially made wooden arbour, strung with flickering white lights and with the figures set against a warm glowing background.

Tom Catesby from the animal sanctuary, sitting with sister Ellie and his lovely mum, turned and put up his hand in greeting. Further along the same pew she could see Austin Ruddick and the familiar bleached white hair of his granddaughter Alice. And in the pew behind them were assorted members of Lucie Wiscombe's large and unruly family. There was no sign of Lucie herself though, and you usually couldn't miss her, with her mane of bright chestnut hair. No Chris either, as he'd already left to spend Christmas with his family in Cornwall and no Tamara; she'd gone off to start her seasonal singing job. Honor didn't think it was her sort of thing anyway. The woman next to her nudged her arm and offered a mint. Honor took one gratefully and then concentrated as Verity climbed the pulpit dressed in her white Christmas vestments.

'Welcome, everyone, to this most happy of days,' the vicar said. 'I think God wanted as many people in the congregation as possible, as He blew most of us up the drive this evening!'

Everyone laughed. Verity was held in fond affection in the town. The church was packed, most never stepped foot in church from one Christmas to the next but they always made an effort for this service. It was considered the traditional start to a Lullbury Bay Christmas.

'Our first reading is taken from Luke Chapter 1, verses 26 to 38.'

Honor listened to the words and let them float over her, the age-old story of an angel appearing to Mary. Then the congregation stood for the first carol 'In the Bleak Midwinter'. She looked around again but there was no Jago. Disappointed, she threw her energies into singing. The service was wonderful. Moving and thoughtful, a celebration of what was to come and a way of bringing the community together. Verity even made reference to the knitted figures outside saying how the mysterious knitting community was enriching the town. Secretly and without expecting any thanks.

After the service was over Honor shook Verity's hand on the way out and thanked her. Pulling the hood of her coat up against the driving rain, she was just about to stand to one side to wait for Avril and Merryn to wish them a Happy Christmas when Lucie ran up to her.

'Oh, Honor, I'm so glad I caught you!' Lucie's hood blew down and her hair flew wildly in the wind. 'Jamie wanted me to get a message to you. They've gone out on a shout.'

The wind snatched Lucie's words from her mouth. Honor went nearer. Something about a shout? But why would Jamie need her to know?

'He told me to tell you Jago's gone out too,' Lucie continued. 'They had no alternative. They're short of crew. Lots have gone away for Christmas and two are stuck on the A35. There's just been a shunt apparently and the road's closed.'

Honor's blood ran cold. She stared at Lucie in horror. 'Jago's gone out on a shout?' she asked stupidly.

Lucie nodded.

'In this?' As if to answer, a howl of wind whipped around the corner of the church.

'A Mayday from a yacht. Sounds like it was trying to get into the harbour before the storm came in.' Lucie gazed up at the dark unrelenting night. Rain poured down her face, soaking her. In the distance they heard the throbbing of a helicopter. 'Coastguard's out too, although not sure for how long in this weather. Look, I'll get back to the station to wait and I'll let you know any more info as soon as it comes in. Okay?' She stopped, seeing the stricken look on Honor's face. 'Or do you want to come with me? Have a cuppa, wait together? It could be a while.'

'No, I need to be with Avril and Merryn. Oh, Lucie, they don't know. They don't know where he is.' She looked at her friend white-faced with worry. 'They don't even know he's volunteered to be crew again.'

'Oh, babe. That's a shocker. Look, check you've got my new number. I've just changed phones.' Lucie pulled Honor back through the crowds leaving the service and into the church porch.

Honor switched her phone back on which she'd turned off for the service and saw she had a voicemail from Jago. Listening to it she heard him say briefly he'd been called out as lifeboat crew. She put her friend's new number in.

'I'll let you know everything just as soon as I can,' Lucie said. 'Will you be all right? Jamie said you and Jago are an item now.'

Honor nodded numbly. 'Turns out he's not married to Avril after all. She's his mum.'

'I know, babe. Haven't had a chance to tell you.'

Honor was too distraught to ask Lucie how she knew. 'I was hoping to see him here at the service but he didn't turn up.'

'Jamie and I were on the way here when his pager went off. He began running back, bumped into Jago and they ran back to the station together. I came on up to let you know.'

'Thank you.' Honor waved her mobile. 'Jago left a message as well. Bit short.'

'They don't always have much time.' She shrugged. 'Plus it's priorities, and we're not at the top of the list. Are you going to be okay? It's never much fun being the one waiting, take it from someone who's experienced at it.'

'I'll be okay.' Honor gasped and put a shocked hand up to her mouth. 'What about Avril though?'

'What about Avril?' The woman herself came into the porch just as Verity was blown back in from outside. She must have overheard the last part of their conversation. 'Is anyone going to tell me what's going on? Lucie? Honor?'

'My goodness,' the vicar said, tidying her hair, 'it's got really rough out there.' She looked from an unhappy Honor to a worried Lucie, and then to Avril whose face bore a mixture of bewilderment and burgeoning anger. Seeming to sum up the situation, she added, 'Can you bear with me, ladies, while I lock up then perhaps we can all go into the vicarage. What do you say to hot chocolate, Merryn?'

'Ace-erooney, yes please.' The little girl looked up from the service programme she'd been studying; she'd been mouthing the words to the carols. Instantly picking up on the tension, she tugged at her mother's hand. 'What's wrong? You look worried. What's wrong, Mummy? Where's Jags?'

Avril shot Honor a look through narrowed eyes and soothed her daughter. 'It's fine, my little mermaid.' She stroked the girl's head. 'We'll go to Verity's and have a nice chat.'

The last few of the congregation were hustled unceremoniously out of the church by Verity, she locked up and then led them next door to the vicarage. The next few minutes were spent getting rid of their wet coats and hanging them on chairs thrust up to the Aga.

They sat down at the vast kitchen table where Verity made a few ineffectual attempts to clear some space. The atmosphere was tense and the harsh fluorescent strip lighting emphasised everyone's white faces. They watched, mutely, as Verity bustled about, filling a saucepan with milk. 'We definitely all need some

NEW BEGINNINGS AT CHRISTMAS TREE COTTAGE

cocoa,' she announced. 'And shortbread. Possibly mince pies! Come on, Merryn, give me a hand.'

When they settled at the table again, mugs in hand and a plateful of shortbread biscuits ignored by everyone except Merryn, Avril began speaking. 'Is this about what I think it is?'

'Avril, I really think–' Honor began. She'd never been so uncomfortable in her life.

'Yes. Jago's volunteered to be crew at Lullbury Bay Lifeboat Station,' Lucie stated baldly. 'And I for one think it's a wonderful idea.'

'Mum?' Merryn questioned.

'It's all right, Mer. Drink your cocoa. Everything will be all right.' Avril turned on Lucie. 'Do you?' she said with steel in her voice. 'Do you think it's a good idea? Then you've never lost the man you love.'

'I haven't, you're right,' Lucie replied. 'I know about what happened to your husband and I'm truly sorry. Really truly sorry. I knew the name Pengethley rang a bell, so I asked Jamie and we googled it. What happened was tragic. An awful tragedy.' She stopped and drew in a deep breath. 'I haven't lost my husband, Avril, but I know the fear. Every time Jamie goes out, even on a nice calm sunny day, I have the fear there's a chance he won't come back to me.'

'Then why do you let him?'

'Because it's what he wants to do. It's what he *needs* to do. Trust me, there have been times when me and the RNLI have fallen out. There have been long evenings when I've been at home while Jamie is out training and I've resented every second he's spending at that,' she hesitated, glancing at Merryn, *'flamin'* station. It even made me hesitate before I married him.'

'If it causes you so much misery he should stop doing it.' Avril stared mutinously at the carved wooden nativity on the table.

Lucie sighed. 'But it's not that simple, is it? They do it because they *have* to. It's like any other emergency service. They have the expertise to go out and save lives. And that's a good thing. It's crossed my mind to ask Jamie to give up.' Lucie shrugged. 'Part of me is jealous of how much of him it takes up. It's all-consuming. But he wouldn't be the man I love and married if he did. He'd only be a shell of my lovely, honourable, brave Jamie. And then maybe, just maybe, I'd stop loving him. So I take the long nights alone, I fill them with things I want to do. I take the waiting for news when he's on a shout and hope and pray he'll come back to me.'

Honor stared at Lucie seeing her in a completely new light. Even though she was a good friend, she'd been guilty of writing the girl off as someone who was all about going out and getting drunk on cider. Now a new respect for her was dawning. Underneath all the jokey banter was a woman of steel.

'And what if he doesn't, Lucie?' Avril met the girl's eyes. 'What if he doesn't come back?'

Lucie swallowed. 'And then I'll deal with the grief and I'll know he died doing something he was being incredibly brave at and trying to help someone.'

'It's not that easy.'

She shook her head. 'Never said it was, Avril. Never said it was. But I'd rather have the Jamie I know for the little time he might be with me than have a lifetime with a man who had been prevented from doing the thing he was called to do.'

There was a silence.

'I lost my husband,' Avril said, with a barely controlled voice. 'I lost him on this night a year ago. How could Jago do this to me?' She put shaking hands up to her face.

'Mummy?' Merryn's lip began to wobble.

Honor moved from her side of the table to Merryn's and put her arms around the little girl. 'It's all right, Merryn. Mummy's upset. But it's all going to be all right.'

Avril removed her hands and frowned at her. 'And I suppose you knew about all of this?'

'Oh, Avril,' Honor replied helplessly. 'I'm so sorry but it wasn't my news to tell. Jago only told me the other evening. He was planning on telling you, I know he was. I don't suppose he thought he'd be called up so soon. He mentioned having to retrain first.'

'It couldn't be helped tonight,' Lucie explained. 'Three car smash on the road into town. Two key volunteers are stuck in the tailback. They'd been visiting family and were on the way back. No one else to call in.'

'Don't be cross with Honor and Lucie, Mum. They're our friends.'

'Oh, I'm not really cross with them, pumpkin,' Avril replied, sounding exhausted. 'I'm cross with your stupid big brother.'

'Why?'

Avril sucked in an enormous sigh, swallowing her anger. 'Because he's joined the lifeboat crew, like your daddy did.'

'Well, that's good.'

'Is it?' Her mother said, surprised. 'How come?'

'He missed it.'

All eyes turned to Merryn. The girl had been staring at them all, listening to proceedings with an avid interest.

'Why do you say that?' Avril asked.

'Any idiot could see it,' Merryn said, scornfully. 'He missed it a lot. It was eating away at him like a maggot. Metaphor?' she asked Honor.

'Simile,' Honor answered absent-mindedly. 'Avril, Jago knew how much it would upset you. He'd agonised over it, but he felt he had to. What Lucie has said about Jamie applies to Jago too. He was trying to find the right time to tell you. He didn't want to do it before Christmas. He thought the day would be difficult enough as it is. He was saving it until after Boxing Day.'

'He should have told me,' Avril sighed again, her anger appearing to deflate into a reluctant acceptance.

'He was worried he'd upset you,' Honor explained gently.

'Of course it would upset me but I would have understood.'

'But you made him promise not to volunteer.'

'You made Jags promise he wouldn't volunteer?' Merryn asked. 'That wasn't a good thing to do.'

'Why, Mer?' her mother asked, puzzled.

'Because he loves doing it. When we take Ivy for a walk around the harbour he always stops and looks at the lifeboat and reads the incident board. He goes all whiskful–'

'Whiskful?'

'Do you mean wistful, Merryn?' Honor asked.

'Yes. Whiskful. All sighing. Gets this soppy look on his face. Actually,' Merryn turned to Honor, chocolate stains from drinking cocoa too enthusiastically around her mouth, 'he gets like that when he talks about you too. He talks about you *a lot*.'

Honor blushed.

Avril ruffled Merryn's hair. 'I was only trying to keep him safe, baby girl. I didn't want him to die like your daddy did.'

'But making Jago promise isn't going to bring Daddy back, is it?'

'No.' Avril said, nonplussed at the logic.

'It's all about doing a chance, isn't it?'

'What do you mean, Mer?'

'It's like when I ride Holly's pony at her house. Holly's my best friend from school,' she explained to Verity. 'She's got ponies and puppies. They're sausage dogs.'

'Ah yes, I've heard about her,' Verity spoke for the first time. 'So, what's this about taking a chance, Merryn?' she asked.

'I've been learning to ride.'

'You've what?' Avril half reared out of her seat.

'Stay cool, Mum. It's like I said. About doing a chance. I wear a hat to keep my head safe and a body protector thing and I go slow in the marriage.'

'Marriage? What are you on about, Mer?'

'Menage?' Honor put in. 'Do you mean the enclosed outdoor space the Carmichaels have?'

Merryn nodded enthusiastically. 'Yes. Holly and her mum walk Pasco round ever so slowly. Once they know I'll be okay I'm going out on a hack.'

'Well maybe, after I've had words with Ciara, and then we'll see,' Avril said. 'She had no right to teach you to ride without asking me first.'

'Ah, Mum, that's the point. I do a chance but a *safe* chance. I wear the right stuff, do training and everything and I'm safe. There's only a teeny chance I'll fall off.'

'But it's a chance too many.' Avril gathered up her daughter in a fierce hug. 'You and Jago are the most precious things in my life. What would I do without you both?'

'But riding Pasco makes me happy, Mum.' Merryn's voice was muffled against her mother's chest. 'And I got to know about horses cos I want to be a vet.'

Avril released her and gave her a watery smile.

'And being at the lifeboat makes Jags happy. We don't stop you doing things that make you happy.'

'You don't but I'm not going to come to much harm at the Knit and Natter Club or working at the bookshop, am I, pumpkin?'

'You have to cross a road to get there.'

'And?'

'You look both ways?'

'Of course I do.'

Merryn grinned. 'See. Doing a safe chance.'

The other women laughed.

'Think she may have scored on the logic there,' Verity said. 'More cocoa anyone?' Everyone said yes so she and Merryn got up to make some more.

Avril flashed a tearful glance at Lucie. 'I agree with every word of what you said earlier. But,' at this her voice quavered, 'it's not easy, is it?'

Lucie reached out and the two women clutched hands.

'I'm sorry I was sharp,' Avril apologised.

Lucie shook her head. 'You weren't and, if you were it's understandable. Me and my big mouth. Going where angels fear to tread and all that.'

'Idiom,' Honor supplied before Merryn could ask. 'Avril, when Jago told me what happened to your family and then explained he'd volunteered, I asked him why he'd done it when he knew the anguish it would cause you.' She took the woman's other hand.

'What did he say?' Avril's eyes were bright with unshed tears.

'He said he wanted to honour his father. He wanted to do something his father would be proud of.'

Avril squeezed their hands. 'And he would be,' she whispered, tears spilling from her eyes, a sob shuddering through her body. 'He would be.'

Verity came to stand behind them and put her hands on Avril's shoulders. The women stayed linked for a while, unspeaking, hands and bodies joined in mutual support and comfort.

CHAPTER 35

'LONELY THIS CHRISTMAS' – MUD

As the women emerged from the front door of the vicarage, a gust of wind knifing up the street nearly knocked them off their feet. It was still raining, but not as hard.

'Come on, I managed to find a parking spot earlier, before the church service,' Honor said. 'I'll drive you round to Christmas Tree Cottage. It'll save you getting wet.' They trooped into the side street where Honor had squeezed her little car in between two others in a feat of parking of which she'd been ridiculously proud. Now the car stood lonely and abandoned on an empty street lit by an amber streetlight. As Avril got in the passenger seat, Lucie and Merryn piled in the back, having to shift various boxes and bags out of the way.

'Sorry, guys,' Honor said, as she switched on the engine. 'Blame my mum. She donated her entire Christmas food-buying frenzy to me.'

It was a short but unpleasant drive along the front to the Pengethley's house. Honor inched along, peering out for debris on the road and thinking she should have gone the back way. Even though the radio blasted out Greg Lake's 'I Believe in Father Christmas', they could still hear the sea raging and crashing onto the shore. The wind pounded at her car and once she had to stop as a high wave drenched it. The evening had a vaguely apocalyptic feel and, unsurprisingly, there was no one else in sight. Honor's heart thudded in hollow fear that somewhere, out at sea, Jago was in a tiny lifeboat tackling the elements.

Avril told her to park slightly up the hill on next door's driveway, explaining the Pengethleys only had a small parking space and their neighbours were away for Christmas. Honor let her passengers out and they dashed in out of the storm. Making sure her car was in gear so there was no chance of it rolling down the steep hill, she followed. Illogically, as Lucie had told them Jamie would text to let them know when the lifeboat was back, she hoped Jago would be at the house waiting for them all. Looking impatient. Wondering where they'd all been.

He wasn't.

A volley of barking sounded from the depths of the house. Merryn dragged Lucie into the sitting room demanding she help untangle the Christmas tree lights and Honor stood, feeling useless, in the hall.

'Here.' Avril thrust their coats at her. 'Can you hang them up? I'll let Ivy out into the garden and then put the kettle on.'

Honor had driven past the house often and had walked past it most days on her commute from school. It stood nearly at the bottom of Harbour Hill, sideways on. God-Almighty Hill was a good nickname for the steep climb. It killed the thighs if you had to walk uphill. She'd often had to stop to catch her breath and rest her legs and had taken the chance to admire what she could see through the un-curtained windows, but she'd never been inside.

Its name was a misnomer. It wasn't really a cottage at all any more, but a large square Victorian house. From the central hallway which led off the porch with its jumble of coats and boots, a snug sitting room was on her right, from where she could hear Merryn and Lucie unboxing lights. She turned left into a family room come kitchen diner which had a conservatory leading off, beyond which there seemed to be some kind of boot room. A door at the back was open and the wet salty air blowing through told her it led to the garden. It was a modern room and not in keeping with the outside, but it was light and bright and welcoming.

Avril wiped the dog's paws down and then let her through where she greeted Honor briefly and then scampered off to find Merryn. 'Just stopped raining, thank goodness, although still windy. You'll have to forgive us, we're still not properly unpacked.'

'It's lovely.' It was. With its white-painted walls, high ceilings, and doors leading to the conservatory it managed to be both stylish and cosy. Hung against the conservatory windows were examples of Jago's glass art. They'd be stunning in daylight with the sun streaming through.

Avril washed her hands and flicked the kettle on. 'When we saw this room, we couldn't resist the house. It's only got a tiny parking space and garden but Jago has the top floor to himself, so it suited us. It's not really a cottage though, is it?'

'No,' Honor agreed.

'Jago tells me you and he have got close.'

The swerve in conversation took her by surprise. 'Yes.' The answer came out questioningly, on a rising note, as if she was asking for approval.

'Don't look so worried.' Avril came to her and hugged her hard. 'I'm thrilled. He needs a nice girl like you. And you're definitely staying for Christmas Day, aren't you?'

'I'd like to, but only if you're sure?'

'Absolutely. Can't have you on your own at Christmas. And you may as well stay tonight too, the bed's made up.'

'Actually, I've got my things in the car. I was late for the service and went straight there. I haven't been back to my flat since driving down from my parents.'

'That's sorted then. We just need…'

Avril's sentence trailed off. Honor knew what she meant. They just needed Jago to come home.

'Now, 'Avril continued, more briskly, 'I don't know about you but as well as tea, I need something to eat.'

'I'll go and unpack my car now, shall I? The least I can do is donate my mum's leftover Christmas food. She bought three panettoni. Three! No idea why.'

'They're Jago's favourite, so he'll be delighted.' Avril cast an anxious glance through the windows and out into the black night and Honor knew what she was thinking.

'Shall we make sandwiches?' Honor suggested, in an attempt to occupy their minds. 'I've a mountain of turkey in a cool box in the boot and mum's home-made cranberry sauce too. If we make a pile, the men can have some when they…' she faltered.

'When they come back,' Avril stated firmly. 'Good idea. You unpack your car, I'll make the tea and cut some bread.'

After Honor had brought her stuff in Merryn took time out from untangling lights to show her the guest room. 'It's the smallest bedroom,' the girl explained. 'Mummy has a nonsweet but you'll have to share my bathroom. My bedroom's the one with the big light up heart on and Jago lives upstairs. He doesn't like me going up there very often cos he says I mess his workstation up. Mum says come down quickly so we can eat.'

Honor unpacked quickly and when she returned to the kitchen, the others were sitting around the breakfast bar sipping tea. An enormous pile of sandwiches stood in the middle.

'Can I have one *now*, Mum?' Merryn pleaded. 'Now Honor's here.'

Avril fixed her daughter with a stern look.

'Please may I have a sandwich?' Merryn amended. 'Please.'

'You may.'

The others laughed, desperate for something to ease the tension.

'I can't believe the amount of food your mother's provided.' Avril took a sandwich but left it untouched on her plate.

'I know. She forgot they were going on holiday today. Bought enough for six and then some so I ended up bringing it back with me.'

'So, tell us who the six are.'

'Mum, Dad, my big sis Blythe, her little girl and husband. Blythe's second baby is due next month.'

'Lovely. And will your parents be back from their holiday in time?'

'No, they're away for over three months. It's unfortunate timing but they'll see the baby when they come back. They live close to my sister.'

'Ugh. Babies.' Merryn wrinkled her nose, a sandwich poised mid-air. 'I'm not having one. I'm having puppies instead.'

Lucie laughed. 'I'm with you all the way, kid but good luck with the biology on that.'

'Why?' Merryn demanded.

Sensing the conversation was in danger of going in an interesting direction, Avril asked where Honor's parents had gone on holiday. It was inconsequential talk, but it steered the women's thoughts away from their men out in the towering black seas and kept Merryn's mind off impossible conceptions.

Honor told them her parents' itinerary and promised to show Merryn the route on the computer later.

'If they're cruising from Southampton they might be delayed by the storm,' Avril observed.

They ate silently for a moment dwelling on the horrors that might be happening. It seemed, no matter how hard they tried to avoid it, the conversation returned to the thing most on their mind. When Honor's phone pinged, they all jumped a foot.

A tense, expectant hush fell over the room. 'Sorry,' Honor said, once she'd read the text. 'It's just my parents. You were right, Avril, they've delayed sailing until tomorrow morning.'

Lucie cleared her throat. 'What are they doing now?' she asked in an over-bright voice.

'Eating dinner.'

'Oh, go on, tell us what they're eating.'

Honor knew no one really wanted to know what her parents were having for dinner on their first night of cruising but dutifully texted them back the question. 'Lobster Bisque, pheasant, and mango and papaya with poached pear,' she reeled off.

'Fabby.' Lucie looked at the plate of sandwiches. Except for Merryn, they'd hardly touched them. Even Lucie, with her legendary appetite, hadn't been able to eat much. 'Jamie and I ate up at the Henville Hotel once. You know, the big posh place just out of Berecombe? It was brilliant. So were the cocktails.' Her voice quavered.

They gazed at the mountain of turkey sandwiches in front of them. It had been a good idea and had kept them busy for twenty minutes but, somehow, no one had the stomach to eat anything.

'I'll put them in the fridge for when Jago and Jamie return,' Avril said.

It was weird how they were all using high-pitched, overly cheerful voices.

Merryn looked suddenly stricken. 'He's been ages. He *is* coming back, isn't he?'

Avril gave her a hug. 'Of course he is! After all, I've got to give him a piece of my mind when he does.'

'Don't think he'll want one,' the girl answered, looking puzzled. 'He's got enough mind of his own.'

'It's a saying, Merryn,' Honor explained. 'Your mum means she's going to tell him off.'

'An idiom!'

'That's right. An idiom. You're so clever.'

'She's too sharp for the knife drawer my mum would say,'

Avril said but there were tears in her eyes. 'What time is it, Lucie?'

'Just gone seven.'

'You'll stay on with us until, well, you know.'

Lucie nodded. 'Yes please, if you don't mind. I usually wait in the flat for Jamie. I can see the station from there, but it's nicer being with people, people who understand.'

Avril reached out a hand. 'Then please stay.' She stood up. 'And now, while Honor and I do the washing up, what about you and Merryn decorate that tree? It's not going to do it by itself. And we'll have the lights switched on and looking pretty for when Jamie and Jago get back.' Her voice broke.

Lucie took one look at her distressed face and propelled Merryn towards the sitting room saying, 'It's my favourite thing ever, decorating the tree. Oh look, Ivy's come to help,' she added, as the dog danced at their feet.

A gust of wind shook the house, wailing down the chimney. It almost drowned out Lucie and Merryn's conversation as they went.

'Blow winds, and crack your cheeks! Rage! Blow!' Merryn sang out.

'Hey, that's cool, kid. King Lear,' Lucie said admiringly.

'I don't know, is it? It's Shakespeare. How do *you* know it's Shakespeare?'

'Because I'm at university and studying it. And that quote is from King Lear which William Shakespeare wrote.'

'Do you think I can learn Shakespeare *and* be a vet?'

'To be honest, Merryn, babe,' Lucie was heard saying, in a dry tone. 'I think you're capable of anything.'

Avril stared at Honor. 'I think Merryn is going to be quoting Shakespeare at her patients. How do you think a poorly Labrador will take it?' She was trying, and failing, to inject some humour into the endless waiting.

'Scrap that. I think she'll run for prime minister,' Honor replied, joining in, desperately trying to lighten the atmosphere.

'Will he come back, Honor? Will my boy come back?'

Honor went to Avril and threw her arms around her. 'He'll come back,' she said through their shuddering tears. 'Of course he will.'

Looking out through the big kitchen window, which again, was streaming with rain, and clutching the angel pendant Jago had made for her, she fervently hoped it was true.

CHAPTER 36

'HOME TO YOU THIS CHRISTMAS' – SIGRID

An hour later, the tree was decorated, Merryn was whiny and overtired and the three women sat on the slouchy sofa in the family room staring glassily and unseeing at the television. Ivy couldn't settle. They'd taken turns trooping out to the garden with her, but it wasn't a wee she wanted. She wanted Jago back.

'Don't we all,' Honor whispered to her on the last abortive visit. Ivy gave her a perplexed look and went to stand in the porch, her nose pressed close to the front door.

'What's the time?' Avril asked for what seemed the millionth time.

Lucie was about to check her phone to tell her when it pinged a text through. 'They're back!' she yelled, making Ivy bark. 'Boat just in. Two casualties rescued. All safe.'

'Thank fuck,' Avril said. She gave Merryn a stern look. 'You did not hear me say that word. Oh, thank God.' She pressed her fingers to her eyes. 'Thank God.'

Honor's phone pinged. Scanning the text she said, in a relieved voice, 'It's the same message.' She didn't read out the final words which made her glow inside. Jago had written,

'Cannot wait to see you and give you the biggest hug. All my love.'

'Right, young lady,' Avril said to Merryn. 'Bed!'

'Aww, Mum, I want to stay up and see Jago when he gets back.'

'If you don't go to bed now, you're going to be horrible tomorrow. And nothing, I mean nothing, is going to spoil this Christmas Day for us.'

'They'll be ages yet, kid,' Lucie added. 'They have to clean the boat down and make it good, deal with the coastguard and the paramedics. Takes a while.' The expression on her face matched her bright hair.

'Muuuuum! It's only nine o'clock.' There was defiance in her voice but a wobbly defeatism too. The child was exhausted. 'Promise me Jago's coming home?'

Avril took her by the shoulders. 'Of course, my darling girl. Of course he's coming home. He's down at the station now just tidying up after the shout. He'll pop in when he's back and kiss you goodnight. But to do that, you have to be in bed. Off you go.'

Merryn hugged Lucie goodnight and then came to Honor. Hugging her too, she whispered, 'Thank you for staying and looking after Mummy. I know she said a rude word but that meant she was really, really worried.'

'Oh, Merryn,' Honor replied, hugging her back. 'I think we've been looking after each other and you did the best job of all. You kept us all busy and made us laugh. That's important. I'll see you in the morning.'

'Bright and early?'

'Well, maybe not *too* bright and early!'

'Mum, can I take Ivy up to cuddle?'

'No,' Avril reprimanded. 'Remember the house rule. No dogs on beds.'

'But she got on the sofa earlier and she's not supposed to go on there either.'

'Bed, Merryn! Now!'

Merryn stomped towards the stairs. 'I am more sinned against than sinning,' she called loftily.

'Baileys?' Avril turned to the others, blowing out a sigh of relief.

'Deffo,' Lucie answered. 'It's Christmas. I've usually had three in my coffee by this time on Christmas Eve.'

Avril found the bottle and three glasses and poured them all stiff measures. They collapsed back onto the sofa and sipped contentedly, the tension slipping from their shoulders, a bone-wearying tiredness replacing it.

After a while Avril spoke. 'Did Merryn *really* just quote Shakespeare at us?'

'Soz. That's my fault. We were talking about King Lear while putting the tree up,' Lucie explained.

Honor, feeling a sort of happy hysteria rising, looked at the other two. 'Well, there's three of us. Who's who then? Can I be Cordelia? Wasn't she the good sister? I can't remember. Don't know the play very well.'

'You learn never to say anything in front of Mer that you don't want repeated back to you. Once heard,' Avril said sagely, 'she never forgets.' She topped up their glasses.

'Well, with your Anglo-Saxon language earlier, I reckon that makes you Regan,' Lucie observed. 'Wait until Merryn turns into a teenage horror and that one will come right back and bite you, babe.'

They shrieked with laughter, tears running down their faces. Merryn thumped on the floor to shut them up.

'Regan? Wasn't he in *The Sweeney*?' Avril asked. 'That was my dad's favourite telly programme.'

They collapsed into giggles again and the more they tried to stop, the more laughter escaped.

'Oh, I needed that laugh,' Avril said eventually, hiccoughing. 'Done me a power of good.'

Lucie picked up the copy of the local newspaper, *The Lullbury*

Bay Echo, which had lain ignored on the floor. 'Have you heard Keiran Ascott is moving on up?'

'Don't tell me he's got promoted to the *Taunton Tribune*?' Honor murmured, having trouble keeping her eyes open. 'Not even Keiran deserves that.'

Keiran Ascott was the journalist from the local newspaper. Known for nosing out stories and inventing them if they didn't exist, he wasn't universally liked.

'It's even better than that, babe. He's moving right out of the area. Rumour is, he's got himself a hack job on *The Mail*.'

Honor levered herself up from the squashy sofa with difficulty. 'What? *The Mail*? In London?'

Lucie nodded. She began leafing through *The Echo*. 'Oh, hold on.' She held up the double-page spread. 'Must be his final hurrah. An exposé on the Knit and Natter Group!'

Over a photograph of the knitting group, shouted the headline:

THEY MAY LOOK INNOCENT BUT ARE THESE WOMEN BEHIND THE KNITTED GRAFFITI SPREADING DISCORD THROUGH TOWN?

'Spreading discord?' Avril said indignantly. 'That's awful.'

'It is,' Honor agreed. 'If he's going to work at *The Mail*, he'll have to come up with punchier headlines than that.'

The others giggled.

'Looks like your cover's blown,' Honor added. 'Not that it was hard to guess anyway. And, don't worry,' she patted Avril's hand. 'It's just Keiran stirring things as usual. I don't know anyone who isn't one hundred percent in love with all your knitted stuff.'

'It's only a bit of silly fun,' Avril defended. 'And entirely innocent.'

'It is.' Lucie began to laugh. 'Although it's just as well a certain pagan and senior member of the knitting group hasn't been around lately.'

'You mean Aggie?' Honor said. 'Why?'

'Can you imagine what Aggie would come up with to knit?' Lucie screwed her eyes up in mock horror. 'What with her being rumoured to be a white witch and everything?'

'Now this is someone I've got to meet,' Avril poured more Baileys.

'Oh, don't worry, you will when she gets back from her swingers' holiday,' Lucie spluttered. 'She's hard to avoid.'

'Are you sure Aggie hasn't had a hand in proceedings?' Honor asked, through giggles. 'Now you come to mention it, I thought the middle wise man at the knitted nativity opposite church looked a bit suspect. A bit too pink and interestingly shaped, if you know what I mean.' She began to laugh uncontrollably. 'And those round presents were very unfortunately placed at his feet.'

'Not to mention the bright purple cloak not being the best choice of colour!' Lucie snorted with laughter.

Avril joined in and the three of them were soon rolling around, tears streaming down their faces. They were so absorbed in the silly joke they didn't hear Ivy bark furiously, or the front door open.

'Well,' Jago said to Jamie, as they stood staring at the hysterical women. 'It's nice to see our womenfolk were at home waiting for us, weeping and wailing and tearing at their hair.'

'Jago!'

'Jamie!'

Honor and Lucie rushed at their men enveloping them in hugs and kisses and tears. Merryn came back downstairs and joined in, and Ivy bounced around clumsily, barking. It was chaos.

Eventually Avril took control, got Merryn back to bed, shut Ivy in the boot room and surveyed the men with a critical mother's eye. 'You look exhausted,' she said and went to make the inevitable pot of tea.

'You're back sooner than we thought,' Lucie said to Jamie, hanging off his arm and gazing up at him with adulation.

'Well, we're a pretty slick team once we get going, you know.'

'What was the emergency?'

'Twenty-five-foot yacht aground just past Lullbury Bay Point,' he explained. 'Engine failure and too difficult to get to them via the cliff, especially in the conditions. That storm was wild.' He tutted. 'There were some big seas out there tonight.'

'I've never seen navigation like it,' Jago added. 'Your Jamie is a hero.' He clapped the man on the back.

'Of course he's my hero,' Lucie said, adoringly.

'Are you staying for a quick drink, Jamie? Although it looks like we're out of Baileys,' Jago added drily, with a glance at the empty bottle lying abandoned on its side.

'If you don't mind, mate, I think Lucie and I will make tracks. It's a big day at the Wiscombes' tomorrow.' Jamie grimaced. 'And with that family, I'll need all my wits about me, if only to deal with Eli.'

'Cheek!' Lucie exclaimed. 'And there was me planning on giving you a very special homecoming present!'

Jamie waggled his dark brows. 'Looks like we'd better get off then. I'm on a promise!'

With much laughter, coats were found, more hugs given, and they left.

Honor and Jago stood at the open door and waved them off until they'd disappeared around the corner at the bottom of the hill. Jago looked up at the skies. The black clouds shifted against a dark sky but, in the gaps, stars twinkled serene and hopeful. 'Looks like the storm has blown itself out.' He hugged Honor to him.

'Was it really bad out there?'

'Let's say it's nothing like I've ever experienced. Jamie knows the coast like the back of his hand though.' He shook his head slightly. 'How he got us between the rocks in those seas, I'll never know. The man's a genius.'

'Did it feel safe?'

'It felt as safe as it could be in the circumstances. Calculated risk I suppose.'

'Funnily enough, that's sort of what Merryn said earlier.'

Jago dropped a kiss on the top of her head. 'Did she? She's a clever girl. Thinks too much though.'

'It was in answer to your mum when she found out you'd joined a crew.' Honor grimaced. 'Avril was pretty steamed up.'

Jago let out an enormous sigh. 'I should have told her straight away, before I'd even properly decided. I should have told her how I was feeling. I just didn't want to add to her worries.' He paused and then added heavily, 'How did she take it?'

'I think she was furious. Disappointed. Furious again. And then mostly terrified you might not make it back. We all were.'

Honor felt Jago tighten his hold. They stood for a moment, listening to the wind die down, to the faint sounds of Christmas Eve revelry coming from The Old Anchor pub on the harbour and the clinking of halyards from the dry-moored yachts. And, over all the noises of the night, the never-ending rhythmic roar of the sea. She wasn't sure she'd ever get used to the terror of waiting. Turning to him, she took his face in her hands. He smelled cold and of the sea. 'I'm so glad you came back to me.'

'Of course I came back to you. How could I not?' He kissed her gently and then laid his forehead against hers. 'I need to go and talk to Mum.'

She nodded slightly and released him.

After he went in, she stayed for a second longer, looking out at the glistening curve of tarmac as it snaked down the hill. She gulped in a huge, healing breath of salty air and sent out a silent prayer of thanks, to whoever or whatever was up there, that Jago had been sent back to her safely.

CHAPTER 37

'HAVE YOURSELF A MERRY LITTLE CHRISTMAS' – JUDY GARLAND

'Mum?' Jago stood on one side of the kitchen breakfast bar watching as Avril found a teapot and mugs. 'I'm not sure I want a cup of tea. To be honest, I could do with a stiff drink.'

Ignoring him, she slammed down the mug in front of him. 'How could you do it, Jago?'

He hung his head, feeling reduced to Merryn's age. 'I'm sorry.'

'No, you're not.'

He looked up and met her gaze. Biting his lip, he answered, 'You know what? I'm not.' He knew it would hurt her, but he wasn't prepared to back down. Not after tonight when he'd seen just how vital the service was in Lullbury Bay.

'You are so like your father.'

'In that case I'm glad. I'm glad I'm like him.'

'But he's not here, Jago.' Avril seemed to crumple in front of his eyes. She slid onto a stool and covered her face with her hands, quietly sobbing.

He went around and hugged her to him, hard. Her pain wrenched through him. 'I know he's not here, Mum. I wish with all my heart that he was.'

'I miss him so much, Jago.'

'I know. So do I.' He held her until the sobbing quietened, then tore off a strip of kitchen roll for her to mop up her tears. Finding a bottle of Scotch, he half-filled two tumblers. Pushing one to her, he sipped his own and then toed across a stool and sat down. He drank his whisky and waited.

Eventually his mother reached for her glass, sniffed and put it to one side. 'I don't drink whisky.'

'Drink it anyway.'

She took a tiny sip and grimaced. 'This on top of all the Baileys I've had will make me bilious.'

'You sound like Granny Pengethley.'

She gave him an old-fashioned look. 'I do not sound like my mother-in-law! It's just that the girls and I had a little celebration when we heard you'd got back.'

'So I see.' A smile twitched at his lips. 'There's none left and it was our Christmas Baileys!'

'It *is* Christmas,' she said indignantly. 'Besides, Lucie and Honor have been wonderful to me tonight, they deserved a drink. And, to my shame, I wasn't very nice to them.' Avril tutted regretfully.

'I'm sure they'll understand. It can't have been much fun waiting for news.'

'It had its moments. Where are they now?'

'Jamie took Lucie home, or it may be that Lucie dragged Jamie home.' An amused expression flickered across his face. 'I think she had plans for him.' He was reassured to hear his mother laugh slightly. 'I think Honor is in the snug watching TV. Probably to give us some privacy. She's thoughtful like that.'

'She's a nice girl, Jago. Is it serious?'

'Too soon to tell but yes, I think it might be. I like her very much. We had to get through some stuff, but it's all sorted now. Let's put it this way, I intend to make it serious.'

'What sort of stuff did you have to sort?'

Jago told her about the misunderstanding.

'Oh dear.' Avril managed a giggle. 'I'm not sure I could cope with being married to you.'

'Thanks!'

'You make far too much mess, what with all your work stuff everywhere.' She pointed her glass at his hair. 'And I'd get you to cut that lot off right away.'

Jago tweaked a curl which was hanging low in front of one eye. His hair had suffered in the wind and rain and had now dried into an unruly mess. 'You might have a point.'

She reached out a hand. 'No, don't cut it off. It reminds me of when you were a baby. You had a lovely mop of curls. Your gran said you got them from her.'

'Gran?' he said incredulously. 'Her hair is fine and dead straight.'

'What can I say? With your in-laws you learn to pick your battles.' She huffed. 'Quite flattering really, Honor thinking I could be your wife when I'm twenty years older. Maybe I don't look my age after all.'

'You know you don't, Mum. By the way, don't tell her I've told you. She's embarrassed enough about it as it is.'

'I won't, I promise.' She bit her lip. 'But I should have been more honest with the school. Been more upfront with everything. It might have helped Merryn more. Not led to all that confusion.'

'I think Mer is doing fine.'

Avril nodded. 'You know, I think she is. She's been amazing tonight. Taken it all in her stride. I think she's turned a corner and coming here to Lullbury Bay has helped.' She gazed at Ivy now back in her basket and snoring. 'We've all gone through so much, but I think we're getting there.'

He put his hand on hers. 'I think we are too.' He paused. 'I'm sorry I volunteered before talking it through with you.'

She sighed gustily. 'Oh, Jago, I had no idea you were missing it so much.'

'Yeah. I missed it. It was as if I wasn't whole. I don't think I had chance to think much about it when we were selling the house and dealing with all dad's stuff, and I had the divorce to think about too but, when I came down here and walked past the station most days, it was as if it was constantly pulling me in.' He sighed. 'But I'd promised you–' he let the sentence hang.

Avril blew out a breath and then was silent for a long moment. 'I don't think I had the right to make you promise not to volunteer,' she said eventually. 'It was wrong of me.' She smiled ruefully. 'As well as being honest with the school, maybe we should have been more honest with each other? Why didn't you discuss it with me? With us? I could see you were unhappy.'

'How could I, Mum? I couldn't add to your worries. You had enough on your plate what with moving here, settling Merryn into school.' He scrubbed an exhausted hand over his face. 'I was going to tell you, but I didn't want to do it until we'd got Christmas over with. There'll be enough to deal with just getting through the first Christmas Day.'

'There *will* be lots to deal with tomorrow, but we'll cope. I'll cope. And, hey, we wanted a different Christmas to last year's, well we've already achieved that. New home. New friends.' Avril pulled a face. 'The beginnings of a menagerie, if Merryn has her way.' She regarded him fondly. 'You're not responsible for me, Jago. I'm not in my dotage yet. I've got friends here now, a job I'm going to love. I can look after myself. Besides, I'm your mum, it should be *me* looking after *you*.'

He shuffled his feet. 'But I do feel responsible, and I do want to look after you. And Merryn.'

She reached forward and clasped his hand. 'My darling boy. You've your own life to live. And it seems to me you're going to have a bright future with Honor. I think she's perfect for you. Lighten you up a bit.'

'So you're not still angry with me?'

'Oh I'm still furious. I'm spitting feathers. You, my boy, are taking out the bins and doing the hoovering until the next millennium. Oh, and you can clean out the hamster's cage while you're at it.' She side-eyed him. 'But Merryn talked some sense into me and so did Honor and Lucie. Verity did too.'

'Verity?'

'You know, the vicar.'

Jago gave a small smile. 'Yes, I know Verity.'

'And, at least the next time you go on a shout I'll know to prepare myself. Like I did with your dad.'

'The next time I go on a shout?'

'Well, you're hardly going to give it up, are you?'

'No. No, Mum, I'm not. In fact, Jamie mentioned they're getting a new boat next year and they're looking for a name. He,' Jago bit back the emotion which threatened, 'he suggested the "Kenan Pengethley". I said I'd run it past you first. What do you think?' He looked at her hesitantly, unable to anticipate her reaction.

Avril gazed at him, her mouth slightly open. 'You mean we'd have Kenan here, in Lullbury Bay?'

'I suppose. In a manner of speaking.'

'And, each time you were called out, you'd use the boat named after him?'

He nodded. 'There's only one boat at Lullbury Bay station. It's due for an upgrade. They've been fundraising like crazy and think they'll meet the target by next spring,' he added, worried. He couldn't gauge how she was taking it. 'You don't have to agree, Mum. You only have to say no, and Jamie will pass your feelings back. They'll officially name it during the Blessings of the Boats Ceremony in May. You know, when they hold a shoreline service to bless the boats and,' he paused, swallowing, 'remember those lost at sea.'

'Say no?' Avril exclaimed, her eyes shining. 'Why would I want to say no? I can't think of a better way to remember your dad.' She clutched his hand hard. 'Oh, Jago, I'm not sure I can take much more tonight. It's been such a rollercoaster of emotion. Oh, Jago,' she repeated, and blindly grabbed the kitchen towel and wiped her eyes and blew her nose hard. 'It's the most perfect Christmas present.'

Jago nudged her whisky glass near again. He had the feeling she needed it. She sipped some and shuddered. 'Revolting stuff,' she said, astringently. 'I don't know how you can drink it. It was your dad's tipple too.'

Jago pulled a face. 'And he was to blame for introducing me to a good single malt.'

She managed a laugh through exhausted tears.

'You need to go to bed, Mum. It's been quite a night.'

'You're right, it certainly has.' She began to slide off the stool and an insistent scrabbling came from the corner of the kitchen as the hamster began to run round his wheel. It woke Ivy who growled slightly and stretched. 'Is it ten thirty?' she yawned. 'That's Chestnut waking up. Same time every night. I'd better check he's got food and water. With all the hoo-ha I expect Merryn will have forgotten.'

'Hold on, Mum, that's the time Dad died, isn't it?'

Avril looked at him in shock. 'Thereabouts. I think they called us in to say goodbye at about ten thirty.' She shook her head as if to clear her thoughts. 'If I'm honest, that night's all a bit of a blur.'

'I know he'll never be far from our thoughts but let's make ten thirty on Christmas Eve the special time to remember him. To raise a glass to his memory.'

'It's a wonderful idea.' Avril's eyes were full of tears, but her face shone with a kind of happiness too. 'I can't believe it's been a whole year.'

'We've come a long way in a year. Just think what we've

achieved.' He smiled at his mother. 'What *you've* achieved. I think Dad would be proud of us all.'

She picked up her glass. 'To Kenan,' she said, her eyes glistening. 'He would have been so very proud of you, Jago.'

He met her glass with his own. 'To Dad.'

CHAPTER 38

'DECEMBER WILL BE MAGIC AGAIN' – KATE BUSH

'Ah, here you are. Why are you watching TV in the dark?'

Honor looked up, relieved to see Jago in one piece. His mother couldn't have been too angry with him. 'It's cosy in here with just the Christmas tree lights and the wood burner. Besides, I thought I'd give you and your mum some privacy. I've been watching *Strictly/The Full Monty/The Voice Christmas Mash Up*.'

'Good?'

'Terrible.'

'Ah well, that's Christmas telly for you.'

'Come and sit down.' She patted the sofa.

He collapsed next to her. 'Good to see you've built up the fire.'

'I wasn't entirely sure what to do but it seems to have worked.'

'And the tree looks great. Did you do that too?'

'All Lucie and Merryn's handiwork. We were trying to find things to keep us busy while we waited. Where's Avril?'

'Gone up to bed. She's exhausted. She said to say good night.'

Honor yawned and looked at her watch. 'Oh my goodness. Look at the time. I need to go to bed too. I imagine Merryn is up pretty early on Christmas Day.'

'It's been a while since I spent a Christmas Eve night at home but the last one, when she was about five I think, she was up at three.'

'Oh no!'

'And then again at seven.'

'I really had better go to bed then. After the last few days I need some shut-eye to prepare.'

'Well, you know what children are like at Christmas.'

'Actually, I don't, not really. Blythe and her family don't get to Mum and Dad's until lunchtime usually and I teach children, I don't have them.'

He gave her a penetrating look. 'Would you like some?'

'What, children?' she asked, startled.

'Well, not right now, but maybe some time in the future.'

'Only as long as they have your curly hair and big green eyes.' Emotion choked her as she realised what he was asking.

He inched nearer and kissed her softly. He still smelled of the sea; briny water underlaid with the scents of adrenaline and exhaustion. 'That's settled then.' After some time, he added with a grin, 'Although you might change your mind after the horrors and delights that will be yours tomorrow morning.' He got up again. 'But don't go to bed yet.' He disappeared back into the kitchen and returned bearing a champagne bottle and two flutes. 'I thought it would be nice to have our own celebration.' Placing the glasses on the coffee table, he uncorked the champagne and poured two frothing glassfuls. The firelight danced through the amber liquid.

'I'm not sure I should. We broke out the Baileys when we heard you'd got back.'

Jago laughed. 'That's exactly what Mum said when I plied her with whisky.' Handing her a glass, he said, 'Merry Christmas.'

'Merry Christmas, Jago.' She sipped some. 'Did you and your mum sort things out?'

He nodded. 'We had a really good talk. The talk we should have had a long time ago.'

'That's good. So she's not angry with you anymore?'

'Only because she's insisted I'm on domestic chore detail for the next hundred years.'

Honor giggled. 'I like a domesticated man.'

He came closer. 'Do you now?'

Lifting her face to his for a kiss, she answered. 'I do.'

After another delicious pause they returned to the champagne.

'I was terrified you wouldn't get back,' Honor confessed. 'I kept a brave face on, we were all doing that for each other, but the storm was so bad–' she let the sentence trail off, the fear of losing him returning.

'I'm sorry I have to put you through it.' He bit his lip. 'But you understand it's something I have to do?'

She nodded. 'If I'm really honest, I don't think I'll ever, *ever* get used to having to wait for you, especially if there's a storm like tonight. But yes, I know it's something you're called to do. Lucie made a very convincing argument for why crew volunteer. I've really seen her in a new light tonight. She's astonishingly brave in her own way.'

Jago nodded. 'Thank you for being with Mum and Merryn. It must have made all the difference that you were together.'

'I didn't have much of a choice. Lucie told me the lifeboat had gone out as we were leaving the church service. I think Avril overheard. Next thing we knew Verity had bundled us all to the vicarage for hot chocolate.'

'Was Verity in charge of negotiations?'

'No, she didn't say much. She just let us get on with it. Lucie was brilliant. She said although she sometimes found it difficult, she'd never stop Jamie being crew because she knew it was what he felt he had to do. Then Merryn got all logical and talked about "doing a chance."'

'Doing a what?'

'Taking calculated risks in life. Then your mum got a bit upset about you and your dad and we all had a bit of a female bonding moment. I think Verity probably prayed or blessed us. Then we came here and waited.'

He pulled her to him and kissed the top of her head. 'I'm so sorry you had all that to go through. It was so not the way I wanted Mum to find out I'd volunteered again.'

'Well, it didn't really compare with fighting the high seas and rescuing people in peril.'

'Bravery comes in many forms.' He kissed her again.

Honor cuddled closer. 'What happened anyway?'

'As Jamie said, the yacht had engine failure and had gone aground. We got the casualties off, a couple in their fifties, and brought them back to harbour.'

'What were they thinking going out on a night like this?'

'Good point. They'd sailed over from France to stay with friends for Christmas. Thought they'd get ahead of the storm but it blew in early and has left early by the looks of things.'

'No one was hurt though?'

Jago shook his head. 'Paramedics checked them out and their friends collected them. All ended well.'

'What a night.'

'So, do you think you'll cope with me volunteering?'

'Do I have an option?'

Jago pulled a face.

'Then I'll just have to learn from the old hands like Lucie and your mum.'

'It'll rarely be as dramatic as tonight. I promise.'

'It had better not be.'

'Does that mean you're planning on staying around?'

'Your mum's asked me to stay tonight,' she said, deliberately misunderstanding but enjoying teasing him.

He lifted a strand of her hair, staring at it intently. 'It wasn't quite what I meant. Oh God, Honor, I know I'm not the hottest catch in town and I've only just got divorced and I suppose some might say I don't even have a proper job.' He gazed into her eyes. 'What I'm trying to say, very badly, is I know we've only just met but I'd like to take this further.' He sucked in a breath. 'I think I'm falling in love with you.' He frowned. 'No, scratch that. I *am* in love with you! I love you, my Honor bright. I love you as I've never loved anyone.'

Honor's breath hitched in her throat. She gazed back at him. At the strain and exhaustion the night had etched upon his face, at the tangle of dark curls she was desperate to run her hands through, at his green eyes liquid with emotion. 'I don't know how this has happened, but it has,' she began, haltingly. 'A month ago, I would have said I was resigned to a single life, working too hard because there was no one to come home to, eating at the Sea Spray because I couldn't be bothered to cook for one, *Strictly* being the highlight of my weekend.'

'And now?'

'Now? Oh, Jago, now I wouldn't know what to do if I thought I'd never see you again.' She ran a finger over his collar bone and felt his shiver of arousal. She pressed her lips there and heard him groan. 'I love you, Jago.'

They kissed. With tenderness building to passion and with the promise that this was only the very beginning of something wonderful.

Honor broke away and giggled slightly. She blamed tiredness and the champagne. 'Besides.'

'Besides what?'

'I really, *really* have to teach you how to love Christmas!'

Laughing, he kissed her again. Releasing her his eyes lit on the angel pendant she was still wearing. He took it in his fingers. 'You're my angel, my Christmas angel. Something tells me you've already sprinkled me with Christmas magic. Something tells me this year we'll have the best Christmas ever.'

'I think it will be too. Happy Christmas, Jago,' she whispered, lost in the love in his eyes.

'Happy Christmas, Honor,' and he kissed her.

THE END

ACKNOWLEDGEMENTS

This book began life in a conversation with writing buddy Lynn Forth. Jago Pengethley was born and he fell, fully formed, onto the page. I hope you love him as much as Lynn and I do! Huge thanks to Lynn for reading an early version of his story.

For an insight into all things RNLI, thanks must go to Stuart Morrison, Duty Commander at Tower Station and to RNLI volunteer Andrew Barker, and Georgina Drew. All mistakes are my own.

Thank you to Jane Cable for help with information on lantern workshops and parades, to Morton S Gray for Verity's sweatshirt slogan and to the Facebook Hivemind who so generously discussed the 'god questions'. Too many to mention individually but it was much appreciated.

My gratitude also goes to the wonderfully talented Sue Jones who let me attend one of her stained-glass workshops; it was great fun and gave me a really useful insight into Jago's craft. You can check out Sue's gorgeous work online as Lymelight Glass Studio on Facebook and Instagram.

A thank you must go to the marvellously kind and efficient team at Bloodhound who have worked so hard on the book.

And lastly, dear readers, without you there would be no Georgia Hill books. Thank you from the bottom of my heart for buying, reading, reviewing and sharing the love. Happy Christmas!

A NOTE FROM THE PUBLISHER

Thank you for reading this book. If you enjoyed it please do consider leaving a review on Amazon to help others find it too.

We hate typos. All of our books have been rigorously edited and proofread, but sometimes mistakes do slip through. If you have spotted a typo, please do let us know and we can get it amended within hours.

info@bloodhoundbooks.com

Printed in Great Britain
by Amazon

32267820R00162